"I want an interview—with you."

Ah, hell. Owen wanted to walk away, but Piper looked determined. It wouldn't be so bad, he reasoned to himself, quickly weighing the pros and cons. She probably wanted to grill him about one of the projects she and her parents were adamantly opposing. "A half hour."

"As long as it takes," she countered.

He shook his head. "No open-ended deals. One hour."

"Two."

"Woman, what on earth could you possibly want to talk about for two damn hours?" he said, annoyance getting the better of him. "An hour and a half. Final offer. Take it or leave it."

"Deal." She smiled. "And I get to pick the topic. And you have to cooperate."

She drove a hard bargain. "Fine. Now get the hell out of here."

She frowned and opened her mouth to protest, but the dark look he sent her snapped it shut pretty quickly. One thing was for sure—she wasn't dumb. Whatever she was after, she was likely to get. He wondered if she approached relationships the same way. Heaven help the man caught in her crosshairs. He wouldn't stand a chance.

Dear Reader,

I confess. I'm a sucker for a story where opposites attract. I love the push-pull of a relationship that seems doomed from the start because both characters are stubborn, determined and absolutely certain they know what's best.

When I envisioned Owen Garrett, the gruff but deliciously sweet logger, I knew right away the woman of his dreams was going to be the last he'd expect. And Piper Sunday didn't disappoint. Immediately I loved her quirky sense of humor and easy acceptance of things that might make others balk. I also loved that she refused to let Owen push her around even when he was blustering. Who wouldn't love a pair like these two?

As the last of Mama Jo's Boys, it's a bittersweet ending. I've loved these "boys" as much as my ever-lovin' Mama Jo. I hope you've enjoyed the journey. I know I certainly have!

Hearing from readers is one of my greatest joys. Feel free to drop me a line at my website, www.kimberlyvanmeter.com, or through snail mail— P.O. Box 2210, Oakdale, CA 95361.

Happy reading,

Kimberly Van Meter

Secrets in a
Small Town
Kimberly Van Meter

TORONTO NEW YORK LONDON
AMSTERDAM PARIS SYDNEY HAMBURG
STOCKHOLM ATHENS TOKYO MILAN MADRID
PRAGUE WARSAW BUDAPEST AUCKLAND

Recycling programs
for this product may
not exist in your area.

ISBN-13: 978-0-373-71706-4

SECRETS IN A SMALL TOWN

For questions and comments about the quality of this book please contact us at Customer_eCare@Harlequin.ca.

® and TM are trademarks of the publisher. Trademarks indicated with ® are registered in the United States Patent and Trademark Office, the Canadian Trade Marks Office and in other countries.

www.eHarlequin.com

Printed in U.S.A.

ABOUT THE AUTHOR

Kimberly Van Meter wrote her first book at age sixteen and finally achieved publication in December 2006. She writes for Harlequin Superromance and Harlequin Romantic Suspense. She and her husband of seventeen years have three children, three cats and always a houseful of friends, family and fun.

Books by Kimberly Van Meter

Don't miss any of our special offers. Write to us at the following address for information on our newest releases.

Harlequin Reader Service
U.S.: 3010 Walden Ave., P.O. Box 1325, Buffalo, NY 14269
Canadian: P.O. Box 609, Fort Erie, Ont. L2A 5X3

My biggest thanks go to Bob Berlage
of Big Creek in Davenport, California.
My husband and I thoroughly
enjoyed your crash course on logging practices
in the Santa Cruz Mountains.
Without your help, I surely would've been
floundering. Any deviations from true practice is
no reflection of your teaching,
for you were a great resource!
Thank you!

CHAPTER ONE

OWEN GARRETT TRIED TO KEEP it cool but he'd already crumpled the newspaper in his hand because he couldn't stop imagining it was the neck of one nosy journalist who'd decided making his life miserable was her single goal in life.

He pushed open the glass door of the *Dayton Tribune*'s office and went straight to the receptionist, with a demand to see the editor.

"She's not here." The woman, her name plaque identifying her as Nancy, arched her brow at his tone. "Perhaps I could take a message?"

He ignored her suggestion and barreled forward, too hot to follow the advice circling in his head. "Then, I want to see the general manager. And if that person isn't available, I want to see the publisher. There ought to be rules about what can and can't be printed without verifying the facts. Oh, wait, there are. If I don't see someone right now about this—" He thrust the mangled front page in front of Nancy's face and she scowled but took the paper from his hand. He pointed at the lead story. "Then the next call I place is to my lawyer. This is slander and I want a retraction. *Now.*"

Nancy exhaled softly and she plainly didn't appreciate his tone or his attitude but he didn't care. This was
the third article that reporter, Piper Sunday, had written
about his logging operation that basically painted him
to be the "big bad logger" out to clear cut the forests
without any consideration for the environment, which
was complete and total *crap*. He'd tried to take the high
road, but she'd pushed too far this time.

"The editor is out for the day and the managing editor
is on vacation until next week. However, Ms. Sunday is
here in the office. Perhaps you'd like to speak with her?"
she asked in a voice so perfectly bland it could be taken
only as a rebuke for his own hotheaded blustering.

Speak with Ms. Sunday? Hell yes. He tried to school
his face into some semblance of calm, but he couldn't
quite manage it. "I would *love* to speak with Ms.
Sunday," he said.

Nancy picked up the phone. "Ms. Sunday, you have
a gentleman up front to speak with you regarding a
story you wrote in this week's edition." She returned
the phone with a smile. "She'll be right up. Would you
like to sit and wait?"

"It'd be my pleasure." Except he didn't sit, he stood,
arms crossed and fuming. This morning he'd nearly
choked on a chunk of his granola cereal when he'd read
the lead story—Logger Proceeds With Flawed Harvesting Plan—printed with big, bold type running across
the page and he'd quickly and suddenly lost his appetite
as he'd spewed a litany of curse words that made his
German shepherd, Timber, cock his head in confusion

and then walk away to flop on his bed with a sad expression. Somehow he'd known they weren't going for a walk after breakfast. Instead Owen had raced into town to deal with lying reporters, which was a waste of a perfectly gorgeous spring day in the Santa Cruz mountains. Yet another reason to want to strangle Ms. Sunday.

He'd only spoken on the phone with her once and she'd taken everything he'd said completely out of context. So when she'd called again, he'd ignored her calls. Well, he'd mistakenly thought if he offered no comment, perhaps she'd find a different story to chase after, but this woman seemed to have an agenda and it was to ruin him. She'd run the story without the benefit of his involvement and it made him look like an evil bastard.

A slim brunette, wearing soft, flowing, white linen pants walked into the foyer with a professional smile on her full lips. "I'm Piper Sunday. How may I help you?" she asked pleasantly.

"You can help me by not slandering me and my company. You have balls of steel, woman." He nearly amended the *woman* part when he noticed the white bow tied neatly in her hair. When she had little to no reaction, he introduced himself. "I'm the evil bastard you seem to enjoy vilifying in the press."

"Perhaps you could be more specific…"

"Owen Garrett, owner of—"

"Big Trees Logging," she finished with a slow smile. "And the man who has an aversion to answering phone calls."

"You mean, an aversion to having my words twisted," he countered. "The one interview I gave you turned into a mess in print."

"That's your opinion."

"No, it's fact. And I'm about to sue this newspaper for slander if I don't get a retraction."

"First, if it's anything, it would be libel, which it's not. Second, you'd have to have a court order to get us to do a retraction. Out of curiosity, which part of the article did you take exception to?" she asked.

"All of it."

"That would be a very long correction, if I were of a mind to offer it," she said, crossing her arms. "And I'm not. Everything I wrote is true."

"I say it's not."

"Well, we're at an impasse. However, I would be happy to sit down with you for an exclusive interview for your rebuttal. I'm sure our readership would love to read your side of things."

Owen clenched his teeth. "I'm not kidding around here."

She held her ground. "Neither am I."

He caught the round-eyed stare of the receptionist as she enjoyed a front-row seat of their little drama and remembered himself. He was playing right into Ms. Sunday's game by appearing every inch the bullying blowhard she practically accused him of being in her articles. He dialed back his temper but it tasted like bile going down. "You'll be hearing from my lawyer," he said quietly, not trusting himself to continue.

There was the tiniest frown that betrayed her surprise when he called her bluff but she didn't try to placate him in order to make him change his mind. When she gave him a shrug as if to say "go for it," he swallowed a snarl and stalked from the office.

He didn't even care if he slammed the door. And in fact, he took perverse pleasure in the hope that the sound rattled the windows and echoed throughout the small building.

OH, BOY, WAS HE MAD. PIPER stifled a nervous giggle. "He has a temper, doesn't he?" she remarked to Nancy.

"Yes, he does. And you've riled him pretty good. You sure you want to do that? He just might sue us, and you know how that will upset Mr. Cook."

At the mention of the publisher, Piper shrugged but the kernel of nervousness remained. She couldn't lose her job. She had big plans. Besides, Owen Garrett could holler all he wanted. It wasn't going to change the fact that she'd done her due diligence on all of her articles on Big Trees Logging. She studied her fingernail and frowned at the hangnail she saw. She nibbled at the offending skin. "It's not my fault that I write the stories that put people on the defensive," she said to Nancy, though the receptionist had already returned to her work, which meant she wasn't paying much attention to her. Piper exhaled and walked to her office where she'd been doing her research on the aging computer. A spinning rainbow greeted her on the monitor as the computer wheezed through her request without much success. "Damn archaic piece of junk," she muttered, wondering whether if she gave it a whack like they do in the movies it would miraculously start working. Instead of bitch-slapping her hard drive like she wanted to, she sighed and shut it down so it could reboot.

"Who wants your head this time?" a voice asked behind her. "It must suck to write the stories people love to hate."

She rolled her eyes before turning to face the owner of the annoyingly snarky tone. "Yes, and it must be tiring to have to be the one to write the stories nobody reads."

Charlie Yertz, the bane of Piper's existence, pulled a nasty face but didn't disappear as she'd hoped. Instead, he tilted his head and regarded her shrewdly, saying, "I think you have an agenda with that Big Trees guy."

She affected a bored expression. "An agenda? Pray tell."

"I don't know yet but I'll figure it out."

"You've been reading too many conspiracy-theory blogs," she said, dismissing him and turning her attention to her slowly booting computer. But it was hard to seem absorbed with nothing showing on the screen, so she busied herself with tidying her space. When Charlie remained, she glared. "Can I help you?"

"You're ambitious," he stated as if that were a revelation, which it wasn't. Everyone knew Piper had big dreams of landing a Pulitzer someday.

"Charlie, who knew you had such hard-core investigative skills. Now, go on, shoo. I have work to do."

"So smug. You didn't let me finish. You've been going after Owen Garrett like a dog with a bone. I can understand one story on the logging hunk. But three? Care to share?"

Charlie thought she had the hots for Owen. If it weren't so ludicrous, she'd be offended. He was not her type. She preferred her men cultivated, civilized and sophisticated, not rough, big and completely disinterested in protecting the environment. Oh, lord, if she were ever to bring home someone like Owen Garrett, much less the brawny man himself, her parents would wilt. *Oh! Speaking of...* She made a buzzer sound for Charlie's benefit. "Wrong. However, two points for trying to think outside the box. Oops, actually you didn't. Not really. It's not a huge jump to try and draw a line between two single adults with some kind of cockamamie romance theory. Rest your little brain, Chuck. I'm starting to see smoke."

Charlie's face reddened and she bit back open laughter. It was just too easy with this guy.

"If I find out you're moonlighting behind the paper's back, I'll take great pleasure in ratting you out."

She kept her face implacable as she said, "I'm sure your uncle appreciates your loyalty."

"I am loyal," he agreed, his gaze hardening. "Unlike some."

She resisted the urge to roll her eyes, and instead, checked her watch. "Oh, look at the time. Gotta go. If you'll excuse me, I have a lunch date scheduled."

She moved past Charlie, who was no doubt plotting her death. The irony was that if he managed to pull off the perfect murder, her obituary would end up on his desk and she wasn't sure she felt comfortable with the idea of Charlie being in charge of her last words printed in the paper.

The funny thing was, for once Charlie had hit the nail on the head, though he was far afield with that romance idea. She was on to something with Owen Garrett and, really, it had nothing to do with his logging operation. She was digging into a bigger, better, far juicer story than the environmental angle her parents were pushing her to pursue.

And Owen Garrett was at the epicenter.

Of course, he was oblivious to the part he was going to play in her master plan—the plan where she busted open a decades-old case involving Owen's late father and, in the process, earned herself a spot among the greats in journalistic history. Now that she had him good and riled, when she pulled the bait and switch on him, he wouldn't know what hit him. He'd be so grateful that she was dropping the logging angle, he'd likely tell her whatever she wanted to know about his father.

Well, that's how it played out in her head. Of course, her mother was fond of telling her that she had a terribly overactive imagination, which, coupled with her writing skills, would make her a terrific fiction writer. But she didn't want to write fiction. She wanted to write the *next big story.* She wanted to rub elbows with the likes of Judith Miller of the *New York Times* and Dan Balz of the *Washington Post.*

And Owen Garrett was going to make that possible.

But first she had to choke down a tofu casserole with her parents, when what she really wanted was a triple-decker beef burger with all the trimmings over at Buns and Burgers. She tried not to drool at the thought and resigned herself to a lovely luncheon marred only by the prospect of the menu.

CHAPTER TWO

"I want to sue the newspaper," Owen growled to his lawyer, Scott Everhall. "She refuses to print a retraction without a court order, so let's give her what she needs. I want to go to court."

"Calm down. Let's talk this through," Scott said as he grabbed a fresh tablet to take notes. "What's got you so full of piss and vinegar?"

"Piper Sunday," he spat.

"I read her stuff. She's good," Scott said, then quickly added when Owen gave him a dark look, "Well, I mean, as good as any small-town reporter, I guess. So what's she said that's upset you so much?"

"She wrote that I'm going forward with the east mountain project with a flawed timber harvest plan, which basically points me out to be some kind of bull-headed jerk who doesn't give a rip about the environment or the endangered fairy shrimp or whatever damn bug that's in need of protecting."

"Well, you are going through with the project, right?" Scott asked for clarification.

"I filed all the necessary paperwork and permits. I'm doing everything by the book. I was given clearance."

"Of course, but that's not the point she's making,

right? You're not going to win with her. You know who her parents are, right?"

"No. Should I?"

Scott chuckled. "Well, they're only the king and queen of liberal politics, Coral and Jasper Sunday. They love to take on people like you. I can just imagine how they would enjoy vilifying a logger."

"This is bullshit," Owen grumbled, raking his hand through his hair, feeling as if he were slipping deeper into a mud pit. "So what are you saying? I've got no recourse, because her parents are pushing an agenda and they're using their daughter to get it done?"

Scott shrugged. "I'm not saying anything. I'm just providing information." He leaned forward and flicked imaginary lint from his desktop. "Here's the thing— I'm your lawyer and your friend. As your lawyer, I can drag the newspaper into court and demand a retraction. But in the end, it'll cost you more than it's worth and, frankly, it'll just make you look worse. Hell, maybe that's what she's hoping. Of course, as a lawyer billing you for my time, I'll do whatever you feel is necessary. But as your friend, I say let it go. Don't let this woman get under your skin. You're not doing anything wrong, so stop letting her make you feel as if you have."

"Just let it go?" Owen repeated, not quite sure if he was able to do that, not while he was as mad as he was anyway.

"Well, that's my advice. But you do what you want. I surely won't turn away your money if you're feeling like throwing it down the toilet."

"I think I need a new lawyer," Owen growled, but

Scott knew he was just blowing steam and simply made a gesture as if to say "you can do what you want" before leaning back in his chair, lacing his hands behind his head. Finally, Owen gave it up. "Fine. I'll let it go. But so help me, if I run into her on the streets, I might not be able to play nice."

Scott laughed. "Come on now…she's not bad-looking, you know. You *ought* to play nice. The saying 'you catch more flies with honey' has a certain logic to it. You could do a lot worse."

Owen barked a short, mirthless laugh in response. "I'd rather bed down with a rattler than pretend to like her just to get her off my back." With a wry dig at Scott, he added, "Some of us have standards."

"Suit yourself." Scott smiled, the insult bouncing right off him without causing a scratch. "Is there anything else I can do for you today?"

"No," Owen answered sullenly, his blood still hot from his encounter with that wretched reporter. "I suppose not if you aren't interested in helping me sue the newspaper."

"Perhaps another time," Scott suggested with an amiable grin. "In the meantime, want to hit the links with me sometime?"

Owen glowered. "I don't golf. Stop asking."

"Stop being so stubborn. You might like it."

"No, thanks. I have work to do. You might try that sometime."

"I work. And you'll have evidence of that as soon as you get my bill in the mail."

Billable hours. He swallowed a sharp retort. As the

woman who raised him would say, he had a bee in his bonnet and he needed to chill out. "All right. I'm out of here then. And don't hurt yourself, okay?" he said, gesturing to the paperwork on Scott's desk before heading for the door.

"Stay out of trouble," Scott called out, and Owen waved in response.

Play nice, that was Scott's advice. Some lawyer he was. Weren't they all bloodthirsty, bottom-feeders? Apparently, he had the one lawyer on the planet who had a conscience.

Wasn't he the lucky one. Yeah…lucky wasn't what he was feeling right at the moment.

PIPER FORCED A SMILE AS HER mother dished a healthy portion of bulgur, lentil and tofu casserole onto her plate and tried not to stare at the offending mess as if it were the enemy. She'd been eating this stuff for years; one would think she'd be used to it by now. But once she'd discovered meat, covertly of course, she'd had a hard time appreciating the taste of tofu. Her parents would be devastated if they knew she was no longer a vegetarian, which was why she hid it from them. She imagined if she took up smoking they'd be more understanding than if she told them she had a hankering for a quarter-pounder with cheese.

"Your article was fantastic," Coral said, her voice warm with pride. "You're keeping your clippings, right?"

"Yes, Coral," she answered dutifully. That was another thing about her parents, she'd never called them

"Mom" and "Dad," instead always referring to them by their given names as they believed it was unnecessary to cling to archaic traditions. Her friends used to think it was wild that she was treated like an adult when she was ten, but secretly, Piper had wished she had a bit more of that "tradition" her parents shied away from. It wasn't easy being the only kid in class with parents like Coral and Jasper. She took a bite of the casserole for her mother's sake. It wasn't terrible, the spices helped; but it wasn't beef and that's what she wanted at the moment. "Actually," she said around the hot bite, "I had a visitor at the paper earlier this morning and, boy, was he mad."

Jasper grinned above his own heaping plateful of casserole. "The owner of Big Trees Logging came down to rail at you, huh? How'd that go?"

"As well as can be expected," Piper said with a shrug. *Mad* was an understatement. If fire could've shot from his eyeballs, she'd have been reduced to a smoldering pile of ash. "He's pretty ticked off. He threatened to sue the paper."

"That's so like a conservative," Jasper growled, and Coral nodded in agreement. "Censor the press so that the message is muffled. Don't worry, sweetheart, the truth is on your side."

She wasn't entirely sure of that. She felt a twinge of regret for having to railroad Owen Garrett, but she was playing both sides against the middle for a bigger cause. Sure, she was helping her parents further their own agenda of protecting the marbled murrelet, but in her heart burned a secret desire for bigger things than their little slice of heaven could provide. "Did you know that Big Trees was awarded a green certification for their environmentally sound and sustainable logging practices?" she asked her mother, who only scowled in response.

"Political designation, kickbacks, there's all sorts of terrible things that go on at the expense of the environment, honey." Coral seated herself and dug into her casserole with relish. "Logging disrupts the natural order of things, creates sediment that kills the fish and erosion that causes a landslide hazard. We are stewards of the land, honey, and it's time people remember that fact."

"It also provides lumber that's used to build homes," Piper countered, unable to help herself. "And jobs, so that people can feed their families. And Garrett's company actually improved the Chileaut watershed."

Coral blinked in surprise. "Piper, you know there are plenty of alternative building products out there that are just as good, if not better, than timber for building homes. If we don't make people change, they never will. And who's to say that the Chileaut watershed was improved?" Piper opened her mouth to answer but Coral continued with a knowing expression that Piper found particularly annoying, saying, "Just because some report by some independent water group claims that the watershed quality has improved, doesn't make it so. We don't know if money changed hands."

Piper had a difficult time imagining Owen paying someone off just to get what he wanted. There was something…noble about the man, even though he did scare her a little with that intense stare of his. It was as if he could zero in on her most intimate thoughts with unerring accuracy. She suppressed a shiver. Her mother was still ranting. The fleeting thought came to her to try and set Coral straight with some facts, but she realized in her mother's current frame of mind the effort would be useless.

She adored her parents, but sometimes they were… well, zealots, and she didn't want to spend the rest of the afternoon listening to them tag team her in a one-sided discussion. It was best to nod and agree and then disagree privately. Piper choked down another bite and smiled, ready to switch subjects.

"Do you remember that case involving the Aryan Coalition?"

Jasper paused, his next forkful nearly to his mouth. "You mean, the massacre at Red Meadows? Why would you want to know about that? It's an embarrassing chapter in the town's history, best left alone."

Coral agreed resolutely, her gaze darting. "I was so glad we didn't have a television. I heard you couldn't turn the channel without something being on about it. Your father is right, the memory is best forgotten."

Oh, Piper heartily disagreed. How something so dark and scandalous could lurk in the shadows of the town's history without piquing at least some kind of outside interest baffled her. When she'd found the details, she'd nearly fallen from her chair in her shock and excitement. It wasn't every day you found the ticket to the big time just waiting for you to discover it. The second coup had been when she'd discovered that the local recluse,

William Dearborn, had actually been at Red Meadows when it all went down. It'd been like stumbling across a buried treasure, only the loot had been in plain sight the whole time.

"Well, when I was doing background research on Big Trees Logging, I stumbled across the information that Owen Garrett was at the massacre. In fact, it was his father who was the leader of the Aryan Coalition."

"That's right. I'd forgotten," Jasper said, returning to his paper. "He was just a kid then, about ten or so?"

"Eleven, actually," she corrected her father. "What a terrible thing to have lived through."

"Yes," Coral hastened to agree, but it was plain that the topic unnerved her, which was saying something because Coral wasn't easily bothered. She often viewed most awkward, volatile or embarrassing situations as an excellent opportunity to study human behavior within the constraints of a working civilized society. "It's probably a blessing he was sent to live with his aunt on the east coast. No telling how twisted he might've grown up to be if he'd remained here after everything he went through with that father of his."

"You knew them?" she asked, unable to contain her delight at this unexpected nugget of information.

Coral looked to Jasper, but quickly shook her head. "Of course not, Piper. It's not as if we ran in the same circles. I'm just saying, the leader of a racist cult is hardly what I'd call a candidate for Father of the Year. You never know what he was teaching that boy." Then she added with a mutter, "I'm shocked Owen returned."

"Yeah, me, too," Piper murmured, her mind moving

rapidly. Her parents had definitely shared a conspiratorial look. What did that mean? Dare she ask? Would they tell the truth? Piper decided to sit on those questions for the moment.

"Piper, you've hardly touched your tofu casserole. Are you feeling all right? Are you taking your elderberry? Springtime is notorious for being cold season. You need to bolster your immunity. Oh, that reminds me, are you coming to the planting on Sunday at the farm?"

The annual community garden planting was something her parents orchestrated as part of the sustainable-society project they started when she'd been born. It had turned into a community of like-minded individuals who operated a co-op of sorts. They all shared in the work and then when harvest time came, they enjoyed the bounty equally. "Of course," she answered, swallowing a sigh. Sometimes she felt she lived two lives. One life was for Piper Sunday, reporter, meat-eater, and quite possibly a closet conservative; the other life was for Piper Morning Dew Sunday, vegetarian, environmentalist, love child who was raised on a commune with slightly odd parents. She used to slide quite easily between both lives but lately, she found more in common with reporter Piper than environmentalist Piper and she didn't know how to reconcile that fact. The idea of spending a full day with her former "community" didn't thrill her. She'd come to appreciate the uses of deodorant and razors, two things the women in particular eschewed because it wasn't "natural."

In answer to her mother's question, she took another

bite and then pushed away her plate. "I'm stuffed. I had a big breakfast at the office this morning," she explained, planning to fudge the actual contents of her breakfast, which had consisted of doughnuts and coffee. "I had one of those veggie burritos and it just filled me up. I might not even eat dinner."

Coral nodded in understanding. "Sometimes I cut one in half to share with your father. Would you like me to put some of this casserole in a container for you to take home?"

"No, that's okay," she said, offering a different suggestion. "Why don't you share it with Tia and Rhonda?"

"That's an excellent suggestion, sweetheart," Coral said with a reflective nod. "I should've thought of it myself."

Tia and Rhonda were life partners on the farm who had just adopted a baby together and were struggling with the sleeplessness that came as an accessory with the new kid.

Piper prepared to put her exit strategy in motion when her dad piped in, asking about her love life. "Any prospects?" he asked, a twinkle in his eye.

"Jasper, stop pestering her," Coral admonished, but Piper could tell she was just as curious. "I'm sure if Piper had something to tell us, she would." She looked to Piper for assurance. "Right?"

"Of course. Nothing to report. I'm too focused on my work to worry about dating."

"You know, Farley was asking about you the other day while we were harvesting the seedlings at the greenhouse. He's a great young man. He makes a mean tofu parmigiana."

Blech. The thought turned her stomach more than the idea of dating Farley did.

"A man with shared values who can also cook—you don't find that too often," Coral added, as if sharing a trade secret of some kind.

"Not according to eHarmony.com," Piper quipped, earning a confused look on her parents' part. No television, no computer. All her best jokes lately had been falling on fallow ground. "Never mind. I was kidding. Forget it. Anyway, gotta go." She rose and pressed a kiss to both their cheeks. "Thanks for the grub. It was great."

"See you on Sunday, lil Miss Sunday," her father said with a wink.

"Can't wait," Piper said with a private sigh.

CHAPTER THREE

PIPER SAT IMPATIENTLY OUTSIDE the classroom of Mrs. Hamby's second-grade class, still chafing a bit at her assignment. She wasn't the education reporter but here she was, stationed outside, getting ready to cover a small piece on the Bring Your Parent To School Day.

"Damn you, Charlie, for getting the flu," she mumbled, adjusting the strap holding the camera on her shoulder. However, if there was ever a person she wouldn't mind knowing was doubled over, going and blowing from both ends, Charlie was the top candidate. As enjoyable as the thought may be, she couldn't make her future on pieces like *this*. She doubted Diane Sawyer ever did time covering student-of-the-month assemblies. She had a degree in journalism, for crying out loud, and yet, she'd been sent to chase after second-graders and their parents. She'd really need to talk to her editor about assignments that were a waste of her talent. They had an intern for occasions like this. She had research to do and a council member to shake up.

She'd received a delicious tip that Councilman Donnelly had been caught with another woman. Big whoop—what politician didn't dip his wick in other pots when the occasion presented itself?—except, Donnelly was an outspoken proponent of old-fashioned values. It was enough to make her giggle with anticipation. The look on his florid face when she casually mentioned the woman's name was going to be priceless.

That is, if she managed to wrap up this silly assignment quick enough to catch Donnelly at his favorite restaurant around lunch.

"Ah, crap."

She heard the expletive muttered behind her and she turned to find Owen Garrett striding toward her, his expression as sour as if he'd been sucking on a lemon for the past half hour.

"What are you doing here?" The question popped from her mouth before she could stop it. But she was legitimately curious. Piper knew Owen wasn't married, nor did he have kids, so it begged the question—why was he strolling through the elementary campus?

"Serving some kind of penance, apparently," he answered.

She ignored that. "I know you don't have kids and you were an only child, so that precludes nephews and nieces. So why are you here?"

"So the yellow journalist has done her homework."

"Don't call me that."

"Why? Does it bother you to be called something you're not? I know the feeling, but in this case, I have to disagree. If I were to look up 'yellow journalist' in the dictionary, I wouldn't be surprised if they used your picture under the definition."

"I'm not a yellow journalist, nor have I ever been one. For your information, I've never sensationalized anything just to attract readers. My stories are just naturally interesting," Piper retorted, refusing to let his digs get under her skin. "You still haven't answered the question. I'm not surprised, though. You're the king of avoiding any question that doesn't suit your purpose to answer."

His mouth clamped shut and she stifled the tickling urge to grin in victory. He was too easy to nettle. And she realized she very much liked to nettle him.

Oh, that didn't bode well for her bigger plan. She straightened with a shrug. "Whatever. I don't care why you're here. I'm here for an assignment, not to trade insults with you."

"That's a shame. I was just getting started."

She turned away from him, mentally kicking herself for not remaining on track. She had to be careful around him. He managed to get under her skin in a fairly short period of time.

"I heard you grew up on a commune," he said conversationally to her back. When she refrained from offering a rejoinder, he added, "With a bunch of nudists."

Heat crawled into her cheeks. It wasn't that she was ashamed—the naked body was a beautiful thing—but the way he said it made it sound insulting. And most people found the fact that she'd grown up in an unorthodox household ripe for conversation. Frankly, she was over it.

"Well, we have something in common, then," she quipped, turning to give him a cool look. "I heard you were raised on a racist compound. I guess you could say we were both raised in nontraditional households.

Mine ran around naked and yours fantasized about genocide."

That stunned him into silence but the lock that slid over his expression told her she'd gone too far. Damn her mouth. How was she ever going to make it to the big time if she couldn't govern what fell from her lips? She ought to pull it back. She chewed the inside of her cheek as she raced through a number of different ways to apologize. But before she could settle on the best one—not that he would've accepted, judging by the stony look on his face—the door opened and Mrs. Hamby welcomed them with a warm greeting. Piper scuttled inside, eager to escape the shadowy feeling of guilt that followed.

HE SHOULD'VE KNOWN BETTER than to poke at her but when he'd seen her standing there, looking harmless as a daisy in her white sundress, her brunette bob framing her angelic face without a hair out of place, he'd dearly wanted to push her into a mud puddle. Barring any available mud, he'd settled for throwing a few verbal shots her way.

He'd hit a nerve with the nudist bit but she'd kidney punched him with a shot about his past. The ghosts of Red Meadows were alive and well in Dayton no matter what he did to try and atone for his father's actions.

She was a damn reporter. Of course she knew about Red Meadows. That's why he should've just kept his mouth shut.

It was true he didn't have kids or nieces or nephews

but his office manager, Gretchen Baker, had a daughter without a father and when she'd asked him to do this he didn't see how he could refuse. He'd always gone out of his way to educate the public about logging but he also enjoyed doing what he could to change the town's memory of the Garrett name.

So, it was a little self-serving coming to the classroom today and that damn journalist was bound to see right through him.

Mrs. Hamby, a short round woman with apple cheeks and puffy curls clinging to her head pointed to the tiny desk and chair, indicating that he and Piper would be sitting beside one another.

Piper took one look at that little red molded plastic chair and saw how close they'd be to one another and she opted to stand at the back of the room, citing the need to be able to move around for pictures.

He was willing to bet his eyeteeth she was lying. But that was fine with him. He didn't want any part of him pressed against her, least of all their thighs and shoulders. He caught the eye of Gretchen's daughter, Quinn, and winked when she brightened with a gap-toothed grin the width of Texas. This part he didn't mind at all. Quinn was a great kid. It wasn't her fault that her mom had terrible taste in men. Quinn's daddy took off when she was just three years old and the newest baby daddy—because Gretchen was seven months pregnant—couldn't seem to make up his mind whether or not he wanted to stick around.

"Class, we have very special guests today," Mrs.

Hamby said, her blue eyes twinkling. "Today, we have our mommies and daddies, uncles and aunts, or caregivers here to talk to us about what they do for a living. Remember, we must all show our guests our best manners so that they might want to visit us again sometime. And as an extra-special treat, we have a reporter from the newspaper who is going to do a wonderful story on our special day!" At that, twenty-seven kids turned toward the back where Piper was standing nibbling on her cuticle, causing her to straighten and flash a reluctant smile. Mrs. Hamby beamed at Piper, saying, "Piper Sunday was one of my very first students here when I came as a young teacher and it's so wonderful to have her here today. She's growing up to be a fine journalist. We might even see her go on to write for the *New York Times* or *San Francisco Chronicle*."

Owen slid his gaze to Piper and caught hers. She seemed to blush a little but lifted her chin with a small smile for Mrs. Hamby's benefit. He didn't know anything about what it took to get to a big metro area paper but he suspected it didn't involve biased reporting or Bring Your Parent To School events. So, in his opinion, she had a snowball's chance in hell of making it anywhere other than little ol' Dayton. She'd be writing about the dangers of riptides for tourists and preschool recitals for the rest of her life. Heh. That actually lightened his mood a bit. Just to throw her off, he sent her a blinding smile.

And it worked. She nearly dropped her writing pad.

Perhaps this day was salvageable.

PIPER SCRIBBLED A FEW NOTES and snapped a few pictures but she was on autopilot. Another part of her brain was processing that smile. From a purely objective place, she could see a certain rugged handsomeness to the man. When he wasn't scowling hard enough to bring on a thundercloud, Owen Garrett wasn't so hard on the eyes. She wondered what relationship he had with the cute kid who'd introduced him. She'd said Owen was her mom's boss and friend. Hmm...translated, that meant boyfriend.

He was sleeping with his office manager. What a jerk. Her mouth tightened as a wave of indignant—*something*—washed over her. She shouldn't be surprised. A man like Owen Garrett probably had to kick women out of his bed on a regular basis. He made a good living raping the land of its resources—okay, *rape* was probably a harsh word, but given her pique, she wasn't in the mood to be politically correct—and he was unattached, which meant no ex-wife hanging around or siphoning from his paycheck. In other words, he was Dayton-delicious as her girlfriends would say.

It was a good thing she had higher standards. A girl could easily lose her focus around all that muscle and brawn. Speaking of, was it really necessary to wear that tight, artfully faded T-shirt that clung to his broad chest like a lover draped across all that hard skin? There were children around, for crying out loud. She pursed her lips and pretended to scribble some additional notes, when in fact, she was just tired of looking at him, which was a problem only she seemed to have as a quick glance revealed plenty of mommies caressing him with their eyes.

Eww.

And, naturally, he didn't seem to notice the effect he had on the estrogen in the room. Why were some good-looking men oblivious to their charm? She drew a deep breath, glad it was nearly over. The next time Charlie couldn't make it to work, she was going to insist their editor see a doctor's note.

And unless he had Ebola, Charlie better have his skinny ass at his post.

Finally finished, she tried slipping from the room, eager to return to the office to write the silly story so she could get back to real journalism, but she was waylaid by an unexpected cute factor.

As the adults said their goodbyes and filed from the room, the little girl launched herself at Owen with the unabashed enthusiasm of the very young. He didn't miss a beat and hefted her slight weight without blinking. She buried her face into his neck and he reciprocated with a tight hug. Before Piper put much thought into her actions, she snapped a quick picture of the scene.

"Thank you for coming, Owen," she heard the little girl whisper, and he murmured something back that Piper didn't quite catch.

Oh, dear. She didn't want to see that. She ought to delete the picture right now before her editor saw it. She already knew from her gut that it was a great shot. He was under her skin again. Without even trying. She snared a look by a single mom who was eyeing Owen as if she wanted to give him a tongue bath. She was tempted to tell her "Go for it, honey, he's all yours" but her mouth wouldn't open. A little fact she refused to examine too closely. Instead, Piper edged past the two and nearly ran from the room.

CHAPTER FOUR

OWEN RETURNED TO THE OFFICE where Big Trees Logging administration did the magic of keeping the business afloat and immediately Gretchen was full of questions. "How'd it go?" she asked.

"It went great. Thanks for asking me to go," he said, moving to the stack of mail he hadn't had the chance to sort through just yet.

"I was going to ask Danny, but Quinn wanted you," she said, almost apologetically.

At the mention of her newest boyfriend, the guy who knocked her up and then decided he needed space to think things through, made Owen want to scowl and say something rude but he held the urge in check. Gretchen had a soft heart and would likely get hurt feelings if he said what he felt right at the moment about the guy who'd bailed on her and their unborn child. "Yeah, not a problem," he assured her, moving to his office. He paused as a sudden thought came to him. "Oh, and I've reconsidered my earlier request to send all calls from Piper Sunday to voice mail. Send any and all calls straight to me."

Gretchen's mouth pinched as she rubbed her distended belly. "Why for? So she can print more lies about you and Big Trees Logging? You ought to sue her and the paper for slander."

"You mean, libel." He grinned at Gretchen's protectiveness. "I wish my lawyer agreed. Unfortunately, it's more trouble than it's worth. I just want to put the whole thing behind me. We're better than that anyway."

"Of course we are," she agreed, nodding vigorously. "But still…seems wrong that she's going to get away with being so mean."

"She's just doing her job, I suppose."

"That's a matter of opinion," Gretchen said with a glower but finally sighed as she relented. "You got it. All calls from Piper Sunday will go straight to you."

"Thanks, Gretchen." He was midway to his desk when he remembered something else and poked his head out to call to Gretchen again. "Hey, anytime you need something for Quinn…it's no imposition. Just ask. You got it?"

Gretchen's eyes warmed and he half expected tears to follow as her pregnancy had been doing a number on the waterworks. Once he found her crying over the coffeepot when she'd run out of filters. But to his relief, her eyes remained dry, but appreciative.

"I wish more people saw what a good man you are," she said, surprising him. "You act all gruff, but you're really a sweet guy."

Uncomfortable with the praise but knowing it came from an honest place, he simply cocked a grin her way and said, "Don't tell anyone. It'll ruin my rep as a badass."

Gretchen winked with a broad smile. He returned the

grin until he realized he had a missed call from Mama Jo. He frowned and quickly punched in the retrieval code.

The beloved voice of his foster mother sounded in his ear as she left a short message, wondering if he might be able to come visit soon, perhaps before the heat of summer got too bad. Since it was only spring, he smiled at the request even if a twinge of guilt followed. He hadn't been home in a long time. He tried to go once a year but he'd been swamped as of late and the time seemed to get away from him.

Piper Sunday didn't know everything about him. She knew only the surface stuff. Everyone knew that his father was killed in an FBI raid at the compound at Red Meadows. They also knew that his father was the head of the Aryan Coalition, a racist group with ties to bad things.

After it'd all gone down, he'd been sent to live with his only living relative, his aunt Danica on his mother's side in West Virginia. But he'd proven to be too much of a handful for his aunt and she'd relinquished custody of the boy she'd never truly known anyway to the state. And he'd landed in the care of Mama Jo, a petite black woman with more heart and wisdom than anyone he'd ever met.

It's also where he'd met his two foster brothers, Thomas Bristol and Christian Holt. He missed them all so much it was like a fire in his gut but he had a job to do here and he wasn't about to walk away because it was easier.

Thomas and Christian had thought he was nuts to

return to the town where his name was associated with something so dark and shameful. But he'd needed to give people something positive to associate the Garrett name with and he figured the best way to do that would be to become a productive member of the community.

To his dying day, he'd never forget Mama Jo's advice to him as he broke the news that he was headed west.

"They got trees right here in West Virginia," she'd said when he'd told her he was going to go into commercial forestry in California.

There'd been no sense in dancing around the truth—Mama Jo would see right through it anyway. She'd always had an uncanny sense about those things. It'd made it rough getting anything past her, which was probably why she'd managed to take three universally screwed-up kids and turn them into something useful to society.

"I have to go," he'd said quietly.

"I know you do," she'd said with a sigh. "I just wish you didn't feel the need to prove yourself to a bunch of people who don't matter anyway. All the people who know your heart are right here."

"It's not about me. It's just something I need to do for my dad. The Garrett name doesn't need to be forever associated with something bad."

Mama Jo's eyes had misted and for a second he'd felt like that lost eleven-year-old boy again. She'd cupped soft, careworn hands around his jaw as she'd said, "You're a good son. You do what you feel is necessary to make it right for you. Your daddy is gone and it don't matter to him none. You do this for you. And when you've done what you feel needs doing, you know where home is."

He'd choked up and Mama Jo had wrapped him in a hug that said as much as her words.

Heading back to California, it'd felt as if he were going to battle.

Just thinking of that day so many years ago caused tears to spring to his eyes and, if he wasn't careful, he'd end up a slobbering, bawling mess at his desk.

So when Mama Jo called, he always answered if he could.

"Hello, Mama," he said when she picked up the line. A smile formed at the sound of her voice as her face appeared in his memory. "I just got your message. What's going on? Everything okay? Did you get that package I sent?"

"Sure did. Never seen fruit arranged like that before. It was good, though Christian and Thomas wiped out the chocolate-topped strawberries before I could blink."

"Oh, Mama, you should've smacked their paws as soon as they tried reaching for them," he grumbled. He loved his brothers but he'd paid a pretty penny to have the fresh fruit arrangement delivered across the states. The overnight cold-storage shipping had been nearly as pricey as the arrangement but Mama was worth it. "I just wanted you to have something different for your birthday."

"It was very thoughtful of you and I loved it, don't you worry. But I wasn't calling about the arrangement. I want to know if I can get a commitment out of you to come visit."

She always asked, but there was something else in her voice—an underlying urgency perhaps that gave him pause. "Everything okay?" he asked.

"Does there have to be some kind of calamity for you to visit your family?" she joked, but it didn't escape his notice that she'd sidestepped the question. A trickle of unease made his heart race. "It's just time to come home for a visit. Don't you think? It's been years," she reminded him.

"It's high time," he agreed, but he was looking at his calendar and there weren't too many open spots. Still, he couldn't get himself to just shut her down. "I'll see what I can do, Mama," he offered, but the weight of her disappointment pressed on him to try harder. He flipped his calendar, scanning for any possible leeway. "How about I bring you here for a visit? We could take a drive into the Bay, see the sights…"

"Maybe another time. You let me know when you can come. I'll see that your brothers are here, too. It's time we spend some time catching up."

"Okay," he agreed, but he didn't know how the hell he was going to manage it. "Everything okay? You sound funny."

"Never tell a lady that, son," she admonished. "Take care, honey. I love you."

"I love you, too, Mama," he murmured, still troubled even as he disconnected. He'd have to call Thomas. His older brother always knew what was going on with Mama. He was the only one who'd stayed behind, getting a job with the local FBI office out of Pittsburgh.

He'd recently moved back to Bridgeport with his wife, Cassi.

In Thomas's case, he'd married his childhood sweetheart—eventually. Before the happily-ever-after happened, he'd been hell-bent on putting her in federal prison. From the stories he'd heard, Cassi had communicated her displeasure with that idea by repeatedly punching, kicking and scratching Thomas each time he tried.

As for Christian, he'd managed to fall in love with a woman on the run from a real bad character that had, for all intents and purposes, enslaved her for his own gain.

His brothers had a knack for finding the most difficult women on the planet and then falling in love with them. He was going to buck that trend. If he didn't, he might end up shackled to someone like that reporter.

He waited for the shudder. But when it came, a shiver of awareness followed and that freaked him out more than finding a rattlesnake in his toilet.

PIPER DONNED A BIG, FLOPPY HAT to shield herself from the sun and exited her car, scanning the farm for her parents. She found them laughing and talking with Tia and Rhonda as they fawned over the new baby. She trudged that way, each step reminding her to stow her annoyance at being pulled away from spending time at the library going through the archived newspapers on microfiche, because she truly loved these weird, left-to-center people with all her heart.

Tia exclaimed when she saw Piper. "There she is.

Little Miss Intrepid Reporter. Come here, you, and give me a hug," Tia demanded with mock seriousness. "For a while, I started to think you'd forgotten all about your friends and family in your quest for journalistic fame."

"You're a hard bunch to forget," Piper said, returning the embrace. "How's the new baby?"

Tia glanced down at the sleeping baby tucked into a beautiful antique pram that Tia likely rescued from a garbage heap somewhere and the corners of her mouth tipped in a gooey smile. "She's perfect."

Rhonda smoothed a lock of jet-black hair from the baby's porcelain China-doll face. "More than perfect. Divine."

Piper smiled indulgently, but held her tongue. She'd never understood the baby thing. To her, the kid looked like any other newborn. Sort of smooshy and wrinkly. And helpless. Piper couldn't even commit to a fish, much less a kid. "So what's her name?"

"Echo Breeze," Tia answered, sharing an adoring look with Rhonda.

Echo. Whatever happened to traditional names like Mary or Nicole? She'd often wished her parents had picked something a little less out there when they'd named her. The kids in school had teased her mercilessly. She gazed down at the baby with a rueful expression. *Good luck with that name, kiddo.* "She's cute," Piper acknowledged, then moved to her parents with an expectant expression. "So what's the plan? I have an appointment later today and can't stay the full day."

Her mother frowned but seemed to understand.

"We'll start with the seed blessings and the offering to Gaia and then we'll start planting. It's a shame you can't stay. Farley was going to sing at the banquet."

"Yeah, bummer," Piper said, nodding, yet inside she chortled at her luck. Farley sang like a boy whose balls hadn't dropped yet. She found it odd, and not in a good way.

"So what are you working on these days?" Rhonda asked. "I read the piece on Big Trees Logging. Fantastic. It's about time someone called that sucker out for what he's doing to the land under the guise of legitimate business. Hopefully, a follow-up piece is on the horizon."

"Actually, that was the third piece and I've run out of steam on that angle. I've been working on something different now." Something far more interesting. She smiled. "But don't worry. There's always something to uncover."

"You bet there is," Rhonda agreed vehemently. "With the amount of corruption out there, you could find things to write about for years. However, I'm sure your parents told you about the tree-sit that's coming up, right?"

They hadn't but she'd had to cut their conversation short during lunch, so that could account for her not knowing. "They might've mentioned it," Piper murmured vaguely, mildly troubled at the prospect. Tree-sits always made her nervous. If people were meant to sit in trees, God would've given them feathers. Her aversion to heights wasn't phobic but she certainly wouldn't volunteer to shimmy up a tree unless her life was in danger.

"Well, it's going to be great. We have a good group this time."

"Are they really that effective?" Piper wondered out loud, earning a quizzical look from Tia that made it seem as if Piper had just uttered something in a foreign language. "I mean, you go up in the tree, you manage to shut things down for a few days at most until Big Trees Logging manages to find a way to get you to come down." She'd never truly subscribed to the ecoterrorism bent of her parents' group but what could she do? They were her family.

"Of course they're effective, particularly when we have our very own reporter to capture everything, right?" Tia smiled but Piper could only return a wan imitation. She was beginning to feel more like a tool to further the personal agendas of her "family" than an actual journalist. Not for long, a voice whispered in her head, bolstering her flagging spirit. Soon, she'd have the biggest story this town had ever seen.

"Well, tree-sits aside, this town seems to have more than its share of corruption from philandering politicians to drug-trafficking," Piper said. "It's not hard to find people doing things they shouldn't, it's finding people who will go on record with their proof."

Tia and Rhonda agreed, but Piper could see their interest level had slipped. The baby made some kind of gurgle—or a burp—and they both dissolved into cooing, doting mommies with a one-track mind, effectively forgetting the grown-up talk in the blink of an eye.

Somewhat relieved, Piper went to search for her

parents, who had slipped away to mingle before the blessing ceremony.

She found them in a cool, shaded spot, enjoying fresh lemonade.

"I can't wait to have grandkids," her father said, surprising her.

"Well, you're going to wait a long time," she quipped, shuddering at the thought of being a parent. "My biological clock is set to snooze, so don't start picturing little heathens just yet."

Her father nodded but he was plainly disappointed. "Of course, sweetheart. I was just saying…looks like a cool gig."

"Yeah, I'm sure it is." For someone else. "But I'm nowhere near ready for that kind of commitment. Besides, I can't be thinking about kids when I'm chasing after big stories."

Her mother agreed, nodding resolutely. "That's right, Piper. Keep your eye on the prize."

Yep. Although she didn't think she and her mother were on the same page as far as the prize went. However, that was a fight for a different day. "I think I need some lemonade, too," she announced, but as she turned she found herself face-to-face with Farley. "Oh! I'm sorry, I nearly ran you over," she said, trying hard not to let her lip curl in distaste. Why her parents thought he was a good catch she'd never understand.

If Piper had one word to describe Farley Deegan it would be *lanky*. In fact, he reminded her of Charlie Yertz, and that wasn't a compliment in her mind.

Farley was at least six feet tall and probably weighed

one hundred and thirty pounds soaking wet. He always seemed to slink when he walked and when he touched her, she was overwhelmed by the urge to wash. He wasn't that bad, really. In fact, at one time she'd been briefly charmed by his gentle manner and passive nature, but as she'd matured, she found him…annoying.

And the fact that he was clearly eyeing her as the most suitable candidate to bear his progeny made her want to run, screaming, the other way.

The idea of Farley's penis… Ugh. It was too much to even fathom.

The awful part? She'd already seen it because, as Owen so mockingly put out there, a community of nudists had raised her.

And Farley had gleefully chucked his clothes whenever possible.

At the thought, she tugged her mom's shirt hem and leaned over to whisper, "The blessing will be performed fully clothed, yes?" When Coral nodded, she didn't hide her relief.

Farley, on the other hand, was quick to show his disappointment. "That's a shame. It seems highly appropriate to be nude as the day we are born when asking for bounty from the earth."

"Yes, well, it's a little on the nippy side and we wouldn't want anyone to shrivel up unnecessarily," she said, unable to hold her tongue. She received a look from her mother for her uncustomary sharpness and she exhaled loudly. "I'm getting lemonade."

"I'll go with you," Farley announced, making Piper want to groan, but what could she say? She forced a tight smile and started walking briskly in the hopes that it might curtail conversation. No such luck. Farley loped alongside her with ease and started yammering. "You look great, Piper. You blossom more and more into a beautiful woman each time I see you."

"Thanks, Farley," she said, and simply to be polite, added, "And you seem to get taller each time I see you." And more annoying.

"When I see you, it's nearly impossible not to remember what good times we've had together." She cringed inside. If he had the gall to bring up the time they... "You know what I particularly enjoy remembering?" Oh God. He's going to do it. She walked a little faster. He slipped his hand into hers, causing her to startle and jump a little. He took advantage in her loss of momentum and pulled her close even as she resisted. "Your lips were like drops of summer rain dancing on mine. It was like...heaven."

Her cheeks fired with intense heat and she tugged her hand out of his grasp. She took a quick glance around to make sure they were relatively on their own then glared at Farley, who was watching her with confusion at her obvious rejection. "Listen, Farley, I don't feel that way about you. Once, when I was a teenager, I thought you were *mildly* cute. But I've grown up and we don't suit. Please stop trying to make something out of nothing."

"We had a connection," he persisted, his brown eyes going melty and gooey again. He grasped her hand and put it to his heart. "I felt it here. I know you did, too."

"Stop it," she snapped, jerking her hand away. "You're embarrassing yourself. Go find a connection with someone else. I'm not attracted to you in that way and I don't relish hurting your feelings but you have to take a hint. It's not going to happen with you and me."

His mouth hardened. "We *do* suit. In time, you will see that. But I'm patient. I'll wait."

She groaned. "What's it going to take? Trust me, if you wait, you'll wait your life away, because I'm not interested. I've changed and you deserve someone who will appreciate your particular beliefs and way of life." She was trying to be nice but he just wasn't getting it. She didn't want to pull her ace because it was also an H-bomb but she didn't see that she had a choice. "Farley, I stopped being a vegetarian years ago. I'm a…meat eater."

His eyes widened at her admission, which was exactly what she was going for. She didn't like to think of herself as cruel but she did register the smidge of enjoyment she gained from his look of horror. "Meat? How could you?" he asked, pained.

She shrugged. "What can I say? I like a juicy steak."

He shuddered in revulsion and she nearly crowed. "See? We don't suit. Stop wasting your time on me and find someone who likes tofu."

Piper thought she'd won but then the look on Farley's face made her uneasy. He had the look of a man on a mission, like he was going to make it his job to bring her back to the fold. Oh, Lord, please not that. He clasped her hands in earnest and she wanted to stomp her feet in frustration.

"Piper, you've just lost your way. You can come back to us. I'll help you, my love. You just need to remember that you're eating a living being and think of the terror that animal must've felt at its last moment before slaughter. I know you're not capable of that kind of cruelty."

Ugh. She pulled away. "Farley…leave me alone."

She was thankful when he stayed behind.

CHAPTER FIVE

PIPER MANAGED TO AVOID Farley for the rest of the day, a small fact she was immensely grateful for, but there was no escaping her thoughts.

She couldn't blame Farley entirely for his misplaced affections. At one time, she had thought Farley was cute enough, but really, thirteen-year-old girls have no true appreciation for what makes for an attractive male and that fact shouldn't be held against her for the rest of her life.

It was safe to say she'd changed in more ways than just her penchant for meat. During the blessing, her thoughts had wandered to Owen and it was a full minute before she realized the route and quickly redirected.

Her gaze drifted covertly over the crowd, taking in the people she'd known her whole life, and while she loved them to pieces, there was the distinct feeling she sat apart from them. At one time she'd felt completely at home eating tofu and sunbathing nude. Now, she didn't know if that was her path.

Her father caught the unhappy sigh that escaped before she could stop it.

"What's wrong, peach pit?" he asked.

"I'm just preoccupied," she answered, which was

only slightly untruthful. "I'm sorry I'm not great company today."

He pressed a kiss to her forehead. "Pah. You're always good company. And you know, don't worry about that stuff I was saying about grandkids. I'm plenty young enough to wait a while longer. Just not too long," he teased, eliciting a rueful smile on her part.

"No promises, but I won't rule it out. How's that?"

"Sounds like a good compromise."

"Jasper…I was wondering…the other day I got the impression that you and Coral knew more about the Red Meadows incident than you wanted to let on. What was I picking up on?"

He frowned and pulled away. "Nothing. Why?"

An odd, uncomfortable tingle buzzed the back of her skull. She'd never known her parents to lie to her, about anything. Yet, she couldn't stop the nagging certainty that her father was lying to her. "Dad?"

She only used the traditional name when she wanted to get their attention. It worked. Jasper shook his head, faint agitation in the movement. "Honey, why are you so curious about the Red Meadows stuff? It's a terrible shame on the town of Dayton. We all would just like to forget about it."

"I imagine it's hard for Owen Garrett to forget," she murmured, glancing up to meet her father's troubled gaze.

"We all have crosses to bear," he said simply.

"Yeah, but some are heavier for others, wouldn't you say?"

He shrugged. "That's the way it goes."

"Why should a son bear the sins of the father?"

Speculation glittered in Jasper's eyes. "Where is this coming from? This sudden need to know all about Red Meadow? It happened when you were just a baby. It's ancient history by now and best left there."

"I don't know about that."

"Why?"

"Well, I've been doing a little digging and—"

"Stop."

She stared. "What? Why?"

"Because nothing good will come from dredging up that mess. There were too many people who were hurt, ashamed and broken after that incident. I don't want you anywhere near it."

"I don't understand—"

"Just do as I ask," he demanded sharply, startling her. He collected himself to add more gently. "Please."

All her life, she'd known her father as the kindest man on the planet. Yet, with the topic of Red Meadows between them, he seemed to harden. She didn't know what to make of this version of her father. She glanced at her mother, who was chatting with another community member, and wondered what hid behind the laughter of the two people Piper trusted the most.

The thought scared her as much as the knowledge that she wouldn't stop until she found out.

OWEN'S CELL PHONE BUZZED on his desk, set in motion by the vibration and he caught it before it danced right off the desk. He frowned when he saw it was Gretchen.

"What's up, Gretch?" he asked, noting the late hour.

But instead of Gretchen, he heard the frightened quiver of seven-year-old Quinn on the other line. "O-wen," she said in a tight whisper. "Can you come get me? I'm scared."

He stood and grabbed his keys. "Sure, honey. Where's your mama?" he asked, keeping his voice calm even when a bad feeling had started to crawl down his spine. "Everything okay?"

"Nooo," she wailed, letting loose with a stream of babbling that he couldn't hope to piece together until she stemmed the tears.

"Hold on, honey, I can't understand you when you're crying. Tell me what's going on. Where's your mama?" he asked again.

She sniffed back the tears and answered in a watery voice. "He took her."

"He who?"

"Danny. And he was real mad. They were yelling and mama was crying," she said, lowering her voice as if she were afraid that Danny might hear her. "And he hit her in her tummy. Mama was hurt real bad I think. And I'm s-scared that he's going to come back and get me, too. Please hurry, Owen."

"You got it, sweetheart. But I want you to do something for me until I get there, okay?"

"Uh-huh," she agreed, listening.

"I want you to walk over to Mr. Peters's house and wait for me there, okay?"

"But Mama said not to leave the house when she's gone," Quinn said, worried.

"That's a very good rule and I'll tell your mama that I said it was okay just this once."

"Okay," Quinn said, her tone solemn and trusting. She sniffed again. "Do you think Mama is going to be all right?"

"I hope so, sweetheart. Now, hang up and walk to Mr. Peters's right now. I'm leaving the office and I'll be there in fifteen minutes."

Quinn hung up and he pictured her running through the dark to the elderly neighbor's house, a man Owen knew would keep her safe until he got there. As he ran to his truck, he dialed 9-1-1 and quickly told the dispatcher the situation.

His mind raced with the bare bits of information Quinn had given him but he tried not to let his imagination paint the worst picture possible. It wasn't as though a seven-year-old was the best source of information but there was an ominous feeling at the base of his skull that he couldn't shake.

A punch to the gut when a woman was in her third trimester... He didn't know much about babies but he had a bad feeling that it spelled tragedy.

Damn it, Gretchen, I told you he was bad news.

IN A LIGHT DOZE AFTER SLUGGING down a half-pint of creamy mint-chocolate-chip ice cream, Piper nearly jumped at the shrill beep of her portable scanner as EMS crews rolled out on a call. She blinked and rubbed the sleep from her eyes to focus on the time. Geesh, nearly eleven o'clock at night. She listened to the call, contemplating just following up in the morning and dragging herself to bed, until she heard "possible kid-napping, scene unsecure" and suddenly all remnants of sleep evaporated. She hopped from the sofa and ran to her bedroom to tug on her jeans and sweatshirt. Within minutes, she was on her cell phone to dispatch getting the location of the incident and then she was in her car, barreling toward what she hoped was something big.

She pulled up to a residence flanked by deep forest growth in a neighborhood sparsely populated by older homes typically used as rentals. She recognized the address for a few disturbance calls she'd read in the police log, but nothing major. She didn't normally chase after ambulances on a domestic-violence arrest unless it sounded particularly violent.

She exited her car and was two steps toward the incident commander when a familiar voice turned her around.

"Sniffing after blood?"

She stared at Owen, momentarily thrown off track by his presence at the scene. "What are you doing here?" she asked.

"None of your business."

Her mouth tightened but she didn't have time to play games or trade witty banter. "Fine. Suit yourself. If you're a witness to whatever went down here, I'll just find out myself when I read the report."

In the pale moonlight, the planes of his face seemed to harden and he looked ready to hurl a litany of curse words her way but as she tried to leave, he stopped her again.

"Listen, I need a favor," he bit out, and she turned

slowly, not quite sure she'd heard him correctly. Owen needed a favor from her? How deliciously fortuitous.

"What kind of favor?" she asked, more curious than anything else. "Nothing illegal I hope."

"Don't print this story," he said.

"I don't even know what the story is yet. Why don't you tell me?"

He looked away, plainly wrestling with his desire to tell her to go screw herself and his need to play nice to gain a favor. Finally, he said in a low voice, "Okay. I don't know what's going on but my office manager seems to be missing. Her daughter—"

"The one in Mrs. Hamby's class?"

"Yeah," he nodded. "She called me and said her mama's boyfriend kicked her around a bit and then they took off."

Ouch. Her demeanor softened when she imagined how scared the kid must've been to witness that kind of abuse, only to be left by herself in the middle of the night. Tragic. But a helluva story. And he wanted her to walk away? Impossible. "I have a job to do...I can't just look the other way," she said with a shrug.

"It must be nice to live in a world where nothing bad ever happens and you've never had to make a difficult choice in your life."

Stung, she pulled back. "You don't know my life, so I don't see how you have the right to judge."

"I know if you had an ounce of compassion gained from walking a mile in someone else's shoes, you'd honor my request. There's a scared little girl sitting in my truck, terrified that her mama is hurt or dead. All

I'm asking is that you don't make it worse for her by splashing her tragedy all over the front page of the local rag."

"It's not a rag. We've won several CNPA awards for coverage in our category," she said stiffly, chafing silently at his angry rebuke. So she hadn't suffered through an abominable childhood; it didn't mean she couldn't feel compassion. She chewed her lip, caught between the urge to get all the gritty details and forcing herself to walk away and proving him wrong about her. He didn't realize what he was asking of her. Had Pulitzer-prize-winning *New York Times* investigative journalist David Barstow ever been asked to look the other way while a top story went untold? She shuddered under the weight of her indecision. She ought to tell him *tough cookies* but she couldn't quite get the words to form. As much as she hated to admit it, she squirmed at the thought that he might actually despise her, which if he didn't already he certainly would if she ran with this story. "It's not really my choice," she hedged, still searching for which way to turn. "I mean, the editor makes the determination of what will run or not…"

"Cut the crap. I know if you write this story, it'll be splashed all over."

"Yeah, and if I don't splash it first, I'll get scooped," she muttered, hating the very idea. Top reporters didn't allow themselves to get scooped. They were the ones who did the scooping and left everyone else panting after their sources. She glowered. "So what do I get if I allow this favor? And it's a biggie, so don't try and say something lame like your eternal gratitude."

"I wouldn't dream of assuming you would care about my gratitude," he remarked dourly. "What do you want? And how do I know you'll keep your word?"

"You'll just have to trust me, I guess."

"Fantastic." He glanced back at the truck, where the little girl was watching the scene with wide eyes. Man, that would make a compelling picture. The headline could read Waiting for Mommy or Mommy Come Home. On autopilot, she started to reach for her camera until Owen made a sound in his throat that resembled a growl. *A growl? Are you kidding me?* It was ridiculous—and sexy. "Name your price and keep your trigger finger off that camera," he instructed in a low voice.

She shivered but tried to put on a brave face, even scowling a bit. "Don't make it sound so sordid. I'm not after your money or anything like that." What did she want? Oh, that was easy, she realized with dizzying speed as the words tumbled out. "I want an interview— with you."

AH, HELL. HE WANTED TO WALK away but the woman looked determined, and she wouldn't settle for anything less than a little face time. It wouldn't be so bad, he reasoned to himself, quickly weighing the pros and cons. She probably wanted to grill him about one of the projects she and her parents were opposing. "A half hour."

"As long as it takes," she countered.

He shook his head. "No open-ended deals. One hour."

"Two."

"Woman, what on earth could you possibly want to talk about for two damn hours?" he said, annoyance getting the better of him. "An hour and a half. Final offer. Take it or leave it. I gotta get Quinn out of here. I've wasted enough time as it is."

"Deal." She smiled. "And I get to pick the topic. And you have to cooperate."

She drove a hard bargain. He didn't really have a choice. He'd do anything to keep this story as quiet as possible. "Fine. But I better not hear one peep about this to anyone. You got me?"

"Loud and clear."

"Good. Now, get the hell out of here."

She frowned and opened her mouth to protest but the dark look he sent her snapped it shut pretty quick. One thing was for sure, she wasn't dumb. He figured that wasn't a point in his favor. Whatever she was after, she was likely to get. He wondered if she approached relationships the same way. Heaven help the man caught in her crosshairs. He wouldn't stand a chance.

He climbed into the truck and instructed Quinn to buckle up.

"Is Miss Sunday going to help find my mom?" Quinn asked, surprising him when she remembered the reporter's name from class a few days ago.

"I doubt it, honey," he answered truthfully, that heavy weight of worry returning to his chest. "But the police sure will. They've got everyone looking for her. She'll turn up. In the meantime, you get to stay with me. You think that's all right?"

Quinn's eyes watered. "I want my mama."

"I know you do. And as soon as we can we'll get things figured out. But until then, you're stuck with me, okay?"

"Okay," she answered, her bottom lip quivering so much it nearly did him in. "Thanks, Owen, for coming to get me."

"You bet, sweetheart. You can always count on me."

She nodded and swallowed what was probably a lump of sadness and fear and he was struck by her bravery. This kid was something else.

But he had a bad feeling about Gretchen.

He hoped to God he was wrong.

CHAPTER SIX

PIPER'S MIND WHIRRED faster than a CD-ROM drive as one single thought ran through her head like a ticker-tape parade: she'd finally wrangled an interview with the elusive and extremely private Owen Garrett. She'd overlook the part where she'd used extortion to get it.

By the time she reached her house, she already had a list of questions zooming through her head. Piper grabbed a notepad—she always had extras lying around for when her brain kicked in and couldn't wait—and jotted down her erratic and fevered thoughts.

How much did he remember from that day, she wondered. He'd been a kid. But sometimes a traumatic event seared itself into a person's brain, clarifying and crystallizing the event until it was impossible to forget. She figured watching your father get gunned down in a hail of bullets was enough to traumatize an adult, let alone an eleven-year-old boy.

She tried to imagine Owen as a kid, a serious, tow-headed child with solemn eyes and a mischievous glint that flashed now and then when he thought no one would notice, and her mouth flirted with a smile. He'd probably been a damn cute little kid. Figures, because he'd grown into a pretty good-looking adult.

And why didn't such an eligible bachelor have a missus attached to him? There had to be something wrong with him, possibly something deep and dark and maybe, perverted.

She toyed with the idea. Owen a pervert? She supposed it was possible. But even as she bandied the idea about, testing the theory, she discarded it with distaste. No. He may be a lot of things but she didn't get the pervie vibe from him.

No, she got a distinctly different vibe from him and it made her shudder and made her think of topics that were inappropriate—and highly unlikely—given their current relationship.

She wondered what he looked like without a shirt. He had the build of a man accustomed to hard work. Big, strong hands, roughened from handling axes, saws and power tools. She moistened her lips and noted her heart rate had kicked up a bit. Oh, goody. Attraction. She recognized it for what it was. She grew up with two professors of anthropology. Dissecting human emotion was something they used to do over dinner. So why did she feel warm and fuzzy and just a bit uncomfortable?

Because she was on the threshold of something big, she reasoned. Finally, she was going to sit down and pick his brain.

And she might just be able to find the clue she needed to bust the case wide-open like never before.

And yes, grandiose music played in the theater of her mind as she envisioned that particular dream.

She laughed, her mood lightened considerably, and she almost skipped to bed, eager for the morning.

IF PIPER DRIFTED TO SLEEP with a smile, Owen did the exact opposite.

Now he had two problems. By agreeing to talk with Piper, he was opening himself to a whole new world of grief. There was no telling as to her true agenda. She played a good game about hearing his side of things but he didn't trust the way her eyes had glittered with barely contained excitement when he'd agreed. It'd put him on edge, worse than he already was. And if that weren't bad enough, the situation with Gretchen had him in knots.

The cops still hadn't located that worthless SOB, which meant Gretchen was still unaccounted for. He had a scared little girl camped out on his couch and there was nothing he could offer her for comfort aside from a cup of warm milk. Hell, he didn't even have any chocolate powder he could mix in. His house wasn't made for guests. It was a space where he washed his clothes, sometimes ate and, most times, crashed when he was too tired to keep his eyes open a minute longer.

He scrubbed his hand over his face, feeling each and every year of his life weighing down on him. That sick feeling in his stomach intensified when he thought of how much worse the situation could have been if Quinn had been taken, too.

That sick bastard. Who kicks a pregnant woman in the stomach, much less the woman carrying your child? He couldn't even fathom. In the eyes of the law, his father was scum, not worth the price of the bullet that ended his life, but to him, he'd been a fabulous father and one of the things he'd always taught Owen was to treat women kindly.

"Son, you always got to watch out for the welfare of your woman. She's the weaker sex and the Bible tells us we have to protect them," his father had said one day when he'd gotten his tail chewed for throwing a rock in the general direction of an obnoxious little girl named Patty living on the compound with them.

"Even colored girls?" he'd asked, wiping at his nose and glowering in Patty's direction because she'd started the fight and then run to her daddy when he'd fought back.

His father, leader of the Aryan Coalition, had straightened, glanced around before answering in a lowered voice so only Owen could hear. "Even colored girls, son. A man isn't a man the minute he hits a woman. You got that?"

"Yessir," he'd answered glumly, still angry but not about to go against his father. "Don't seem fair that she started it, though," he'd added, glancing up at his dad.

Ty Garrett had smiled. "Never is, son. It never is. Don't change a thing."

Owen roused himself from the memory. It was hard to reconcile that image of his father with the one everyone else harbored. He shook off his melancholy. No sense in crying over the past. Not right now, anyway. He had bigger problems.

"Gretchen…" he muttered to himself, checking one last time on Quinn, who was fast asleep. "If you manage to make it through the night, you'd better promise me you'll break up with this bastard."

He turned off the lights and resigned himself to a restless night.

OWEN GOT THE CALL AT 3:00 A.M. that Gretchen had been found alongside the road, bruised and bloody, unconscious from a vicious blow to the head.

But she was alive.

He listened as the police officer gave him as much information as he knew, which wasn't a lot aside from the fact that she'd been beaten and left for dead like roadkill.

"Danny Mathers did this," he said in a low tone so as not to wake Quinn.

"We'll find him," the officer assured him. "You can see her tomorrow if the doctor thinks she can have visitors. Is her daughter all right with you for a few days?"

He glanced over at Quinn, a small bundle curled on his lumpy sofa, and he nodded. "Yeah. No problem."

"Good. If you change your mind, we can call social services but since you're her emergency contact, we figured the girl was safe with you for the time being."

"What about the baby?" he asked, his throat tight, almost afraid to know.

There was a long pause and then the officer said, "It doesn't look good." He rattled off a case number for reference in case Owen needed it later and hung up.

Returning to his bedroom, he fell back into bed and wondered how the hell he was going to run a business without Gretchen at the office and with Quinn at his heels.

Ah, hell, he thought just as his eyes fluttered shut.

That reporter was coming tomorrow.

Shit. The day had just officially gone from bad to worse.

PIPER TOOK GREAT CARE in choosing her wardrobe that morning. She'd bounced from bed five minutes before the alarm went off, the spring in her step mirroring her excitement, and after enjoying a hearty breakfast of eggs and bacon—God, how she loved bacon—she showered and donned her most professional attire. She wanted her outfit to reflect her drive and ambition and she wanted to appear confident and smart, a sharp-witted shark accustomed to swimming in a pool filled with other maneaters. Except, it took her five outfits to achieve that look and even as she stood before the mirror, she wasn't sure if another change was in order.

She twisted to stare at her backside, fretting that the powder-blue pencil skirt wasn't aggressive enough of a color *and* it made her butt look enormous. But it had a matching jacket, she lamented to herself even as she prepared to shrug out of it. Black, she thought, seizing her favorite slacks and blazer. Too austere? She didn't want to seem as if she were going to a funeral. Piper blew hair from her eyes and stared at herself, standing in matching pink bra and panties. Well, at least her undergarments were sharp.

Finally, she was dressed—hopefully for success—and ready to leave. She grabbed her extra notebook and her camera and left for Big Trees Logging administrative offices.

But when she arrived, she was disappointed by Owen's absence. The office was locked up tight and there was no one around to even question. She frowned and muttered something that would make a sailor proud and contemplated her next move. A deal was a deal, she groused, glancing around the deserted office. Well, if he wasn't going to meet her, she'd meet him. She just happened to know his home address. The internet was a beautiful thing, particularly when one knew what to look for. She smiled and climbed back into her car. Owen was going to learn that she didn't give up easily.

OWEN HAD JUST CLOSED HIS front door, harried and worried that Quinn was going to be late to school, when he turned and found Piper striding down his front walk, a determined expression on her face.

"Did you forget something?" she queried, seeming to miss the sack lunch clutched in his hand and the little girl trailing behind him as they made their way to his truck.

"I didn't forget. Just a little busy at the moment," he said curtly, adding over his shoulder. "No need to chase me down like the damn paparazzi."

She scowled, obviously taking offense at the term, but she also had the grace to notice Quinn. Her frown eased and something akin to guilt flushed her face. "I didn't know you'd still have…um…"

"Her name is Quinn," he answered, reaching down

to lift the girl into the truck. "And we're late for school. We'll have to table this until later."

"Later when?" she asked, concerned. "I'm ready now."

"Well, I'm not." The engine of his diesel truck rumbled to life and she scrunched her nose at the sound. He glanced at her ride—a hybrid of some sort—and he resisted the urge to smirk. She probably didn't think too highly of his truck. "Later."

"No, wait," she exclaimed, running after the vehicle as he slowly pulled away. "When? I need a date and time. A commitment! Owen! I swear to God I'll run that story with all the gory details if you don't stop this instant and talk to me instead of running off with some lame excuse."

The truck growled to a stop and idled loudly. Owen's brows pulled together in a harsh line. "We had a deal," he reminded her.

How was it that he got more handsome when he looked ready to tear someone's head off? Mainly hers as of late? She pushed that annoying thought aside and took a step his way, going so far as to stand on the running board and to get right into his face. "That's right. We did. So honor it."

A tense moment passed between them and she half wondered if she hadn't pushed too far and she was a heartbeat away from getting tossed as he peeled away. Just when she thought she might have to back down, he jerked his head toward the passenger seat and instructed her to "Get in or get off."

She jumped down and scrambled to the passenger

side and climbed in beside Quinn with a sense of triumph.

"Thank you. I—" she started amiably until Owen cut her off by switching the radio on and drowning her out with a blast of country music.

By way of explanation, he said, "Interview's not yet," and then, tucking his arm out the window, he tuned her out as effectively as if he'd left her standing alongside the road.

Oh, and she hated country music. Was it possible that he knew that? Quite possible and he was loving the advantage.

So much for swimming with sharks.

Right about now she felt like a guppy—and it had nothing to do with her outfit.

CHAPTER SEVEN

OWEN RETURNED TO HIS truck after escorting Quinn safely to her classroom. He didn't feel comfortable only dropping her off when things were so touch and go with that asshole Danny still at-large. He had no idea whether Danny might try and come after Quinn but Owen wasn't taking any chances.

Piper sat primly in his truck, back straight and hands clasped in her lap as if she were unsure of how to relax. She always looked so perfectly put together. That was one thing he noticed about her. Every detail appeared painstakingly thought out and planned, which to him seemed contradictory to the image he had of her hedonistic childhood. When she wasn't badgering him, she was a little on the cute side. *Snap out of it,* he said to himself when he realized where his thoughts were headed. It'd been a long while since he'd dated anyone serious and, because he didn't have the time—or the inclination—for casual dating, there'd been a drought of sexual activity in his bedroom.

And his hormones had picked a cherry of a time to remind him of that fact.

He climbed into his truck and tried not to look at her.

"So are you ready now?" she asked.

He turned to her, forgetting his seconds-earlier decree to stay focused on the road rather than her for the time being. "You're something else, you know that?" he said, his tone hard. "Do you ever think of anyone other than yourself? Quinn is going through something you can't even imagine yet all you can focus on is your story. You haven't even asked if Gretchen has been found."

She drew back imperceptibly and her eyelashes fluttered as if she were trying to find an acceptable comeback yet found herself struggling. She moistened her lips and the slight motion drew his reluctant attention to the soft fullness of her pink lips. Totally clear of make-up of any kind, she had a dewy freshness about her that made his mind wander into dark corners before he realized where he was going.

"I'm just doing my job and, since you'd already removed the possibility of doing the story on Gretchen, I had moved on," she said finally, her chin jutting out, but her eyes held a wounded softness that he found incredibly intriguing. Sweet and charming yet hiding a dagger behind her back. That was Piper Sunday. He needed to stay reminded of that fact before he found himself stuck and bleeding. She glanced over at him through a thick curtain of lashes, adding stiffly, "I'm assuming she's been found. I haven't heard any chatter on the scanner that would support the fact that they were still searching for her." When he grunted an affirmative, she nodded and tacked on, "I'm glad she's been found. How is she?"

"You don't need to patronize me. I know you don't care, and your fake concern is insulting."

She glared but shifted in her seat as if his words had illuminated an uncomfortable truth. "Of course I care. Are you going to tell me or do I have to find out through the grapevine?"

He could only imagine the tangled network that comprised the local grapevine and he didn't want to take the chance of Piper getting hold of bad information, so he told her what he knew. "She's pretty banged up. The guy who did this left her alongside the road to die. I'm not even sure if the baby made it."

"I didn't know she was pregnant," she murmured, peering at him oddly. "Is it...your baby?" she ventured hesitantly.

At that, he nearly did a double take. His kid? "She's my office manager," he said in a tone that communicated what he thought about dating employees.

"It's not against the law," she said, but the way her shoulders relaxed told him she'd been tense over the possibility he'd been shacking up with Gretchen.

"That's not how I operate," he grumbled, annoyed at how a minute thrill chased the knowledge she'd been apprehensive over his dating choices. He risked a short glance her way. "I draw the line at employees and cousins."

That last part was meant as a joke and he was relieved to see her crack a reluctant smile.

"So why is her daughter with you?" she asked. "I assumed because you were there for her at school that maybe you and her mom were a couple."

"I was just helping Gretchen out. She's a good woman with questionable taste in men. And Quinn's a great kid."

A slow smile lifted her mouth but she appeared perplexed by the information. Someone must've been filling her ear with bad press when it came to him, for she seemed suddenly adrift. "That's very nice of you," she finally said.

"Yeah, sometimes I take a break from ruining the environment to be kind to someone else," he quipped, turning to face her. "Listen, we got off on a bad foot. We don't have to be enemies. I'm prepared to let bygones be bygones if we can start fresh."

"And what does that entail?" she asked.

"What do you mean?"

"I mean, I still have a job to do. Are you still willing to do the interview?"

"Of course," he stated.

"Okay. Then I'm willing to accept those terms," she answered with an efficient nod that went as a perfect accessory to her flawless look. He wondered if she let herself go wild in the bedroom. And then because his mind had already sparked the question, his imagination provided the imagery. His groin tightened as he saw in his mind's eye a bed-tousled Piper in a sea of tangled sheets with a wicked, come-get-me-bad-boy smile. Hell, that's not helpful at all, he chastised himself. "Shall we head to your office to get started?" she asked, her eyes bright and cheery with expectation.

But he didn't want to be stuck indoors. It was part of the reason he'd gone into forestry. He hated being rooted to a desk for eight hours. He needed fresh air and a distraction. He started the truck and pulled onto the highway.

"Speaking of jobs, I have one, too. You want your interview? You have to tag along with me to the job site."

"And where's that?" she asked, trying to appear unconcerned by his announcement.

He grinned and pulled onto the highway. "Up on the mountain. Where else?"

PIPER'S GAZE DROPPED to her pretty heels, and she swallowed a moan at how ruined her new shoes would be after tromping after Owen in the Santa Cruz mountains. "Are you sure the office wouldn't be more appropriate for an interview?" she asked, hoping to appeal to some sense of logic but to no avail. In fact, he seemed quite amused by the idea of her trailing after him dressed as she was in a tight silk skirt and ultra-feminine white chiffon blouse with fluttery georgette sleeves.

"You want the real deal, you got it," he said, that damnable grin returning so that he looked rakish and delicious at the same time.

She huffed a silent breath and counted to ten. He was trying to get her to back out, to get her to relinquish their deal without losing face. Well, he didn't know who he was dealing with. Piper had once won a staring contest even when a bug had landed on her nose. She wasn't one to give up, no matter the obstacle. She liked to consider it one of her more impressive traits that would surely lead to success later down the road.

Her mom liked to tell her she might need therapy to overcome some of her "obsessive tendencies."

"What about Gretchen?" she asked. "What if she needs you? Shouldn't you be close by?"

"Already called the doc early this morning. No visitors who aren't family until she's out of ICU. Besides, I need to keep busy," he answered. "And the job doesn't run itself. Gretchen wouldn't want me crying at my desk, wringing my hands. She'd tell me to get my ass out there and make the money that helps pay her salary. That's just the kind of woman she is."

"Sounds like she's...quite the woman."

"She is."

Piper heard the pride in his voice and she felt a tiny pinch of jealousy. It wasn't that she didn't have a great support system—her parents were her biggest fans—but for a small, infinitesimal moment she wanted to hear him say something about her with that tone. And that wasn't going to happen. Not now, not ever, because even though he talked a good game about making nice, after she wrote the piece on his father and the Red Meadows incident, he likely wouldn't want to speak to her again.

She worried her bottom lip, unsure why that bothered her. You had to break a few eggs to make an omelet, she reminded herself. To get to the top, you had to step on a few heads. She was sure there were plenty of clichés she could lean on to support her belief but even as she repeated them in her head like a mantra, it only served to intensify the lonely feeling filling her chest.

Focus. She needed *F.O.C.U.S.* Piper cleared her

throat and brought out her notepad. "I can take notes while we drive," she announced brightly. "Like background stuff."

"Background? What do you mean?" he asked, wary.

"Well, like a bio. Stuff you'd put in a eulogy."

"That's morbid."

"True, but it serves an excellent purpose. It's like the highlight reel of your life. A synopsis, if you will."

"What's on your highlight reel?" he asked, throwing it back to her.

She waved away his question with an airy chuckle. "That's easy and stuff you already know. Raised on a hippie nudist commune by two anthropology professors. Boring. End of story."

"In that one sentence alone I have a million questions."

She smiled. "Ah, too bad you're not the one doing the writing. Now, back to you."

"All right. Ask your questions."

"Start with your childhood," she suggested casually, though her palms had begun to shake with her excitement. It was one thing to read about something but to have someone who went through it personally is completely different.

Owen focused on the road, his mouth losing the sensual softness she'd been trying really hard to ignore and she knew he was struggling with what to share and what to leave out. She could either use the direct approach and flat-out bring up the Red Meadows incident or she could take the circuitous route. She opted for the latter. He needed loosening up.

"How about we start with Big Trees Logging. How did you end up the owner?"

He visibly relaxed once she pulled the focus from his childhood to his livelihood. "That's easy. An opportunity came up to purchase the company from the previous owner, who had made some bad investments and was nearing bankruptcy. I had a background in forestry and I'd always known I wanted to return to Dayton at some point."

"You were raised by your aunt, right?" she supplied, hoping to impress him that she knew some of the obscure details. But he surprised her when he shook his head.

"My aunt gave me over to the state, said I was too much of a handful for a single woman who'd never raised kids. A woman named Mary Jo Bell, or as we call her, Mama Jo, raised me. She's my true family. Along with my two brothers, Christian and Thomas. They're all still back east in West Virginia."

She digested this unexpected piece of information. He'd lost his father and then his only other family had abandoned him to the state foster care system. How awful. She imagined Owen, a sad, grief-stricken boy thrust among strangers. A low, melancholy ache thrummed an odd tune in her chest, something she didn't recognize or know how to process. "So you love this foster family?" she asked.

"Oh, yeah. I miss them a lot."

"So why do you stay in California?"

He crooked a grin. "My brothers ask that question all the time. I stay because I like it here."

An internal sensor went off and she instinctively knew he wasn't being entirely truthful. He stayed for more than the scenery. She wondered what it was and made a note to dig a little deeper later. "Must be hard, though," she surmised, holding her breath even as she tried to remain nonchalant. "Being without your family, I mean."

"Yeah. It doesn't get any easier. But a man's gotta make a living and that's what I do here."

"Plus, I imagine it's nice to return to your hometown…" she fished for more information, hoping he'd latch on to the bait.

But he didn't. He simply shrugged and then offered a noncommittal nod. "Yeah, it's nice."

Nice. What a perfectly *blah* word. And totally discordant with the vibe she was getting. Interesting.

"Married?" she threw out there to catch his reaction, and she wasn't disappointed.

"Not me," he answered without hesitation. In fact, he answered like a man who gave that particular hangman's noose a very wide berth.

"Afraid of commitment?" she guessed, dissecting his reaction with a clinical eye. Why else would someone like him be chronically unattached? Judging by the hungry looks he'd received by the mommies in Mrs. Hamby's class that day, he probably had to beat women off with a stick. "So you're more of a wham-bam-thank-you-ma'am and don't-let-the-door-hit-you-on-the-way-out kind of man?"

He scowled. "I don't really want to talk about my personal life," he said, which told her she'd hit a nerve. *Interesting.* She made a note of it as he continued. "I'll answer whatever questions you like about the logging industry and any current jobs, but as far as my dating history...I'd rather keep that private. I doubt your readers want to know about that crap anyway."

"I beg to differ," she disagreed, omitting the part where *she* was most interested in the information. "It makes you more of a person."

"More of a person?" he repeated. "What does that mean?"

"Oh, well, you know, it humanizes you. Instead of just the big, bad logger, you're the man who shops at the local market and loves to eat Chinese food. I did a story on the mayor once and you know what people remembered the most? The fact that he loves musical theater and used to dream of being on Broadway before his life took a different turn. See? Who knew the mayor could sing? Now, his voters know."

"Yeah, well, I'd prefer my personal business—particularly my dating habits—to remain private," he said, unwilling to budge on that score. She blew out a short breath and scratched out some notes. A pregnant pause rested between them as Piper tried to think of ways to get him to open up. An idea came to her and she snapped her notebook shut with an easy, inviting smile. "Okay, so tell me off the record, then."

CHAPTER EIGHT

OFF THE RECORD? HE shot her a wary look. "Do reporters ever actually do anything off the record? Or is that just something you say to get people to trust you?"

She shrugged. "I can't say what other reporters do. I can only say what I do. If I say it's off the record, I mean it."

"How about this…for every question I answer, you answer one in kind."

She frowned as if she didn't think that was a fair exchange but he was curious about what made Piper Sunday tick. She agreed with a slow nod but he could tell she wasn't quite sure if she should. He liked her uncertainty. It put them on a far more even keel and that was always a good thing during negotiations of any sort.

"So why do you want to know so much about me? I'm hardly interesting," she said.

"I guess I'll find out if that's true for myself."

She exhaled a long breath and shook her head as she smoothed her skirt and straightened the seat belt so it rested perfectly across her chest. "Fine. I'll go first," she volunteered. "What do you want to know?"

"Any brothers or sisters?" He figured he'd start off with the easy stuff.

"No. But before you start to think that I spent my childhood alone without playmates, rest assured, I was never alone being raised in a tight-knit community." She didn't hesitate when she said, "My turn. What happened to your mother?"

He spared her a short look. "My biological mom died in a car accident when I was about two years old."

"That's terrible. I'm sorry."

He didn't remember her, so the pain wasn't raw like when he lost his father. There were times, during private moments, when he wished his dad were still around for advice. Mama Jo had definitely filled the void left by his mother but there were some things he would've rather shared with his dad. His dad had been an ace when it came to offering counsel. He'd had a way about him that made people listen. The FBI had called him "dangerously charismatic." Owen pulled off the highway and onto a county road that would turn into a forest service access point. "You might want to hold on, it'll get bumpy in a minute," he advised, slowing as the paved county road gave way to hard-packed dirt. Out of his peripheral vision, he saw her clutch the handle on the passenger side while the other hand held her notebook.

"Where are we going exactly?" she asked as they jounced along the dirt road.

"A piece of private property along the lake. Owner sold us twenty acres for harvesting." Before she could interject, he added, "And yes, I have all the required clearances and permits. And no, there's no old-growth, so take a chill pill." He slid a sidewise glance her way. "Are you always so tightly wound?"

"Is that your question?" she said, returning the look.

He laughed. "Stickler for the rules, I see. Okay, no, that's not my question, because I think I already know the answer."

"I'm not uptight if that's what you're thinking," she retorted, but her cheeks had pinked an interesting shade.

"We'll see. Tell me what it's like to grow up on a commune."

She sighed as if the question annoyed her. He suspected she got asked that a lot. He could commiserate. His unique childhood often sparked curiosity, too. He was just as reluctant to share. "It was like anyone's living situation until I realized I was different. When I was little, it was bliss. I was never alone, we always had big barbecues and everyone brought something. We had a community garden where everyone got to share as long as they helped with the work. It was great. Then as I got older and started to realize that not everyone lived as we did, I started to wish we had a more traditional family structure. I mean, what kid doesn't know what cake tastes like until they're in the eighth grade? My parents never allowed processed sugar in the house and the only sweetener we used was natural honey raised from the bees on the farm. And then the first time I tried a hamburger I was in college."

"You were a vegetarian?"

"Yeah, my entire childhood. My parents still think I am," she added with a slightly guilty tone. "But I found I love meat and I don't like tofu. I despise it, actually, and I have to choke it down every time I visit my parents."

"Why don't you just tell them? You're an adult. I'm sure they'd respect your choice."

"No, they wouldn't. They'd lecture me on inhumane slaughtering techniques and constantly remind me that I'm eating something that once had a face. You have no idea how that can kill your appetite."

He couldn't imagine going without meat in his life. "That's rough," he acknowledged with a chuckle. "But I'm guessing there are worse secrets to have."

"Not in my family," she muttered darkly, before returning the focus to him. "Nice try with the whole deflection technique. Kid gloves are coming off, Owen Garrett. It's time for the hard questions."

Owen pulled off the road and grinned. "Then I'm lucky that we're here. You can wait in the truck or come with me, but you have to wear this if you step outside." He grabbed a spare hard hat from his backseat and handed it to her. She eyed it with dismay, probably imagining the havoc it would wreak on her hair, but when she sensed he wasn't going to relent on the topic, she placed it gingerly on her head. He smiled good-naturedly. "Excellent. Let's go. I'll show you what we're doing."

SNEAKY MAN, SHE THOUGHT, tripping after him, her heels sinking in the soft, springy grass floor as they trudged up the mountain toward the sound of saws buzzing and men shouting above the din. She'd ended up sharing more than him and the whole point had been to get him to talk. She'd have to be more on her game. He wasn't easily managed. She couldn't just smile prettily and get him to gush all his secrets. She didn't know why she thought it would be that easy. He wanted something for his information, as evidenced by his bargain. Within minutes, sweat trickled between the valley of her breasts and she was breathing heavily. "How much farther?" she asked, wobbling on her heels. "I didn't exactly wear the right hiking attire, as you can see."

"Not far," he assured her, holding out his hand as she nearly toppled over. She hesitated, but it seemed like good sense if she didn't want to fall on her tush for the sake of her pride. She accepted his hand and swallowed a gasp as a wild, arcing thrill chased her nerve endings and ignited her senses in a totally unfortunate way. She swallowed and avoided his gaze, afraid she might see that he knew she'd had some kind of reaction to his touch. She needn't have worried, though, he seemed focused on the climb and not on the fact that they were holding hands.

They reached the top of the ridge and Owen pointed, saying, "There's my crew. Right on schedule." He noted her heavy breathing and he lifted a brow at her. "You okay?"

"Fine," she wheezed, holding her side. Traversing the uneven terrain was far more of a workout than the mountain-hike simulation on her treadmill, but she wasn't about to admit that to Owen. "Like I said, I wasn't prepared to go hiking today. I would've been more properly dressed if I'd known." With that, she sent him a dark glower, clearly communicating that she knew he'd done this on purpose to put her off but he accepted her answer and, to her surprise, he started to explain what was going on. "You see over there, the timber fallers went through a few months ago and cut the trees that were marked by the forester; the skidder readies the timber for the helicopter, which is coming later this afternoon out of Oregon. That's some precision work. If you've never seen heli-logging, you're missing out. Did you know back in the day they used to haul the wood out using something called a steam donkey? I have an old black-and-white picture of one back at the office I could show you. Logging's come a long way since the days of clear cutting."

"Which was outlawed in the Santa Cruz mountains in '72," she murmured, coaxing a begrudging smile from Owen with her knowledge. She knew what he was doing, trying to feed her positive PR on the logging industry. What he didn't seem to realize was that she already knew how logging had changed and contrary to what he believed, she wasn't the enemy. Besides, she had her eye on a bigger story than logging practices in the Santa Cruz mountains. "That's all well and good but I'm not really here to talk about the logging industry," she said.

"You're not?" He frowned in surprise. "What are you here to talk about, then?"

She drew a deep breath, nervous excitement starting to build as she readied the speech she'd rehearsed earlier for this very moment. "Well, it seems—" she began, until his sudden motion halted her momentum.

"Hold on a sec," he said briefly, before grabbing the walkie-talkie she hadn't noticed hanging on his belt loop. "Yeah, I'm here on site, up on the ridge," he said to whoever was on the other end, likely his foreman. She couldn't very well interrupt him, so she simply listened unabashedly as he gave orders and direction, answering questions and putting out proverbial fires and a smidge of respect blossomed for the man. He knew his job the way a master craftsman instinctively knew how to create magic with his tools. In her head, she heard her parents' voices, ringing with distaste when his name or company was mentioned, and she couldn't help the frown.

"So how do you know so much about logging?" she asked when he'd ended his conversation, lured by curiosity that had nothing to do with the story she was working on and had everything to do with the growing kernel of unprofessional interest she felt.

"I used to be a timber faller. I've logged forests all over the United States. I also knew I wouldn't be able to fall trees for the rest of my life. Eventually, my body was going to give out, so I learned everything I could from the ground up."

Smart and in ridiculously good shape, she noted to herself. So why was he still single? Let's face it, in a small town, pickings could be frightfully slim and when there was a bachelor like Owen Garrett on the market, there was likely to be plenty of hungry single women chasing after him. Yet, she hadn't managed to unearth any old girlfriends she could question. Whoever he had dated in the past certainly wasn't around Dayton, because by all accounts, the man was married to his job with little time for anything else.

Owen returned his walkie-talkie to his belt loop and gestured for her to follow. "Where are we going now?" she asked, only just now able to breathe normally.

"Somewhere that's out of the fall zone and a little quieter."

That sounded promising, she thought, eagerly following after him. They emerged into a clearing with a tributary creek, swollen from the snow runoff, that fed its icy water to the lake. White two-eyed violets dotted the field with delicate starry false Solomon's seal peeking among the lush overgrowth.

"I found this spot while surveying the property for harvest last year," he said by way of explanation. "Nice, huh?"

It took her breath away. She smiled. "Very."

"Will this work for our little interview session?"

Oh, yes. On impulse, she slid her camera from her shoulder and snapped a few pictures. "I think this will do," she said, kicking off her heels with a groan as her protesting toes felt immediate relief from being freed. She settled on the soft meadow grass and tucked her feet demurely underneath her skirt before lifting the uncomfortable hard hat from her head and placing it beside her. She grinned at him and patted the ground beside her as she readied her notepad. "Shall we?"

OWEN TOOK THE SPOT OFFERED and then questioned his good judgment for bringing her along to his private spot. The drowsing warmth of the sun made him want to stretch out and catch a few Z's seeing as he didn't sleep worth a damn last night but he remained upright and instead grabbed a blade of grass to chew. "So what do you want to know?" he asked, noting for the first time the tiny freckles that danced across the bridge of her nose like fairy footprints. Well, he already knew she was cute, but he wanted to grumble to himself for noticing that small detail. No sense in belaboring the point. He glanced at his watch. "Better hurry. We only have an hour or so before I have to get back to town to pick up Quinn and check on Gretchen."

At the mention of Gretchen, Piper's expression sobered and she seemed to move quickly into reporter mode. Pen poised and ready, she moistened her lips before beginning, and the small inconsequential movement dried the spit in his mouth and caused him to ask, "Are you married or something? I mean, do you have a guy waiting for you somewhere?" She startled at his sudden change in direction from business to personal and he could tell it had rattled her, probably more than she would've been comfortable with him knowing. That was okay, he was more ridiculously drawn to the chocolate sheen of her hair than appropriately on guard from her questioning and that made *him* uncomfortable. However, he sensed a chink in her armor and he wasn't above taking advantage of the unexpected benefit.

"Why?" she asked.

He lifted a shoulder in a lazy shrug, enjoying throwing a curveball her way just to see how she handled it.

"You're the kind of woman who always has someone on the hook."

She stiffened. "What's that supposed to mean?"

"Come on now…you're certainly not blind. I'm not going to pretend to be, either." Hell, he was playing a dangerous game. His groin tightened as if to prove the point but he liked getting her all riled up. He figured, turnabout was fair play after all the sleepless nights she'd given him with her coverage in the past few weeks. The way he saw it, payback was coming. He just hadn't imagined that she'd offer up the opportunity so easily.

"I…" She stopped, consternation in the purse of her lush, totally kissable lips, and he almost let her off the hook, but she answered staunchly, "Do not have time for romantic attachments right now." She slewed her gaze his way. "I'm sure that's something you can understand, given the all-consuming nature of your profession."

"True. But I make time to go out now and then," he lied through his teeth. The last time he'd been on a true date, the presidential administration had been different. The truth, in this matter, was inconsequential and it didn't bother him one iota that he was purposefully goading her into sharing personal information about herself.

"If you're doing this to catch me off guard, it won't work. I'm a professional, not some easily flattered intern. Good try, though," she retorted, though Owen caught a subtle softness to her voice that belied the harshness of her words.

He chuckled. "You give me too much credit. Fine, have it your way, then. One more question, though…"

"I think we should get back on topic," she disagreed, her wary gaze contradicting the tentative touch of her tongue against her lips as she tried to regain control of the conversation. Wasn't she aware of how seductive that one little gesture was? Perhaps. Perhaps not. He didn't know her well enough to know if she were doing it for effect or innocently. Either way, it fired his blood in the worst way.

"Where's the harm in answering one question? You seem to know everything there is to know about me…."

"Not everything," she admitted with a small shrug. "I wouldn't be sitting here with you if I knew everything I wanted to know." When he conceded her point, she seemed to give a little. "All right. One question and then we're back on topic, if you please," she grudgingly said, raising her index finger to add in warning, "Just one."

"Why no time for dating? You look a little young to be married to your work." Speaking of…how old was she? He knew he was older, but he'd never been a good judge of those things. These days, a guy had to check driver's licenses before committing to a date with a woman for fear of breaking the law with some precocious teen who looked more womanly than was prudent around hot-blooded men. He eyed Piper, trying to guess her age in spite of his terrible skills in that department, then gave up and asked plainly, "How old are you?"

She offered a small, playful smile. "Afraid you're here with an underaged girl pretending to be an adult?" she asked sweetly, seeming to enjoy that she'd zeroed in on his thoughts exactly.

"Maybe," he allowed gruffly. "So?"

"Do I look like a teenager?"

He did a quick perusal, trying not to let his gaze feast on her pert breasts, which he was fairly certain would fit perfectly in his palm and his mouth, and looked away. "No," he said, adding tightly, "heaven help me if you are."

She laughed, the sound tripping down his spine and pooling in his groin as she assured him she was not a teenager. "I'm ten years younger than you but no kid. Rest easy. You look about ready to pass out."

He released a shaky breath but smiled. She'd turned the tables on him so quickly, he hadn't seen it coming. He straightened and tossed the grass he'd chewed to shreds. "You never answered my question…why don't you date?"

"Oh, that's easy. I don't see the point. Or, well, it's just that I'm very driven and I have goals that may collide with personal attachments."

"What kind of goals?" he asked.

She met his stare without an ounce of jocularity as she said, "The Pulitzer."

"Lofty," he murmured. "And a boyfriend might prevent you from attaining it?"

"One might," she allowed. "When you're in a relationship, your head gets muddied with emotion. I've seen too many women give up their dreams for the sake of a relationship and I don't want the complication. Or the drama. Like I said, I'm focused."

He chuckled. "Yeah, I can see that."

"Right. So back to the interview. Tell me how—"

"So, if you don't casually date, as you put it, and you don't date seriously…how do you…get any…*quality* time with anyone?" he asked, amused by the sudden blush staining her cheeks as his meaning sunk in. He found her reaction interesting, given her background.

He half-expected her to tell him to mind his own business, which she probably should've anyway. Hell, he'd pretty much told her the very same thing in the truck on the way over here but she surprised him with an answer. "I don't—I haven't— What I mean to say is— Well, I don't worry about those things because I don't know what I'm missing. And I prefer it that way. Keeps me focused."

His jaw went slack. Had she just admitted she was a virgin?

His stunned silence caused her to add defensively, "I'm proud of my virginity. It sets me apart from those around me and I'm glad. I don't have to worry about an unwanted pregnancy, STDs or emotional baggage." She became flustered as if just realizing she was sharing more than she'd intended and she huffed a short breath, determination in the set of her jaw. "We've wasted too much time talking about unprofessional things. Let's return to the topic at hand, please," she instructed in a strident tone that may have been bitchy if not for the high patches of pink riding her cheeks that transformed her from cute to radiant beauty in an instant.

Untouched. The word and its meaning floated through his mind and he startled at how much it turned his crank. He'd never been that guy, crowing and beating his chest at the idea of breaking in a virgin, but when he looked at Piper the idea gave him an odd, almost frightening sensation in his chest.

"Owen?"

Her questioning tone brought him back to the moment and he gestured for her to continue. "I'm just waiting on you," he bluffed, hoping she didn't see right through him.

"Here's the thing, originally I'd thought I would try to win you over into my confidence but I've since learned that you aren't the kind of man who can be easily cajoled into giving out anything you're not prepared to give, so I'm going to be straight with you."

Warm, lusty feelings evaporating, Owen regarded her shrewdly, awaiting her true intention. His initial gut instinct had been right. "I'm listening," he said by way of encouragement.

She hesitated a fraction but plunged forward, admitting, "I'm doing research into the Red Meadows incident and I would love to hear your side of things."

He pulled away, feeling as if she'd punched him upside the head. Why couldn't people just let it go? What was with the fascination with his own personal tragedy? He climbed to his feet. "Check the newspaper archive. I'm sure you can find plenty of information there."

She followed, not bothering to put her shoes back on. "I've read all the newspaper clippings. I've read everything in the local paper and even in the regional newspapers but I need to hear it from you, someone who lived through it."

"I was just a kid," he answered flatly. "My memory is hardly reliable. Sorry to disappoint you."

"I hope you're wrong about that," she said. "You weren't too small to remember the details, Owen. My guess is you remember everything quite well, which is why you don't want to talk about it."

"Nice theory, even if it's wrong."

He'd hoped that was the end of it, but she wasn't ready to give up. Her tenacity might've been impressive if it weren't being directed at him. He tried to start walking, signaling the end to their idyllic pit stop but she swung around in front of him, her hand on his chest. "Wait," she pleaded, her gaze searching his. "I think I have something you're going to want to know."

"Oh? And what could that be?" he asked. She held his stare, not backing down an inch. "Come on, out with it," he demanded, ready to be finished with the interview.

"I think I may have found proof that your father was innocent."

CHAPTER NINE

CORAL SUNDAY TAPPED her fingers idly against the windowsill, restless to the bone. She'd always worried that this day would come but she never suspected it would come with the encouragement of their daughter.

Jasper walked in, his mind occupied elsewhere and she fought the spurt of jealousy for his ability to focus on the present rather than the past.

Well, his leisurely day was about to end.

"We should think about sending Piper to New York to see your sister," she announced, causing him to glance up from his reading. He peered at her from above his glasses and frowned in annoyance at her interruption. "She needs to get out of Dayton for a while."

"Why?" Jasper asked. "And you hate my sister."

She ignored the part about his sister and continued, the idea germinating inside her head quickly. "She needs a change of scenery and New York would likely capture her imagination. This town is too small for her to grow professionally. We need to foster her talent and I don't see that happening here with the limited resources available to her."

"I say we should let her decide what she wants to do with her life and in what direction she wants to go,"

Jasper said with a shrug, and attempted to bury himself in his reading again but Coral wasn't having it. They needed to be a united front or else it wouldn't work.

"Jasper," she said sharply. "This is serious."

"Good gravy, woman, what is eating at you today?" he asked. "I'm trying to read this fascinating editorial on modern man and you're ruining my enjoyment with your strident tone."

"You know she's digging into the Red Meadows incident and she refuses to let it go."

Jasper waved away her concern. "I talked with her at the planting last Sunday and I think I've convinced her to move on. She's an inquisitive young woman and she couldn't help but poke around a little. However, when she finds nothing but what was reported in the news, she'll move on. Stop worrying, Coral. You'll give yourself an ulcer." His expression softened as he suggested, "Why don't you go make yourself some fresh mint tea. We have some in the cupboard and it's really good. Settles the stomach and the mind."

She didn't want tea. "Don't manage me, professor," she said brusquely. "And you underestimate your daughter. She's like a bulldog with a bone when she gets something into her head. I don't think she's going to drop it and move on at all. And what are we going to do if she discovers the truth?"

Jasper pursed his mouth and his gaze clouded as if he were remembering something distasteful and she knew he was reliving that awful day. They'd done so much to put the past behind them. Neither wanted to see it resurrected. "Let's wait and see," he said finally.

"I'm not comfortable waiting for her to dig up our dirty secret. I'd rather she not know at all. If we send her away before she can finish her research, we won't have to cross that bridge."

Jasper heard her this time but he wasn't ready to make the move just yet. "It's going to be all right. This is all going to blow over, just like it always does. Trust me."

Coral eyed him with a cold stare. "Make sure that it does," she said. "I won't lose my daughter over this mess."

"You won't have to," he promised, but Coral saw the apprehension in his gaze.

The ghosts of the past were rising again. And Coral could feel their phantom fingers reaching for all she and Jasper held dear.

OWEN STARED AT PIPER, stunned. "What did you say?" he asked in a harsh tone, causing her to take a faltering step away from him.

She swallowed. "You heard me. I've found inconsistencies in some of the statements given by eyewitnesses to your father's death at Red Meadows. And well, my gut says there's more to the story than everyone has been told."

"You said you had proof."

"Okay, that part might've been a mild embellishment to get your attention," she said sheepishly, rushing to explain when he looked ready to walk. "However, I wasn't lying when I said that I've found some things that I think you ought to take an interest in."

"Such as?"

"A hunch."

"A hunch," he repeated, dismissing her claim with a sharp exhale of breath. He sidestepped her, and she had no choice but to retrieve her shoes and hard hat and follow.

"Aren't you the least bit curious about what I'm saying?" she asked, tripping after him. She yelped when the sole of her foot connected with a sharp rock but she limped on, reaching out to grab the back of his shirt and haul him back. "Listen to me. I know what I'm talking about. Something doesn't add up. Didn't you ever wonder? I mean, think about it. The official story goes that Ty Garrett was shot down when he tried to shoot an FBI agent during the raid at Red Meadows."

He turned and glared. "I know how it goes. I don't need a play-by-play."

She continued, undeterred. "But I've found something that suggests a different story."

"Which is?" he demanded impatiently.

"I'll admit it's not much, and that's why I plan to keep looking, but I found someone from the Aryan Coalition who said that your dad was actually working for the FBI when it all went down and that the shooting was a cover-up."

Tense silence filled the air, the only evidence of Owen's turmoil being the subtle flare of his nostrils. "Who is your source?"

She crossed her arms. "You know I can't reveal my sources."

"This is a bunch of horseshit," he muttered, disgust

in his tone. "You're unbelievable, you know that? Why don't you play around in someone else's tragedy and leave the skeletons in my closet alone."

"I'm not going to stop," she called out stubbornly. "With or without your help, I'm going to keep digging, because I'm not going to walk away from the biggest story this town has ever seen. I just thought you might like to find out the truth. Maybe even clear your dad's name in the process."

CHAPTER TEN

OWEN STOPPED. CLEAR HIS DAD'S NAME? Wasn't that what he was trying to do when he'd returned to Dayton and took over running a legitimate business? He busted his ass every day trying to change the public perception of the Garrett name. Would he ever be able to wash away the stain left behind by his father's association with the Aryan Coalition? He'd do anything to be able to walk down the street without wondering if the covert stares and whispers were simply a figment of his paranoid imagination or if people were still judging him by the actions of his father.

Ty Garrett hadn't been a bad man—but he'd done a bad thing and sometimes in a small town they were one and the same. Hell yes, he wanted to do what he could to clear his father's name. He wanted people to know the side of Ty Garrett he'd known, not the caricature of evil that was painted of him after the shit had gone down at Red Meadows.

"How exactly do you plan to accomplish this?" he asked finally. "And, assuming you get the information you're looking for, what do you plan to do with it?"

Emboldened, she said, "First, I want to hear your side of the story. I know you were a kid but I want to see if your account of the incident matches what the official report says."

"Official. You mean, what was printed in the papers?"

She shook her head, a gleam of triumph in her eyes. "I got the FBI report."

"How'd you manage that?" Not even he had a copy of that report. "Can I see it?"

"One thing at a time," she said, her expression lighting with pleasure at his interest. "When can we sit down and do the interview?"

"I thought that's what we were doing now."

"Well, we would've if you hadn't spent so much time asking me personal questions. Now, it's nearly time to go." She pointed at the dainty watch perched on her slim wrist. "Quinn will be done with school in about thirty minutes, which is barely enough time to get back to town."

He startled at the mention of Quinn and a guilty flush followed. He'd completely forgotten about the kid. Some guardian he was turning out to be. "Crap. You're right. Let's get moving. I don't want her to be left alone at the school." They started the hike back to the truck and he offered a short thanks for keeping on an eye on the time. "I appreciate it," he said gruffly. "I'm not used to having a kid to watch out for."

"Me, neither," she admitted blithely, trudging beside him without her shoes this time, which seemed to make it easier for her to maneuver the terrain without the hindrance of the spindly heels. "But I have a thing for remembering details. I was an excellent babysitter back on the farm and there were plenty of kids running around to get enough practice."

He let that information settle for a moment while he processed what she'd shared about her theory. The temptation to shut her down was strong. He wasn't keen on ripping open old wounds, particularly when there was no guarantee that anything good would come of it, but he couldn't deny she'd dangled a pretty juicy carrot in front of a man hungry for redemption. He trudged along the terrain, helping her up a steep incline, then tried to fill the silence with something, anything other than the chatter in his head.

"Must've been pretty wild growing up on a commune," he mused. "Is it true about the nudist part?"

"Yes," she answered without hesitation. "But it's completely voluntary. It's not like everyone is required to shuck their clothes or else they get kicked off the island. That's a *Survivor* reference," she supplied unnecessarily. He stared, bemused, as she explained. "I love that show. I never got to watch television as a kid, so I kind of turned into a junkie in college. I caught a lot of marathons over the weekends. Now I never miss a season. I even thought about auditioning but I couldn't fathom spending that much time without being able to shower."

He openly appraised her, crooking a short grin. Yeah, he couldn't quite see that, either. "You're not much of a camper, eh?"

"Owen, my entire childhood felt like camping. I prefer my lifestyle with all the conveniences of modern technology like a dishwasher, washing machine, toaster oven…"

"Toaster oven?"

"Yes. I prefer English muffins in the toaster oven as opposed to the toaster because the toaster always burns the edges and a toaster oven crisps everything perfectly."

"You're a very precise woman, you know that?"

"You're not the first to tell me that," she acknowledged. "Which do you prefer?"

"I like whatever is hot and easy." He hadn't meant to sound dirty but by the way her cheeks bloomed and her eyes widened, he knew that's the way she'd heard it. He knew he ought to clarify but he kind of liked the way she got all flustered at the idea. What could he say? He had a bit of a bad boy in him.

They reached the truck and made the drive back to town. Owen returned her to her parked vehicle and before she climbed out, she pinned him with her steady stare—the one he was quickly learning meant she was in ruthless-reporter mode—and insisted on nailing down a date for the interview. Before he could offer a word, she threw down a few rules. "It can't be somewhere in the woods like today and it can't be at a bar or something like that. I need someplace quiet so outside noise doesn't get in the way of the recording."

"Recording?"

"Of course. I wouldn't want to simply rely on memory for something this important. You don't mind, do you?"

"Would it matter if I did?"

"Not really, but it seems courtesy to ask. Besides, it's for your own protection, as well. This way, you'll know that you're being accurately represented."

An alarm bell trilled in his head. "Whoa…wait a minute. What do you mean by *represented?* I thought you just wanted to hear my side? Are you writing about this?" She hesitated and he took that to mean yes. He swore, then shook his head. "No. I don't care what you uncover. I don't want my family's name thrown around in the media again."

"Owen, be reasonable. How else are you supposed to clear your father's name? By word of mouth?"

She had a point but he didn't care. She didn't know what it was like to be talked about every time she turned around over something as awful as the Red Meadow incident. "No."

"We made a deal," she reminded him, her mouth tightening. "And you're backing out."

"I agreed to talk. Nothing more."

She chewed her cheek in thought and that plainly calculating look in her eyes made him leery but she relented with a deliberate shrug, saying, "So serious. What's to write about? It's ancient history. I'm just curious. For my own sake."

"Don't you have anything better to do with your free time?" he asked, finding her exploration into past history *for fun,* just a bit odd.

She offered an enigmatic smile. "We all have our quirks."

"Yeah, I guess we do," he agreed, even though he smelled a pile of something steamy. However, aside from the local rag, he couldn't imagine who else would be interested in Dayton's little embarrassment, so he felt marginally safe in letting down his guard. "Fine. But I better not find this interview on the internet somewhere."

"My we think highly of ourselves," she teased. "Why would I post an audio file on the internet? Boring. This is just for me. I promise."

He supposed he could live with that. "Since you have so many rules, why don't you suggest where we should meet."

She brightened. "Excellent idea. How about right here?"

"My home?" he asked.

"Yes. You live alone, right?"

"At the moment." He enjoyed the subtle flash of a scowl that crossed her features for the simple reason that her reaction fed his ego. "How about we meet at *your* house? Or maybe your farm?"

"The farm? Why would you want to meet there?" Before he could answer, she moved on with a firm shake of her head. "No. That's not a good idea. My parents would not enjoy that at all. They don't seem to like you very much. Though, I don't really know why. Anyway, no, it should be your place. Besides, if you have any photos of when you were living with the Aryan Coalition, I would love to see them."

He did have photos. Somewhere. He supposed he'd have to look for them tonight. "Fine. Tomorrow then?"

She nodded, pleased. "Tomorrow."

Owen watched as she walked barefoot back to her car, tossing the heels into the passenger seat before she climbed in. He'd spent the afternoon with Piper Sunday. And he was going to spend tomorrow with her, too.

Oddly, the idea didn't make him want to run the other way.

And he knew it should.

PIPER'S STEP BORDERED ON A JIG but she couldn't help it. She breezed into the newspaper office and went straight to her desk, still elated that she'd managed to convince Owen to work with her.

"You're looking chipper. What's the occasion?" Charlie asked, lounging against the doorjamb, his back rounding in a slouch. "Anything you'd like to share?"

"With you? No. It's personal."

"Ah, personal. So you and Garrett are having a thing?"

She looked at him sharply. How did he know she'd been with Owen? "I don't know what you're talking about," she retorted coolly. "Go bother someone else with less work to do. I'm busy."

"So busy that you missed your interview with Councilman Olivo?" he inquired with fake concern. Her gaze flew to her large-format calendar and there it was in bright red pen. She gasped and he chuckled at her distress. "Yeah, he called, looking for you. Seemed pretty pissed off that you'd stood him up. You know how he gets. But I'm sure it's fine."

Darn it. She'd meant to put the appointment and the phone number in her cell phone, but she'd been distracted and put it off for later, except later seemed to have passed by without her notice. "It's here some-where." How'd she forget such an important interview? How completely appalling. Top professionals kept a myriad of dates and times and other important details in their head and yet she'd managed to blow off a major player in the city of Dayton because she'd been intoxi-cated by the possibility of interviewing Owen. Damn it.

"For such a persnickety personality, you have the organizational skills of a homeless person," Charlie observed, causing her to whirl and hiss at him.

"Don't you have anything better to do than bother me?"

"Not presently."

"Well, I don't have time to listen to your crap. Go pester someone else."

"Why would I do that when pestering you is not only fun but also beneficial?"

"Beneficial? How so?"

"Because seeing you so riled gives me joy, which in turn causes a sweet endorphin rush and when that happens, my blood pressure lowers, which is beneficial to my health."

"So happy to help," she said drily. "Now, get out of my space before I file a harassment claim against you. I don't care if your uncle owns the paper or not—rules are rules and you're creating a hostile work environment for me."

Charlie's mouth pinched and his laughter faded. Un-fortunately, she didn't have time to enjoy her victory.

She found the Post-it she was looking for, but before she could celebrate, Charlie interrupted her again.

"I think the editor might find it interesting that you're doing something on the side that involves Owen Garrett. You know how my uncle, the publisher, feels about freelancing."

Yes, she knew. He'd made it very clear that he expected his reporters to save their best for *his* publication. Any moonlighting could be cause for termination. Technically, as long as the publication wasn't in direct competition with the newspaper, legally, he really couldn't say what she could do with her off time; however, with California businesses subscribing to the at-will employee rule, basically, the publisher could fire her for whatever he wanted if it suited him, as long as it wasn't *obviously* against the labor laws.

And that included moonlighting.

With only one newspaper in town and most newspapers in the immediate area in a hiring freeze, she couldn't afford to lose her position at the *Tribune*. Damn Charlie for knowing it, too.

She turned. "What are you talking about?" she asked, blinking in what she hoped appeared as confusion.

"Don't go all Bambi eyes on me. I know you've been doing all this after-hours research on the Red Meadows raid. You're not the only one who pays attention."

She shrugged. "What's your point? What I do on my own time is my own."

"Yeah, but you're not just doing this stuff on your own time. You're using company time to do your research."

"Prove it. In the meantime, get out of my space. You're contaminating the energy with your negative, slimy self. It's a wonder they let you around kids, Charlie," she said, secretly holding her breath. She couldn't show weakness around the little worm. He'd run to his uncle for sure.

Since she didn't cave or quail, Charlie had nothing to build on. Frustration laced his tone as he exited, saying, "You're going to slip up and when you do…I'll be there."

As soon as he was gone, she exhaled. *Crud.* He was hot on her tail. She'd need to be more careful around the tattletale. No more sneaking off to do research.

She sighed and prepared to make up a plausible excuse for blowing off the biggest ego in Dayton.

CHAPTER ELEVEN

OWEN WALKED INTO THE HOSPITAL, Quinn at his side, with a large bouquet of flowers in his hand.

"Do you think she'll like these flowers?" he asked Quinn in an attempt to lighten the mood. Quinn had been quiet since he'd picked her up from school and that wasn't like the little chatterbox. She worried her bottom lip and the usual sparkle in her eyes had been replaced by fear and trepidation. He wished she didn't have to go through something like this. It wasn't right for a kid to have to deal with the kind of violence Quinn had seen.

Quinn nodded in answer as they rounded the corner to Gretchen's room, where she'd been downgraded from intensive care to a standard room earlier that afternoon while he'd been with Piper.

He peeked inside and swallowed when he saw Gretchen lying against the white pillow, her eyes closed. He looked to Quinn and put a finger to his lips with a "shh," and they padded silently into the room.

Owen placed the bouquet vase—which happened to be in the shape of a stork, because that's all the florist had on such short notice so late in the afternoon—on the small bedside table, and tried to hold back the wince when he caught Gretchen's battered face. "Oh, man," he breathed, taking in the full extent of her injuries. She'd been beaten within an inch of her life it seemed. He was afraid to look at her belly. It was hard to tell with the blankets covering her if her stomach had lost the basketball roundness she'd been sporting a few days earlier.

"Mama," Quinn whispered, tears clogging her voice. She stared up at Owen, looking for answers he didn't have. Quinn tried again. "Mama? It's Quinn…"

Gretchen's eyes opened but her gaze remained bleary and unfocused. Quinn approached the bed and gently touched her mama's hand. It was enough to make Owen choke up. God, he hoped to hell the cops had found Danny and put his ass in jail for what he'd done.

"Owen," Gretchen's voice sounded like she'd eaten gravel for breakfast. She smiled weakly at Quinn. "Thanks for taking care of my girl."

"You don't even have to ask," he said gruffly. "How are you feeling?" If the way she looked was any indication, she probably felt like crap. She made a small expression that said "eh, I've been better" but she attempted a wider smile. She was a trouper. Now for the hard question. He swallowed and gestured toward her belly. "What about the baby?"

She nodded. "Baby is fine. It's another girl." Gretchen said to Quinn. "You're getting a baby sister."

"A sister?" Quinn's voice brightened. "Does that mean I get to name her?"

Gretchen nodded. "That was the deal. Better put your

thinking cap on. It has to be the most perfect name ever because she's been through a lot already."

"Oh, it will be," Quinn promised fervently then sobered, the worry returning to her voice. "When are you coming home, Mama?"

"Soon, sweetheart," Gretchen answered. "Can you do me a favor, sugar?" Quinn nodded. "Can you go ask the nurse for some more water for me. I'm pretty thirsty and my pitcher is empty."

"Yes, Mama," Quinn said, grabbing the pitcher and disappearing from the room.

"That was a ploy to get her out of the room, wasn't it?" Owen asked. "What's wrong?"

She closed her eyes and winced as she tried to move a little. "Cops haven't found Danny yet. I'm scared of what he might do when he finds out the cops are looking for him. The house is leased in his name. I can't go back there. I don't know what to do. Can you keep Quinn for a few more days until I figure out where we can stay? I know it's a lot to ask and I'll understand if you say no. I just don't know who to turn to." A small tear escaped and slid down her cheek. He hated to see a woman cry and he'd do anything to keep it from happening.

"You can stay with me," he offered, his mouth working faster than his head. He wondered what Piper would think of another woman moving into his house. He supposed she wouldn't care two figs, since they weren't anything to one another. Gretchen stared, uncomprehending. "Yeah, well, it's nothing fancy but it'll do in a pinch. I've a spare bedroom you can share with Quinn. We'll get this figured out. I don't need you worrying about your safety with that asshole out there. My house is at least safe even if it's not the lap of luxury."

"Why would you do this for us?" she asked, blinking back tears.

"Because you're a good employee and I don't want the hassle of training someone new," he joked, but there was some truth to his blithe statement. He didn't have time to interview and then babysit someone new when Gretchen was the best office manager he'd ever had. If he had to put her up for a few days, it was worth his sanity and his productivity.

She smiled around her cracked lip. "Well, you have a point there," she said. "Then, I accept your offer. Thank you. We appreciate it."

"No problem." It felt good to help, but he had to know one more thing. "Is it over between you and Danny Mathers?" he asked, then gestured at her injuries. "What happened? I figured him for a loser but not a violent one."

She drew a shuddering breath and more tears leaked down her face. "It's definitely over. He tried to kill me. Said he didn't want the baby and it was my fault for pressuring him into fatherhood. He didn't care if we lived or died. How could I have been so blind?"

"We've all made bad calls in our life," he said, trying to offer some kind of solace but rage had kindled in his gut at the new information. "The police talk to you yet?" he asked, his voice rough.

She nodded. "I gave a statement about an hour ago." Her unhappy frown gave way to more tears. "I never imagined he could be so cruel. I just thought he had cold feet and he'd come around but I never suspected… Oh, God, Owen, he could've hurt Quinn, too. I get sick to my stomach just thinking of what he could've done to her if he was willing to do what he did to his own child."

Owen didn't have any words of comfort that wouldn't sound disingenuous so he remained silent and let her cry it out. She gingerly wiped away the remaining tears and he handed her a fresh tissue for her nose. "It's going to be all right," he assured her, all the while entertaining dark fantasies of mayhem against Danny Mathers. Heaven help the man if Owen got a hold of him before the cops did. In the meantime, he'd do whatever he had to to keep Quinn and Gretchen safe. "We'll get everything figured out."

She flashed him a watery smile and shook her head. "If only people knew the real you. They'd forget about all that other stuff, you know?"

He thought of Piper and the possibility of clearing his father's name. Wouldn't it be great to be able to walk down the street without feeling as if he had to defend his every action? Hell yes. Maybe he'd even get the fresh start he'd been trying to achieve since moving back. The idea was enough to make him yearn for the future in more ways than just safeguarding his livelihood. He crooked a smile at Gretchen. "I told you to keep that on the down low. I don't want my secret to get out," he teased, reaching to pat her hand softly. "Get some rest. I'll check in on you tomorrow. Don't worry about Quinn. I managed to figure out the school scheduling thing and everything is fine."

"You're awesome," Gretchen said, smiling with true relief. "I'll find a way to make it up to you."

"You just focus on getting better. We'll figure everything else out later."

She nodded, her eyes drifting shut as she succumbed to the fatigue he read in her expression. The burden she carried, he couldn't imagine. It was easy for him to say that she'd better drop the SOB who put her in the hospital but his dad had once told him "the heart wants want the heart wants and sometimes it defies reason."

He hoped to God that Gretchen's heart wanted nothing to do with Danny Mathers from here on out but he knew better than to assume anything.

PIPER FINISHED HER MORNING yoga and with music blaring, she spent an extra ten minutes exfoliating so that when she shaved her legs they'd be extra smooth—not for any particular reason but if Owen happened to notice, that wouldn't be too awful—and since she lived alone, she didn't bother covering with her towel when she was dried.

Still humming, she crossed the hallway and went into her living room with the intent to grab some orange juice in the kitchen but she shrieked when she realized she wasn't alone.

"Farley! What are you doing here?" she asked, her hands flying to shield her breasts and private parts. "Good God! Close your eyes or turn around, please."

Farley chuckled and made a show of covering his eyes but then peeped through his fingers. "Ah, gotcha," he teased but when she continued to glare at him, he sighed and did as she asked.

The nerve, she fumed as she jerked a robe over her body. She was going to have to talk to her parents about Farley. He was getting out of control. She stared Farley down, hoping he read the fury in her eyes as she said, "This is unacceptable. You can't come into my home like you own it or something. I'm within my rights to call the cops, you know."

"I apologize," Farley said, the seeming picture of contrition but there was something else lurking in his gaze and to her mind it looked suspiciously like delight at catching her naked, which only caused her temper to spike even higher. She was about to pick up her cell phone and report him when he said, "But I think I may have found something of importance to you."

"Yeah? Such as?" she asked warily. She couldn't imagine there was anything Farley knew that she didn't already. It wasn't as if Farley were a fountain of untapped knowledge.

"First, a kiss…" he suggested, and she balked.

"Are you serious?"

"As a heart attack," Farley answered with a grin.

"Farley…you have ten seconds to get your butt out of my house before I report you to the cops for breaking and entering, peeping and whatever else cops charge people with for generally annoying the crap out of a person."

"One kiss?"

She held up her fist. "How about a knuckle sandwich?"

He grimaced, disappointment evident. "It's a box," he answered dully, all play leaching from his tone as he continued. She almost felt sorry for him. She imagined it was hard to be in love with someone who didn't feel the same for you. "I was busy cleaning out the old shed behind the greenhouse and found a box of stuff you might want to sift through."

So far she wasn't intrigued. "And why would I want to look through an old box?" she asked, irritated.

"Because it's full of your old things from when you lived on the farm. I guess your parents forgot about the old shed. It's got some little mementos and stuff I thought you might like to hang on to. It's in the car. I'll leave it on the porch for you."

She suppressed another wave of annoyance but she held her tongue. Farley looked fairly miserable and she wasn't cruel. Attempting a smile for old times' sake, she said, "Thank you, Farley. I'll check it out. I appreciate you letting me know."

"Of course," he said, his adoring grin returning. "Happy to help."

She pointed toward the door. "Now, out. And don't pull another stunt like this or, I swear, you'll regret it."

"My apologies," he murmured, his cheeks reddening. "I didn't think you'd mind…given as how we were both raised on the farm."

"Well, I don't live on the farm any longer and I do mind. I mind very much."

He nodded and ducked out, closing the door behind him.

Piper rolled her eyes to the ceiling and blew out a

short breath. What was she going to do with that love-sick man? Honestly…

For a moment, she imagined that instead of Farley standing there it had been Owen. She sucked in a tight breath and she laughed shakily. Wow. That was… telling.

Well, all she could say about that was thank God it hadn't been Owen standing there after all.

CHAPTER TWELVE

OWEN HELPED GRETCHEN from the truck, worried about her every move, every wince.

"You okay?" he asked for the tenth time in as many minutes as they walked slowly to the front door. "Maybe I should carry you. Or maybe I should've rented a wheelchair." He bunched his brows, mentally berating himself for not thinking ahead. "I could go back and get one for you if you need…"

"I'm not going to let you carry or push me," Gretchen said, determined even though her bruises stood out in the sunlight. Her rounded belly protruded stubbornly in spite of her ordeal. She picked her way toward the door, waving him away. "Stop hovering, Owen, before I go insane. I'll be fine. Just go open the door for me."

"Right." Owen rushed to do as instructed. He was way out of his element. He'd never had much experience with caregiving though he'd spent enough time smoothing over the rough spots his brothers had often left behind with their high-spirited ways. The irony that Thomas had gone into law enforcement within the FBI never failed to amuse him. He held the door open for Gretchen and escorted her to the bedroom that would be hers and Quinn's for the time being.

He wasn't lying when he'd told her it wasn't fancy. He'd always imagined that Mama Jo would spruce it up when she visited but he hadn't been able to persuade her to come to California in all the years since he'd packed up and moved from Bridgeport, West Virginia. The sparse room seemed a mirror to his life, he thought irritably. Of course, he'd imagined things a lot differently at one time. He gestured toward the closet, eager to put his mind back on task. "Make yourself at home. I have extra blankets in the closet and don't hesitate to ask if you need something."

Gretchen absently rubbed her belly, an echo of sadness in the slow, soothing action, and a memory long buried rose to the surface.

A woman he didn't know—wouldn't dare talk to—and his father.

It'd been summer and they'd left the compound to pick up supplies, but they'd taken a detour to a place he hadn't recognized. His father had instructed him to remain in the old Ford truck as he went to the door of the small cottage.

She came to the door wearing a cream gauzy sundress that dusted her bare knees. Her rounded shoulders matched the subtle rounding of her belly. Her hands caressed the bump even as she and his father began to argue. He couldn't hear what they were saying, but his father seemed very frustrated. Tears were streaming down her face. She reached up to touch his father on his cheek, the motion loving yet urgent, and Owen's eyes widened in shock. Then his father lightly touched her stomach. Owen's confusion warred with revulsion.

The woman was black.

And his father was touching her with kindness...even desperate longing. No, this was wrong, he thought. His father would explain.

But Ty hadn't explained. When Owen had questioned him, almost demanding an answer, his father hadn't been able to say much more than, "Not everything is as it seems, so just mind your own business and keep it to yourself, son."

Owen hadn't mentioned it again. Not that he'd had the chance.

Two days later, the woman was dead and a week later, so was his father.

"You okay, Owen?" Gretchen queried now, catching a remnant of that disturbing memory in his gaze. She reached out to him, worried. "You look like you just saw a ghost or something. You're white as a sheet."

He chuckled at her observation, waving off her concern. "You don't need to be worrying about me. You just focus on healing. I'm fine. I promise," he assured her when she refused to be mollified. He loved that about Gretchen—she was always considering others before herself. Except, he wished she'd put herself first before that jackass roughed her up. Maybe if she'd done that, she might've walked before it was too late.

"Should I make something for dinner tonight?" she asked, and he immediately balked.

"Woman, what part of *rest* don't you understand?" he asked, shaking his head when she frowned and began to protest.

"I have to do something to earn our keep here,"

Gretchen said, resolute determination in her face. "I'm no freeloader."

"No, you're pregnant and injured. That constitutes needing a little pampering. I'll pick something up on my way home each night. No cooking. Besides, I don't even know if I have much more than one pot and a skillet. Not sure you could make much of a meal with that."

That seemed to make some sense to her and she backed down, but Owen had a feeling it was only a temporary concession on her part. Gretchen had a mind of her own when it came to certain things. He suppressed a sigh and gestured. "Do you need anything else? I have to head back to town for a few things."

"We're good. Thanks again, Owen," she said, the sincerity in her voice hard to miss. He was pleased to help but he wasn't accustomed to having two extra people, let alone those of the female persuasion, running around in his space. He'd deal but it would take some getting used to. No walking around naked he supposed. He chuckled at the idea of telling Piper that she wasn't the only one who enjoyed walking around in the buff when no one was around.

There was something to be said for the caress of a cool breeze on the backside, he mused with a smile of private humor.

When he'd been a timber faller back in his early twenties he'd often come home covered in sawdust from the day's work and instead of tracking all that mess into the house to clean later, he'd just shuck his clothes at the door and walk in naked as a jaybird. Usually he'd been so bone-tired from a day of falling trees that he'd tumbled, exhausted, to the couch. He'd often wake around seven in the evening to shove some food down his gullet, shower and go back to bed to start all over again the next day at the crack of dawn. He missed a lot of things about just being an employee but he didn't miss the back-breaking work of being a faller. If he'd continued in that profession, he'd be listening to a surgeon tell him he was due for a hip and knee replacement at the ripe age of thirty-six.

He climbed into his truck with one last glance toward the house, feeling odd to leave the girls alone, but he had to get supplies if people were going to be staying for any length of time. At the present time, he barely had enough to support one person, let alone three. Hell, he didn't even know if he had a full roll of toilet paper.

PIPER SLID THE BOX FARLEY BROUGHT onto her kitchen table and started to rummage through it. She found a few items she expected, such as dusty school projects and papers with good grades circled in faded red ink—she'd always been an overachiever, even as a child—and then she found something that was plainly out of place with her childhood mementos.

She frowned as she lifted the stiff leather-bound journal and blew away the dust to get a better look at it. She knew for certain it hadn't belonged to her. She opened it gingerly, staring at the odd collection of notes and photos. She thumbed through the faded pictures, her puzzlement growing when she didn't recognize a single person in the bunch. She slumped in disappointment. Someone at the farm must've accidentally thrown this in with her stuff, mistaking it for their own box. She grabbed the stack of photos and prepared to return them to the safety of the leather volume but curiosity got the better of her and she started to thumb through the pages. She hadn't become a reporter for nothing. The pages were dated but not by year or day-by-day. The penciled scrawl, faded almost to nothing, drew her attention. She flipped to the last page and read a barely legible scribble. She squinted at the script and made out *M. LaRoche*. Grinning with delight at her unexpected treasure, she settled in to read the private thoughts of a stranger, written long ago.

Piper surmised it was written by a woman, someone who was in love.

"Ohh, my favorite," she murmured, grinning. "Let's see what we have here…"

But her grin faded as she continued to read. Soon it became clear this was not a love story. It was a tragedy.

"It hardly seems possible in this day and age but there is hatred and prejudice alive and well in this town. I never thought I'd come face-to-face with such thinking but the "purists" came to visit me today. They're disgusting, awful people and they scare me. I have to tell T but I can't right now. He said soon, though, everything is going to work out. He's got a plan. I trust him but I'm worried. Those people…if they find out what T's doing… it could be bad."

The entries ended abruptly on May 25. Piper sighed, frowning in thought. The "purists" she imagined were another name for the members of the Aryan Coalition. From the research she'd done thus far, the members were zealots who believed only those with pure blood, as in no ethnicities, were superior. Ugh. The very idea, Piper thought. It was a good thing the Aryan Coalition had disbanded after the Red Meadows incident. She couldn't imagine people with those kinds of beliefs still acting like this.

It was difficult to picture the seething racial hatred that the Aryan Coalition supported flourishing in a place as easygoing in nature as Dayton. Yet, it had. In fact, there were people arrested that day who were grocers, postal workers, day-care providers…everyday people.

And of course, there was Ty Garrett. Carpenter by day, and white supremist leader by night. She tucked the journal against her side and rose from the floor. She wondered if her parents knew who the journal might belong to. Her parents would likely chastise her for not dropping the research into Red Meadows like they'd suggested. Her normally placid father had actually spoken sharply to her the other day over her research. She bit her lip and her gaze went to the journal in her hand. No, she supposed she needn't mention the journal just yet. She wanted to see what she could find on her own first.

She checked her watch. There was still time to get to the library and check out the archives before she was scheduled to meet Owen at his place. Humming to herself, she grabbed her purse and stuffed the journal inside. Hopefully, she could find something that might tie the diary to someone in town she could identify. Maybe she could even return it to whoever this M. LaRoche was…it was a happy thought that made her smile. Imagine this mystery person's surprise to have their long-lost journal returned. Perhaps, if she found the owner, she could ask why the entries stopped so abruptly. Her curiosity had been well and truly piqued. "I do love a puzzle," she murmured as she locked up her house. Hopefully, if she managed to find M. LaRoche, she could get her to share her experiences with the purists. It might shed some additional light on what actually happened that fateful day at Red Meadows.

Two hours into reading back issues of the paper, looking for news clippings of the Red Meadows incident, Piper leaned back in the chair and stretched. She felt permanently hunched from poring over the small type. She'd found several small interesting tidbits but nothing groundbreaking. She checked her watch and her stomach muscles jumped in anticipation. It was nearly time to meet with Owen. She told herself the butterflies in her tummy were simply because she was finally getting the interview opportunity she'd been wanting, not because she was looking forward to seeing Owen himself.

She gathered the copies she'd made with a pleased smile, yet when she started to lift the bound archive to return it to its shelf, a sudden thought came to her. Acting on a whim, she returned the volume to the table and opened it to May of 1984, the year of the Red Meadows raid. She wasn't sure what she was looking for but when she read a small headline buried on the second page of the last issue in May, an uncomfortable tingle in her stomach caused her to plop down in her chair.

A young, black woman was found dead in her home, the victim of an apparent botched robbery. Police found the home trashed and the woman, Mimi LaRoche, dead from a single gunshot to the head. She'd been six months pregnant.

M. LaRoche. Piper was willing to bet her eyeteeth the *M* stood for *Mimi*.

She was carrying the diary of a dead woman in her purse. She read on, noting the woman, Mimi, had been a student at San Jose City College, majoring in fine arts.

"Are you all right, dear?" the librarian asked, noting her change in mood.

"Do you remember the murder of a young woman who was six months pregnant right before the raid at Red Meadows?" she asked, hoping the librarian, who was a fossil in the town of Dayton, might remember something that wasn't put in the newspapers.

Mrs. Huffle, her facial features going slack as she searched her memory, suddenly came upon something and the recollection was enough to pull a sad frown. "Oh, dear, that was a sad, sad day. Nice girl. She used to come in to do her studying. She was going to be a painter or something. Something artsy, I remember that. They never found who did it. Right shame, I tell you."

"The police never had any leads?"

"Oh, well, I don't know about that. Nothing they were going to follow up on. Not during those times anyway."

Piper recalled the fearful passages in the journal and asked, "Was it because of the Aryan Coalition?"

At the mention of the racist cult, Mrs. Huffle's softly wrinkled face pinched in open disgust. "Oh, those people were for rot. Screws loose, all of them. Going on about the 'pure race.' Pure poppycock, if you ask me. I, for one, was relieved when the FBI came in and cleaned house. It was well overdue. They were ruining this town."

"Do you remember if Mimi LaRoche was seeing someone? I mean, she was pregnant. She didn't get that way on her own."

Mrs. Huffle shook her head. "I never saw her with no one. I just assumed she might've had a friend at the college. Such a pretty girl, though. She had those Cajun looks, you know with that rich brown skin and pale green eyes? She was a looker, for sure. Sad business." Mrs. Huffle sighed, then peered at Piper. "Why all the questions all of a sudden about this stuff?"

"Just curious," she answered, not ready to share her true intentions with anyone, not even sweet Mrs. Huffle. "I was doing research into something else and came across the news clipping."

Satisfied with her answer, Mrs. Huffle nodded with a twinkle. "You've always been a curious cat. Probably why you make such an ace reporter. I do love reading your work, though."

"Thank you. That's nice to hear." She accepted the

compliment and made her way to the door until one more question popped in her head. "Mrs. Huffle…is there anyone who still lives here, aside from William Dearborn, who knew anything about the Red Meadows incident?"

Mrs. Huffle cocked her head, a slightly puzzled expression on her face as she answered, "Why yes, dear…you ought to know the answer to that question. Your parents, of course. They were there when it all happened."

CHAPTER THIRTEEN

THE FALSE SMILE SHE'D PASTED on her lips fell the
moment she hit the car. Mrs. Huffle's bombshell had
made her head ring with an explosion of denials and
head shakes, yet she'd never known Mrs. Huffle to lie
about anything. Besides, the old woman had assumed
her parents had shared this whopper of a secret with her
long ago, which obviously they had not.

And why hadn't they? Her parents had always been
open and honest with her—at least, she thought so. This
new information put things in a skewed light that she
couldn't make heads or tails of, no matter how she ma-
nipulated the angle. Her parents at Red Meadows? She
thought of the time line. Back then, her parents were
teaching at the same college Mimi LaRoche was attend-
ing. Had they known her? Would they tell her the truth
if they had? Before this, she would've assumed that her
parents never lied to her, but now, she wasn't sure what
to think.

And the biggest question of all, why were her parents
at Red Meadows? They openly hated racial prejudice
and whenever the topic was raised about the incident,
they reacted negatively. She thought of her father and
how he'd changed before her eyes when she'd brought

up Red Meadows and how her parents seemed to hate Owen Garrett. A sick feeling started to churn in her gut. It was all too much to fathom but tiny pieces were starting to slide into place, revealing a bigger puzzle that needed solving. But how? It wasn't like she could just sit down with her parents over a cup of mint tea and ask about their involvement with a racist cult back when they were younger. Especially after her father's initial reaction to her interest.

For the first time in her life, she was afraid to go to her parents. She worried her bottom lip, unsure of what to do next.

The distinct feeling overcame her that if she continued from this point, things might never be the same. She thought of her nearly idyllic childhood, the happy, carefree times spent at the farm surrounded by love and acceptance. She tried to imagine how her gentle, accepting, and totally nonviolent parents could be affiliated— in any way—to the Aryan Coalition and one question pulled at her: did she want to know?

A long, agonizing moment passed before she had her answer. Her parents had raised her to ask questions. She couldn't stop now. Whatever was lurking in the closets needed to come out. No matter what she found.

OWEN HAD JUST PUT AWAY the supplies from his trip to town when he heard someone pulling into his driveway. His pulse jumped a little when he saw Piper's little hybrid sedan parked neatly beside his giant truck. He couldn't imagine driving that tiny matchbox of a car without losing some kind of manhood points. A decent-size dog, such as Timber, wouldn't even fit in the front seat.

He watched from his kitchen window, which fronted the drive, as Piper, wearing a peach skirt that flirted with her knees and dainty brown girly shoes, picked her way to the front door, navigating the gravel of his driveway gingerly. Damn, there was no denying she was prettier than a picture with never a hair out of place. He stared down at his rough and calloused hands, the seemingly permanently dirt-stained pads of his fingers, and felt like an ogre fantasizing about the princess in the castle. Hell, it was probably just as well. He liked his women busty, ballsy and uninterested in a commitment—Piper was the antithesis of those qualities.

So why did just seeing her make his spine tighten? A sharp rap at the front door precluded the opportunity to give the situation much more thought, which was probably a good thing.

He opened the door and there stood Piper, yet instead of the sunny sparkle of determination he usually saw in her eyes, he saw agitation even though she was trying to hide it.

"What's wrong?" he asked.

"What makes you think something is wrong?"

"Answering a question with a question is usually not a great way to throw someone off your tail," he advised her, ushering her into his home. She glanced around his surroundings, but offered little comment. What could she say? He knew he didn't have much to look at in the way of furnishings. He'd never cared before. Now, he wished he'd put a little more thought into the niceties.

"Where would you like to do this?" she asked.

The bedroom, his dirty mind supplied almost immediately. He was immensely grateful the thought hadn't spilled from his head to his mouth. "The kitchen table?" he offered, and she nodded. "Can I get you anything to drink?"

"I'm fine," she said, taking her pen and pad out, all business.

He heaved a silent sigh, not crazy about this idea of dredging up old memories but he figured if it helped prove his father wasn't the devil the town thought him to be, he'd suffer through it. He pulled up a chair and gestured for her to start. "Let's get this over with," he said with a sigh.

A tiny smile played on her lips. "Don't be such a sourpuss… I promise to be gentle."

Their eyes met and he could've sworn electricity jumped between them in a flash. She must've felt it, too, because she straightened and seemed a little flustered, as if thrown off track for a moment. "Right. So, let's start at the beginning…."

Just then Gretchen's voice floated in from the back bedroom and Piper's head swung around in confusion. "Who's that?" she asked, not missing a beat.

"Ah, it's Gretchen."

"Your office manager?" she said, her stare narrowing in suspicion. "I thought you said there was nothing going on between you?"

"There's not," he answered gruffly as he rose to see what Gretchen needed. "Wait here," he instructed, but Piper ignored his request and followed close on his heels. He gave her an annoyed look, saying, "Woman, don't you ever do as your told?"

"No," she answered evenly. "Haven't you ever heard of the saying 'well-behaved women rarely make history'?"

"Well, you're well on your way to making a name for yourself, that's for sure," he grumbled as he entered Gretchen's room. Piper followed without apology, as if she had the right to know why he was harboring a woman in his house. He found her actions mildly amusing but he wondered at her motivation. Was it possible she was jealous? That seemed improbable but it gave him a faint rise in his heart rate at the thought of Piper feeling possessive over him. Ah, great. Things were going from bad to worse in that department.

Gretchen's stare registered shock, then narrowed in distaste as she saw Piper at his side. "What's she doing here?" she inquired, not pulling any punches.

Piper came forward. "I'm interviewing Owen about what he remembers from the Red Meadows incident," she answered easily, not the least bit put off by the glacial stare coming her way. "Why are you staying with Owen?"

"That's between me and Owen," Gretchen retorted, glancing away as if dismissing Piper. Owen had to swallow a grin at the open animosity Gretchen had for Piper. He knew it came from a protective place and he wouldn't fault her for it. Besides, Piper seemed able to hold her own against the feisty blonde, so he didn't see the need to intervene. And would it be totally wrong for him to admit, he was flattered by the attention? Yeah, it would. So he kept his mouth shut. Gretchen continued, saying, "I called the bus station and changed Quinn's bus stop from our place to here. I hope that's okay with you?"

"Staying long, I see," Piper said, inserting herself back in the conversation. She looked to Owen. "It's fun playing house, isn't it? Insta-family. Sweet."

"Yes, it is. Owen is a very good man," Gretchen said, nearly baring her teeth at Piper before returning to Owen with an adoring smile. "What would you like me to make for dinner? I was thinking mashed potatoes and grilled pork chops. Quinn loves them."

"Girl after my own heart," he said. "Pork chops sound good to me, just let me know what you need and I'll help."

"How domestic," Piper murmured, cutting her glance away from Gretchen, her mouth tightening just enough to give away her irritation. "Who knew your office manager was a regular Rachael Ray. I wonder what other talents she's eager to show you."

Gretchen cocked her head and offered a saccharine sweet smile. "Wouldn't you like to know? Fortunately, it's really none of your business."

"Touché."

Owen spared Piper a short look that said *cut it out* and nodded to Gretchen, ready to separate the two women before they really unsheathed their claws and someone ended up a casualty. "That's fine. Is there anything else you need?" At the shake of her head, he nudged Piper from the room and grabbed the door to close it behind him as he informed Gretchen he'd be a while. "Get some rest," he instructed her, and closed the door but not before catching a glimpse of pique on Gretchen's face.

"I didn't realize you were running a halfway house," Piper said, walking in front of him so that he had a nice view of her backside as it twitched enticingly beneath the flirty peach skirt. He made it a point to avert his gaze before his mind took another unscheduled detour.

"I would say there's probably a lot you don't know about me," he said.

"Not for long," she said in a husky murmur that fired his blood.

"We'll see," he said. She turned as if to return to the kitchen but he didn't want to be indoors. He gestured to the door. "Follow me."

PIPER HESITATED. ONCE AGAIN, she wasn't exactly dressed for an excursion into the wild. He saw her reluctance and cracked a grin that she felt down to her manicured toes, which were peeking out from her wedged, open-toed sandals. Oh, that was dangerous. She smoothed her hair and followed, hoping she didn't end up falling on her face.

"And where are we going?" she asked, closing the door behind her. "I think this qualifies as a reneging on our deal," she said, chasing after him.

"Don't worry, we're not going far," he promised her, actually offering his hand to steady her on the uneven terrain. She accepted his help, secretly delighting in the rough, hard skin scraping against the delicate softness of her hands. She wondered what it would feel like to have those masculine hands touching other parts of her body. She suppressed a shiver but he caught the subtle motion in the tremble of her hand and he stopped. "Are you all right?" he asked, concerned. "If you really don't want to be outside, we can go back in the house. I just didn't want our conversation overheard... It's personal, you know?"

Yes. She got that. A spark of heat trailed the realization that he was going to share those personal things with her, not Gretchen. *Yeah, because first you blackmailed him and then you enticed him with the possibility of clearing his father's name, not because you're having a tender moment,* a snarky voice reminded her. *Stay focused.* She pulled her hand from his grasp. "Outside is fine. Where are we going?" He pointed toward a copse of trees near a creek that poured into a deep watering hole framed by granite boulders. "Wow, not bad," she breathed in surprise. "You can't even see this from the road."

"I know," he said, grinning. "It was the main selling point of the property. Reminds me of being a kid in West Virginia. My brothers and I used to hit the swimming holes regularly in the summer. We played hours of Drown the Rat. It was our favorite game."

"I'm not much of a swimmer," she admitted, though that water looked nice. "But I'd love to put my feet in." She shucked her shoes and settled on the bank to slip her toes into the freezing water. She immediately removed them. "That's *so* cold," she announced unnecessarily, catching a grin from Owen. "You could've warned me that the water is like ice," she grumbled, and he shrugged in response. Oh, she was beginning to like that grin far too much. The way his lips tipped at the corners should be a crime. Tucking her feet under her, she opened her pad and readied her pen. "Whenever you're ready, Mr. Garrett," she said, indicating it was time to get serious, which a small part of her, she could admit, was lamenting. She rather liked the idea of spending a lazy day here with Owen by the creek. Her imagination was doing a fair job of presenting all kinds of unprofessional pursuits and she needed to nip that kind of thinking in the bud. She hadn't come so far only to get derailed by her own hormones. However, if she were of a mind to throw away all her hard work and single-minded focus on a wild night of debauchery, she could see herself making a beeline for Owen Garrett. He was, in a word, hot stuff.

OWEN SETTLED BESIDE PIPER in the cool shade of a towering redwood but didn't know where to start. For one, he was distracted by the subtle scent of Piper's hair as the light breeze lifted the dark brown strands, making it the first time he'd ever seen her hair less than perfect. It stirred his imagination to see what a bed-tousled Piper looked like. Just the thought sent his mind racing and awakened his, uh, other parts. "So what do you want to know?" he asked, irritably.

"No need to be snippy. You agreed to do this," she reminded him.

"Sorry. Talking about this stuff puts me on edge. It's not exactly good times we're dredging up here," he said, and understanding dawned in her eyes. Soft, cocoa-brown eyes, he noted, doing a small double take. He looked away. "Ask your questions. I'll do my best to answer, but you have to promise me something…" He paused, and she waited expectantly. He figured it was a good sign that she hadn't immediately balked at his request. "If you find something that pertains to my father in your research, you'll let me know."

She smiled, the picture of perfection and beguiling sweetness. He had the distinct impression it was a well-rehearsed act, as she said, "Of course, Owen. Let's start from the beginning. What do you remember about the day your father died?"

CHAPTER FOURTEEN

OWEN CLOSED HIS EYES, not sure he was ready to relive that day. He'd spent a lifetime trying to forget.

"It was the first week of June, already hotter than hell," he remembered. "I'd been after my dad to go fishing but he'd been on edge all day. He wouldn't let me go down to the swimming hole, either. He wanted me close by, within his line of sight, he'd told me. I figured I was in trouble for something, because he'd never been one to act like that so it must've been me who'd done something."

"Was your father a strict disciplinarian?" Piper asked.

"Yeah, but he wasn't stingy with the love. He always kissed me on the forehead before bed and told me he loved me. He used to tell me, 'if there's nothing else in this world that's real, know that I love you.' It always made me feel special."

"That's sweet," Piper murmured, pausing in her note taking. "Hard to imagine, given the stories I've heard of Ty Garrett my whole life."

"Contrary to what people may believe, he wasn't a monster," he said. "Before he was Ty Garrett, leader of the Aryan Coalition, he was just my dad and I loved him."

"How'd your dad fall into that role as leader?"

He searched his memory, but came up blank. "I don't remember."

She flipped a few pages in her notebook and read a few lines, "According to my source, Ty Garrett became involved with the Aryan Coalition in 1979, five years before the raid. You would've been around six or so," she supplied, looking up to gauge his reaction.

"That's right. We moved around a lot before that," he recalled. "We settled here and stayed. My dad said there was good opportunity for work with the college campuses so close." He pulled his pocketknife from his back pocket and wandered to the closest tree to grab a suitable branch to skin. "But that was okay. I liked it here. I didn't mind."

She watched as he worked the branch, skinning the outside layer to reveal the smooth wood underneath. "What are you doing?" she asked.

"Whittling. Something my dad taught me. Good stress reliever."

"What are you making?"

"I don't know yet. Maybe nothing. Depends on what emerges from the wood." He gestured. "Keep going. I only want to go through this once, so let's not waste time."

"You were telling me about that day…" she said helpfully.

"Yeah…well, like I said, my dad was edgy all day, like he knew something was going to happen and if it did, he wanted me close so we could hightail it out of there."

"The raid happened around six o'clock that evening," she said. "But the information is sketchy in the hour afterward because, as we all know, it did not go down quietly."

"No," he replied darkly. "It did not." His father hadn't been the only one killed that day. In all, twelve people were mowed down that day. Some were innocent women and children.

"My father tried to get everyone out quietly and safely but something went wrong and suddenly bullets started flying. I don't even know who fired off the first shot but once that happened, the agents raiding the place went crazy until there were bodies and people dying everywhere."

"The news said that your father refused to surrender. That he fired the first shot and, in fact, the agent who shot your father claimed self-defense."

"That's not how I remember it," he said, though the details were hazy. He recalled his father falling, dead in front of him and then as he screamed, he felt someone jerk him off his feet and carry him away. "I saw him gunned down in cold blood but I was a kid, loyal to his father, and who was going to listen to me?"

A tiny excited smile lit her lips. "I think people will with the right evidence. Are you ready for this? My source said that your father was actually protecting *you* when he was shot. The agent had his gun trained on you and Ty took the hit instead."

"What?"

"Yeah, and I don't know why an agent would want to shoot a kid, but something feels fishy to me. Like I mentioned before, my source also told me that your dad was actually working with the FBI to bring the Aryan Coalition down. He was working deep cover, so deep that no one ever knew except those in the Bureau who had to know."

"Yeah, you said that, but what proof is there? Is your source willing to testify to that fact?" Owen asked, unable to keep the bitterness from his voice. His father? Actually one of the good guys? He wanted desperately to believe that but without proof it was useless. "Who said this?" he demanded, his voice trembling from the effort it took not to yell. "If this is true, I need to talk to this person."

She made a gesture as if to say *calm down* and continued, "You know I can't reveal my source, but I can tell you this, I've checked it out and he's legit. However, he's risking a lot in coming forward so I can't reveal who it is."

"Piper…" he warned in a low growl. "You're playing with my life. I need to know."

She ignored his request and said, "Back to Red Meadows… The news reports state the FBI had been trying to infiltrate the Aryan Coalition for years in order to break up their sophisticated drug and gun trafficking network. The FBI recovered a cache of drugs and guns that were worth millions. Apparently, a shipment had been ready to go when the raid occurred. Obviously your dad had someone on the inside he was also working with. Do you remember anyone who seemed particularly close to your dad?"

Unbidden, the image of the pregnant woman rose to the top of his memories and in light of this new information, he wondered if it were relevant. Pressing his lips together, he admitted, "I don't know of anyone at the compound, but there may have been a woman he was close to…but she's dead."

At that, Piper's mouth popped open and she sucked a wild breath as she gasped, "T… She called him T… Oh, I should've seen it…" At his look of confusion, she dug out a leather journal from the depths of her purse. She held it out to him and he took it, flipping it open as she explained. "I found this in a box that had my old stuff in it at the farm and I think the author of this journal was a young woman named Mimi LaRoche. She was murdered a week before the Red Meadows raid. I think…"

"She was my dad's girlfriend," he supplied in a pained voice, seeing the pregnant belly and how his father had been so gentle and reverent with his touch. He shook his head, still unable to process it. "But she was black…my dad was a racist. It doesn't make sense."

"What if he really wasn't? It was an act? You know, like my source said, deep cover?"

"But we were at the compound for five years…"

"He had to make it convincing. Remember how I said they'd been trying to infiltrate the Aryan Coalition for some time? They couldn't take any chances. It had to be all or nothing. Your dad fit the bill. No one knew him, he could pull off the cover without any hitches. It had to be real for you so that everyone would buy it. He probably never imagined it would go on for so long but once he was in, he couldn't get out until it was done."

His head reeled with the implications. "There has to be a record of him working with the FBI, some kind of employment record. Where could I find that?"

Another bright smile followed as she said, "You can't. But I can. What do you think I've been working on? I've submitted a FOIA request for the employment record for Ty Garrett. They have twenty working days to comply and it's likely they'll drag their feet until the last second."

"But if my dad was an agent, wouldn't I have received some kind of death benefit? Life insurance or something? As far as I know, I was tossed to my aunt with nothing. At least she never said anything."

"One thing at a time. First, we have to establish he was an agent. Then we'll figure out what happened to his death benefits."

He nodded but couldn't quite say anything else. His mind was blown. She seemed to realize he needed a minute because she respectfully offered him her silence. In fact, when their eyes met, he saw compassion. He looked away, staring across the creek's edge and wondered if he'd ever known his father at all. He returned to Piper. "So what's in it for you? Why are you digging into this?"

Something heavy warred behind her brown eyes but she gave him nothing. She simply smiled and shrugged. "I can't resist a good story."

He didn't believe her for a second and he called her

on it. "You've been after me for some time. Why are you digging up this story in particular? What's your angle? I already told you I'm not comfortable with you writing about this, so I have to wonder what you have to gain."

She fidgeted with her pad. "It's a pet project."

"That's all?" he asked, peering at her, trying to discern if she was being truthful. "Seems like a lot of work for very little payout."

"Well, that's your opinion," she retorted. "I like having answers and the discovery of this possible cover-up was more than I could pass up. Even if I'm just digging around to satisfy my own curiosity."

She drew a deep breath, flashing him a bright smile, and he wondered if she thought by blinding him with her pearly whites he'd become so dazzled that he didn't notice the tension in her shoulders. "Are you sure that's it?" he asked. He held her stare, willing her to be honest with him, even if he didn't like the answer.

She faltered, then admitted, "I want the truth to come out. I hate the idea that someone might be unjustly accused, and your dad seems to fit the criteria. The Red Meadows incident, as it's called in town, is a dark stain on the community yet no one is willing to talk about it. It made me wonder why. To my knowledge when people are hiding something they tend to want to bury it, which is exactly what happened with the Red Meadows raid. I mean, sure, there were the requisite news reports because hiding dead bodies is difficult, but it seemed too cut-and-dried, too easy. So I started asking around. I found a few people willing to give me tidbits of information that were nowhere near the story that was fed to the press. It fired me up and I wanted to know more. When I found the information about your dad, I knew I was looking at a full-scale cover-up that possibly went really high up the food chain."

"I can appreciate that," he mused, but he had a niggling sense that she'd hoped to win her coveted Pulitzer with his father's story. "But my intuition says you wanted more than just answers to a small-town mystery. You've already admitted to being ambitious. Forgive me if I'm a little wary."

"I won't apologize for my ambition," she said, stiffening.

He shook his head. "I'm not asking you to. But try to imagine if it were your family placed center stage in this tragedy. Would you still want the attention?"

She hesitated, clearly choosing her answer carefully. "If my father was innocent of the atrocities he'd been accused of, I'd want everyone to know and if that meant shouting it from the rooftops, I'd do it in a heartbeat."

"Even if your father didn't want the publicity?"

"Yes, I mean, no." She appeared frustrated with his questions. "We're not talking about me. I've already told you I'm not writing about this in the *Tribune,* so can we get back on task?"

He wasn't sorry he'd somehow touched a nerve. Maybe it would help her to understand how he felt. He wanted answers for his father but he wasn't interested in being in the spotlight over it. He still had a business to run, and stirring the pot—even under the assumption that it might change people's opinions—was a job he didn't want. He wanted answers for himself. He needed to know that the man he'd loved wasn't a monster after all. And for that, he was willing to endure the questions and the painful trip down memory lane.

"My parents might be involved in some way," she said, shocking him with her quiet admission. He could only stare, trying to process what she'd said. She shrugged, obviously troubled. "A source told me my parents were there at Red Meadows when it all went down. It could turn out to be idle gossip. My source wasn't exactly someone I would feel comfortable relying upon."

"Why?"

"Let's just say her memory might be fallible."

"So this person is old?"

"Very."

"Have you asked your parents about it?"

"No."

"Why not?"

She gave a half-laugh that sounded very sad to his ears and he realized she'd been thrown by this information. He could relate.

"Would you believe I'm not entirely sure they would tell me the truth?" she answered with a wry smile. "I grew up thinking my parents were incapable of lying, simply because everything in my household was always so open and nonjudgmental. If it's true…I don't know what it means."

"They might surprise you and come clean," he offered, hating the sadness he saw in her eyes. She had the look of a kid who had just discovered Santa wasn't real. He glanced at the stick he'd been whittling and tossed it in the creek when he realized he hadn't made much progress. He pocketed his knife and held his hand out to Piper. "Let's call it a day. I have to get back and make sure my crews got the work done."

She accepted his help and he hauled her up. He realized he liked the feeling of her hand in his and he might've held on a little longer than was necessary. If she noticed, she didn't comment on it and for that he was grateful. He wanted to thank her for being the nosy person she is and for digging into his business, but he wasn't sure how to say it without revealing too much. For years, he'd dreamed of clearing his dad's name but he'd had no clue as to how to do it. She'd single-handedly poked and prodded the right people to find what he couldn't in all these years.

"For a small thing, you're one helluva woman," he admitted, earning a grin that revealed white teeth that looked perfect for lightly nipping sensitive places.

"And for a tough-talking grouch, you're…not bad, either." She laughed at his chagrined expression at being called a grouch but the sound of her laughter coaxed a smile out of him. She sobered and he sensed she felt the tension between them just as keenly as he did but was fighting it twice as hard, which was saying something. A hunger to taste, touch and feel the petite firecracker demurely dressed in peach and white made his hands clench but he restrained himself. She seemed disappointed but stepped away, putting a respectable distance between them. "Thanks for doing this," she said. "I know it wasn't easy."

"If I finally get some answers…it was worth it."

And that was the truth.

CHAPTER FIFTEEN

PIPER'S MIND WAS BRIMMING with all the questions that still needed answering but she appreciated that these things had to be done in phases. The first go-around had left Owen stunned and her heart went out to him for the revelations. She'd felt a similarly stunning blow when Mrs. Huffle had dropped her bomb. However, she couldn't stop. You had to strike when the iron was hot.

The one thing making her squirm was her intent. She'd been evasive when Owen had asked but she didn't have the guts to admit she fully planned to write the story for a national publication when she had all the facts gathered. She should've been brutally honest and admitted she was going to write the story no matter his feelings and he could either jump on board and be part of the process or stand by the wayside and let the chips fall where they may. But with him looking at her the way he had been, she hadn't been able to get her mouth to actually say the words. It had seemed predatory, so she'd shied away from the truth and now she was disappointed in herself for being such a coward. If she wanted to be a top-level journalist, she had to be prepared to be ruthless, to do anything to get the story.

And yet, she was allowing personal feelings to rule her head.

She needed to work on that. And while she was at it, she ought to work on the wicked attraction growing between them. She couldn't allow herself to slip and let her hormones take the driver's seat.

Properly reminded of her motivation, she walked into her office and found two police officers waiting in the reception area. Nancy's apprehensive expression didn't bode well.

"What's going on?" she asked.

Nancy gestured to the police officers. "These gentlemen said they need to speak with you. I couldn't reach you on your cell…."

She grimaced as she remembered switching her cell off before her interview with Owen. She hadn't wanted to be interrupted. "I was out of cell range," she explained, smiling pleasantly as she gestured toward her office. "I'd be happy to speak with you. Follow me."

She led them to her office and closed the door for privacy. Her smile remained but an apprehensive quiver had begun in her stomach. "What can I do for you?"

The first officer pulled out a small notepad as he asked in a stern voice, "How did you know William H. Dearborn?"

She settled in her chair, her mind working furiously, though she remained impassive. Why were they asking about Dearborn? Finding the old recluse had been a coup in her research. Getting him to talk about his experience at Red Meadows had been like winning the lottery. But the way the officers were eyeing her, she had a distinct feeling something bad had happened to the old coot. "Well, I wouldn't say that I know him, per se, but I've talked to him casually about a story I was working on," she said, being purposefully vague. "Why?"

"When was the last time you saw him?" the officer said, ignoring her question.

She made a show of searching her memory, though in truth she knew the exact date. "Oh, gosh…let me see, maybe a month ago, I guess. Is something wrong?"

"I'd say. He's dead."

Dead? She suppressed a shudder as a goose tripped over her grave. She didn't like dead things. "I'm assuming since you're here it wasn't natural causes and you're chasing down any leads and because I had contact with him, you're zeroing in on me?"

"Something like that."

"Well, I'm an open book. Ask whatever you like. I'm terribly sorry to hear about Mr. Dearborn, though. I hope you catch whoever did this. He was a nice man, once you got past the twelve-gauge shotgun aimed at your face."

"He threatened you?"

She laughed. "He threatened anyone who came onto his property unannounced. But once he realized I was harmless, he settled down. We had a very nice interview. He even sent me home with some fresh herbs he'd grown in his garden." The officers exchanged looks, prompting Piper to clarify. "Totally *legal* herbs. You know, thyme and basil? Makes for really good spaghetti sauce." She paused, then asked, "And just how did you come by the information that I had visited him in the first place?"

"We found your business card on his desk."

"Ah, an obvious sign of guilt," she murmured with a false frown, annoyed and relieved at the same time that they had nothing to go on yet they were grabbing at anything and everything. Not that she was worried. When she'd left Dearborn, he'd been very much alive. However, she was troubled by his sudden death and that was the truth. "Is there anything else I can help you with?"

"What story were you working on?" the officer asked.

She smiled and lied. "Garden growing in the mountains."

"Can I see it?"

"Of course." She went to her computer and pulled up the dummy file of the story she'd written with absolutely no intentions of submitting but made for convincing evidence that she'd actually been working on something for the paper. She'd done it for Charlie's sake—the little cretin was always peeking over her shoulder, looking for an opportunity to get her canned—but, boy, she was glad she had it at the moment.

The officer peered at the computer screen and seemed satisfied. "It is going to run?" he asked.

She affected a sad expression. "Unfortunately not. My editor didn't think it had enough local interest, so he killed it. Oh, well. That's the way it goes sometimes."

"Seems like a lot of work for nothing."

She shrugged. "It's the nature of the business. Anything else?"

"No, we've taken up enough of your time. If we have any further questions, we'll let you know."

She saw them out and, once they were safely in their cruiser and gone, she let out a shaky breath that Nancy caught. "What's going on?" she asked, her eyes as wide as saucers. "Are you in trouble? Oh, the publisher isn't going to like trouble."

She waved away Nancy's concern, though she felt uneasy. "They're just following up any lead they can. William Dearborn was found dead. And not of natural causes."

Nancy's mouth turned down and she shook her head. "Such a shame. You know, before he turned into a recluse, he was quite handsome."

Piper did a double take at Nancy's unexpected comment. "Are we talking about the same William Dearborn? Wild, bushy-haired, mountain-man William Dearborn?"

Nancy nodded. "He was never the same after Red Meadows. Walked away from his wife and son, quit his job… It was all very sad."

She perked and stared at Nancy. "Who was his wife and son?"

"I don't remember her name off the top of my head but I remember the son's because it was so unusual… Farley, wait, no, yes, Farley. I think he and his mom stayed in the area, too."

Farley? Farley Deegan? The bane of her existence was related to William Dearborn? Funny, he hadn't mentioned having a son, but maybe he'd crossed them out of his life after Red Meadows…but why? She peered at Nancy, unsure she had her facts straight. "Do you mean Farley Deegan?" she asked.

"No, I'm pretty sure the boy's name was Farley Dearborn. Unless his mother changed it later. Oh, who knows these days. The mother was a bit…odd."

Odd certainly described Olivia Deegan well. Of course, *odd* was a relative term when describing inhabitants of the farm. "Why'd he leave his wife and son behind?" she asked.

At that, Nancy seemed to remember herself and closed up. "I don't know," she said hastily. "The whole town changed. Anyway, it's probably best to just let sleeping dogs lie. I'm sorry to hear about William Dearborn, but I'm glad you have nothing to worry about with the authorities. I'll make sure Mr. Cook doesn't hear of this little visit." She winked and went back to her work, leaving Piper to wonder if a fountain of information had been underneath her nose the whole time in their mild-mannered receptionist. She'd have to ferret out a way to see what Nancy knew. One thing was for sure, it was becoming readily apparent that Red Meadows affected more than just Ty Garrett. It was starting to feel as if everyone had something to hide.

And that didn't sit well with Piper at all.

GRETCHEN RUBBED HER BELLY and waddled into the kitchen, unable to just sit on her butt and do nothing when Owen was extending his hospitality by taking them in. She checked the kitchen to see what there was to work with and, to her surprise, she found enough supplies to make a decent meal in spite of Owen's claim to the contrary. He was such a good man, she thought, smiling with a sigh. If only he had someone to take care of him. Owen needed a good woman, someone who understood his schedule and his lifestyle. And her mama always said the best way to a man's heart was through his stomach. She grabbed a skillet and placed it on the stove. If there was one thing she was good at, it was getting a man's attention. *It was just holding it that you had a problem with,* her mama's voice countered sharply.

If it weren't for bad luck, she surely wouldn't have any, that was for sure. She also seemed to have a knack for finding the man with the least amount of character to fall in love with. Her love life résumé was pretty pathetic. She swallowed a lump of regret for her past and stared down at her huge belly. "I'm going to find you a good daddy," she whispered, wiping away the tears that gathered at the corners of her eyes. "I promise. No more Danny Mathers types for us. Nothing but top shelf, a hundred percent grade A from now on."

Gretchen shook her head and got to work, glad to have a project to keep her mind from straying too far into dangerous territory.

Danny was still out there. A shiver of fear followed. He didn't know where Owen lived but she supposed it wouldn't take too much effort to find out. She didn't want Owen to get caught in the cross fire should Danny show up wanting her to come back. She had to stop worrying about tomorrow when there was plenty to do today. She kicked Danny from her mind and focused on putting together dinner.

OWEN RETURNED TO HIS PLACE with one of his fallers, Timothy Knox, so as to make it less awkward with just him, Gretchen and Quinn sitting around. He didn't know what he was going to do after tonight but he'd figure that out later.

He opened the door and his nose alerted him to food cooking. "What the…" He sought out the savory smells and found Gretchen setting the table with a smile. "Gretchen, I told you I'd pick something up. I don't want you fussing over a stove in your condition."

Timothy followed, giving Timber a scratch behind the ears, but came up short when he saw Gretchen. His Adam's apple bobbed and he seemed flustered. Owen had forgotten to mention Gretchen was staying with him for a while when he'd extended the invitation for grub back at his place. "Smells good," Timothy said, rubbing his belly as if starved. "Bet it's a fair sight better than that chicken in a bucket you got there."

Owen glanced down at the takeout in his hand and agreed. Whatever Gretchen had whipped up smelled pretty damn good. Gretchen, shooting an unsure glance at Timothy, took the bucket and put it on the counter. "There's always room for chicken. We'll have both," she assured him.

Quinn bounced in, following her nose. "Chicken! My favorite!"

Gretchen grinned. "See? It won't go to waste. Now, go wash up. All of you."

Owen and Timothy went to the sink and made quick work of scrubbing while Quinn took over the bathroom.

The sound of her off-kilter singing was pretty cute, he had to admit.

He took a seat at the table where Gretchen had put out a full spread and he wondered how she'd managed to create so much with so little.

"Gretch…I appreciate…"

"Hush now, Owen, or you'll hurt my feelings," she said, and he buttoned up quick. He looked over at Timothy, who was watching Gretchen with something that looked a lot like longing, and he was struck by the sudden revelation that his faller had a secret crush on his office manager.

And Gretchen seemed oblivious.

How long had this been going on? he wondered. And how had he totally missed it?

Owen shot a look at Timothy and the faller seemed to catch himself, dragging his attention away from Gretchen and back to Owen. "How's things with that reporter? She still giving you hell?"

At the mention of Piper, Gretchen's expression soured. She settled at the table with Quinn and served her daughter before helping herself. "I'd never presume to tell you your business but I've got a bad feeling about that woman," Gretchen said. "She's nothing but trouble. I can see it from a mile away."

Timothy nodded. "I thought your head was going to explode when that last article came out." He snickered. "She sure knows how to rile you up, that's for sure."

Owen smiled. There was no denying that. Except, lately, he was feeling riled in a different sort of way.

"What were you talking about today? I mean, I

thought it was weird that she came here for an interview."

Owen shrugged, not particularly interested in sharing the details about their talk just yet. He wasn't ready for other people to know what was going on. Maybe because he didn't want to hear anything that might discount Piper's theory. Not yet anyway. He'd spent his life wishing he could find a way to clear his dad's reputation and now that Piper may have found a way, he wanted to cling to it. At least, for a little while.

"Are you feeling all right?" Timothy asked Gretchen, the rough-hewn faller looking as uncomfortable as a long-tailed cat in a room full of rockers at the idea of small talk but he was willing to give it a try. "You look good," he added. "'Cept for that black eye."

From the covert stares Timothy was giving Gretchen, Owen imagined Timothy was dreaming of the different ways he'd like to give Danny Mathers an education on how to treat a woman, much less a pregnant woman. It was probably a bloody and messy lesson at the cost of several teeth. He withheld a chuckle and stuffed his mouth with chicken and rice.

Gretchen colored and offered a strained smile. "I'm coming around. Hurts still." She turned to Owen. "But I want to go back to work tomorrow. I can't handle sitting around waiting for nothing."

"What about Danny?" Owen asked, concerned the SOB might try and show up at the office to find Gretchen.

"I can't hide forever," she murmured with a sigh. "Besides, I don't think he will. He's a coward. He knows there's always a handful of people at the office, bigger and stronger than he is." She risked a glance at Timothy and he gave a short nod, his mouth tight.

"He comes around when I'm there, I'll give him the message he's not wanted," Timothy promised, earning a small but grateful smile from Gretchen. "I'd like to see how he measures up against a man. See if he can hold his own when he's not thumping on a woman. Damn, piece of—"

"Yes, thank you, Tim," Gretchen interrupted with a nervous laugh before Quinn caught an earful of colorful language. Quinn giggled and grinned at Timothy and then at Owen, who was struggling to hide his own laughter. Tim, God love him, was as solid as they came but he didn't know much about censoring himself around children.

Tim realized his goof and his ears reddened. "Sorry," he mumbled, before shoveling rice in his mouth.

"Don't worry. I've heard worse," Quinn quipped. "'Specially when Mama came around the corner and banged her toe on the coffee table. She said lots of bad things."

The laughter Owen had been holding back burst forth in a guffaw that had Tim joining in and Gretchen blushing. "It really hurt," she admitted with a grin of her own.

The laughter eased the awkward tension and conversation flowed a bit easier until the subject of Piper came up again.

"So, do you think that reporter is likely to start hanging around?" Gretchen asked, fishing for more information. He shrugged and took another bite. "You know, I wouldn't be a good friend if I didn't at least share my fears about that woman."

"By all means," he agreed, curious as to what Gretchen had to say.

"Well, for starters, she's hyper-focused on her career, which means she'll do anything to get ahead. She's made it no secret that she has bigger dreams than staying in Dayton. She wants to be like some Diane Sawyer or something. I'm worried that she might be using you to make a name for herself."

Owen sobered. Gretchen had inadvertently zeroed in on his secret fear. Piper hadn't exactly answered his question when he asked what her angle was. But he couldn't imagine anyone in Dayton wanted to read anything new about Red Meadows and he certainly didn't want to see it splashed all over the news again. Although he supposed if he wanted people to know his father wasn't the bastard they thought he was, he'd need to release the information somewhere...still the idea of opening up the wounds was a little daunting. There were people who would never believe anything but what they wanted to believe. To some, Ty Garrett would always be the devil.

And no amount of evidence proving otherwise was going to matter.

CHAPTER SIXTEEN

PIPER FILED HER LAST STORY for the upcoming issue and tried to leave the building before Charlie made a nuisance of himself but she wasn't so lucky.

She was just at the front door when Charlie made his appearance.

"Police seem to be interested in your comings and goings after finding William Dearborn with a bullet in his head. Weird stuff," he said, causing her to turn and give him her best I'm-disinterested-in-whatever-you-say look.

"Charlie, if you have a point, please make it. I have an appointment."

He shrugged, but his eyes registered delight. "No point. Just making an observation."

"How'd you know he was shot?" she asked, latching on to that, as of yet, unreleased detail.

"I have sources."

"You're the education reporter. What sources could you possibly have? Unless, of course, there's some breaking news about the rising price in school lunches and the janitor wants to share what he's been pulling out of the trash cans."

He chuckled but there was a distinctly nasty tone to

it. "You ought to watch yourself. You're poking around in things that could get a girl like you hurt."

"Oh? Says who?" When he simply smiled, she turned away in disgust, but only to hide the shiver that had chased her spine. "Go bother someone else, Charlie. You bore me."

She closed the door on his next comment but she felt his stare boring into her back. She'd always considered Charlie harmless... Had she been wrong?

PIPER PULLED UP TO THE FARM and parked, not exactly looking forward to this appointment but she couldn't walk away from the possibility that Farley Deegan was actually Farley Dearborn. Given how Farley worshipped her, she imagined getting the information from him would be easy—if he had any information to give; however, Olivia Deegan might be difficult.

She walked up to the cottage that the Deegans had occupied since she was a child and knocked with sweaty hands. Farley opened the door, a giant smile wreathing his dopey face.

"Hi, Farley," she managed with a smile. "I hope I'm not intruding..."

"You're always welcome. You know that," he said, ushering her inside the small home. The immediate scent of patchouli made her nose twitch but, by the grace of God, she held back the sneeze. "Can I get you some fresh mint tea?" he asked, the picture of a solicitous host, which only made Piper feel worse.

"Tea would be great," she said, glancing around the home, looking for any sign of William in the photos scattered around in handmade frames of shells and rocks and other unusual scavenged items. "Is your mom home today?" she asked casually.

Farley returned with teacups in hand. "No, she's off with the group, making a difference. You know how she is. Nothing stops Olivia Deegan."

"She's a force of nature, that's for sure," Piper murmured in agreement as she lifted the teacup to her lips, wondering how to go about broaching the subject. In the end, she figured direct was best. Setting her cup down, she met Farley's stare and asked, "Farley, are you William Dearborn's son?"

"Yeah." Farley's bemused answer shocked her so much she could only stare. "Why would you want to know that?"

She let out a confused breath, staring at him for being so calm. "Did you know he died a few days ago? Was murdered even?"

At that, Farley looked away and gave a short shrug. "I didn't know him. It's a tragedy he died so violently. But he's with Gaia now, so I don't grieve, I rejoice. He was a very unhappy man in life."

"Why'd he leave you and your mom? And why don't you have his last name?"

Farley quieted, and for the first time in their acquaintance, she saw a different side of Farley. "You know, Red Meadows changed people. Some people were able to pick themselves up and move on…William couldn't seem to do that. William's brother, my uncle Teddy, was among those who died. I think William lived with a lot of guilt. In the end, it was too much. When he left, we came here. My mom thought it would be best to cut ties completely so that we could get a fresh start. The farm enabled us to do that. We changed our names legally and William never contacted us again."

"But you've lived in the same town," she exclaimed, her mind spinning. Did everyone in this town have something to hide? Had she lived her entire childhood with a bunch of strangers? It sure felt like it right about now. "Surely you must've seen each other from time to time. How awkward...and didn't you want a relationship with your father as you got older?"

Farley shrugged. "That wasn't our path. He went his way, I went mine."

"Farley," she began, shaking her head, not quite sure how to wrap her head around everything that she'd discovered in the past few days. "He was your father. And now he's dead. Doesn't that bother you in the slightest?"

Farley met her incredulous stare with a strong one of his own. "We all make choices. He made his. I'm not going to live my life with regret."

She huffed a short breath and set her teacup down for fear of dropping it in her agitation. "Okay, so you weren't close and you didn't want to be. But the fact remains he's dead. Who would want to hurt him? Do you think it has anything to do with Red Meadows?"

"Why would it? That was twenty-five years ago."

She dropped her gaze and nibbled her lip. "Well, I don't know if this means anything, but when I found out that your dad was at Red Meadows and he still lived in town—of course, this was before I discovered there's a handful of people still around—I went to his place to ask some questions. He told me some things that have led me to believe that…well, maybe things weren't reported accurately when it all went down."

"William had begun to lose his mind from the isolation," Farley warned her. "I wouldn't put much store in what he had to say. His memory was likely faulty. He might've even made a few things up. You never know."

"I thought that at first, too, but I have reason to believe that he was telling me the truth and now he's dead. Do you see a correlation?"

Farley paused, then said, "I think it's a stretch. This is Dayton, not San Francisco. It's not like this town has secrets worth killing for," he added with a patronizing chuckle that immediately grated on her nerves, signaling the Farley that annoyed the hell out of her had returned. "But it's so like you with that clever mind to try and find a story no matter where you look."

Piper tried not to grit her teeth. Instead, she directed the conversation back to more fertile ground. "You know that box you brought to me yesterday?" At Farley's nod, she continued, more convinced than ever that she was sitting on the hottest story Dayton had ever seen. "There was a journal in it that didn't belong to me. It belonged to a woman named Mimi LaRoche, a woman who was killed twenty-five years ago, right before the Red Meadows raid."

Farley looked aghast. "How morbid. Did you throw it out? I'm sorry you had to find that."

"Of course I didn't throw it away," she retorted,

unable to keep the irritation from her voice. "It's important evidence that proves my theory."

"Your theory of widespread deception in the town of Dayton?" he said with another deprecating laugh that made her want to do something rash. And particularly painful on his end. Sensing her rising blood pressure, he tried to mollify her, saying, "Listen, I think you're chasing a ghost story, but it seems important to you, so it's important to me. How about this… I will see what I can find out about that journal, such as how it winded up in your things, and if I find anything, I will let you know."

She relaxed a little, realizing that he was making an effort. "Okay," she agreed, yet added a caveat. "Please call first before just showing up. I don't want a repeat of the other day."

Farley's grin said he wasn't sorry at all for catching her in her birthday suit, but she supposed she'd let him have that one. As much as Farley annoyed her, he'd been a friend for a long time. It wasn't his fault she could never see him as anything but the boy she grew up with when he'd, at some point, fallen in love with her.

She rose and prepared to leave, but Farley stopped her at the door. "I miss hanging out," he admitted, all traces of the annoying Farley gone. "Since you left the farm, I never see you anymore. It'd be nice to get together once in a while. Even just as friends."

Piper nodded. "I'll work on it," she promised.

He accepted her answer with a smile. "See you around, then."

She started toward her car but then noticed the farm

was oddly quiet. Usually, it was bustling with activity. The quiet was unnerving and it signaled that something was going on. She turned to Farley, a question in her eyes. "Where did you say your mom went?"

Farley cracked a grin. "The tree-sit, remember? They're staging a protest against Big Trees Logging. Gonna shut him down for as long as possible. Didn't your mom tell you?"

She winced, her immediate thought going to Owen and how fired up he was going to be when he found his operation shut down. "I gotta go," she said, rushing to her car. She had to talk some sense into her parents before they ruined any chance for her to get more answers out of Owen.

Damn. Damn. Damn!

OWEN LISTENED TO HIS FOREMAN, Wesley Butcher, pepper his rant with swearwords above the crackle of the radio and once Owen caught the gist of the information, he followed with a blue streak of his own.

"They've shut us down, Owen," Wesley ground out. "They were here first thing this morning before first light. And there's a bunch of those tree-hugging liberals up the tree, too. You better get over here, pronto."

"I'm on my way," he said, shoving the half-eaten sandwich Gretchen had made for him into the trash. He wouldn't have time to eat it now and it would likely go bad sitting in his truck. He called out to Gretchen, letting her know where he was going in case she needed him, whistled for Timber who came bounding, and tore out of there, spitting gravel in his wake.

This was just perfect, he thought sourly. He should've known something like this was coming. That group had been entirely too quiet as of late. Obviously, they'd been mobilizing for a bigger event. Had Piper known this? Had she been running interference, keeping him busy so they could slip in unnoticed?

The thought raised plenty of ugly questions and one thing was for sure, if he saw a certain reporter she was going to get an earful.

Owen arrived in a cloud of dust, throwing his truck into Park so hard the transmission protested but he was too pissed to care. He strode into the clearing with Timber loping beside him, past the silent and waiting skidders and loaders, and their operators. He went straight to Wesley, who was staring up at the cluster of ecoterrorists with a jaundiced eye worthy of a crusty pirate. "You call the police?" he asked.

Wesley nodded in disgust. "For all the good it does. They're just gonna yell at them with a bullhorn and order them to come down, which they're gonna refuse. We're gonna lose a full day of production. Damn it!"

He clapped a hand on Wesley's solid shoulder and gave the short, compact man leave to take a breather. "I got this," he said, agreeing with Wesley the day was shot. "Why don't you guys go crack a beer. I've got some cold ones in the truck."

Wesley gave a final look at the tree-sitters who were perched on a platform about thirty feet in the air and walked away in search of a cold one, saying, "You're the boss."

He called out to the tree-sitters, "You're breaking the

law, you know. Don't you have better things to do than make the lives of honest folk miserable?"

An egg came sailing his way, narrowly missing him as he sidestepped the bio-missile to have it shatter messily on the ground. Timber sniffed at it before walking away, disinterested. Owen silently fumed. Maybe he should've let it hit him. Then he could've had them arrested for battery, too. Laughter followed and he gave them a middle finger.

The sound of another car pulling up caused him to turn and, when he saw Piper climbing out, camera in hand, he wanted to put his hands around her neck and squeeze until her head popped off.

OH, DEAR. HE WAS REALLY MAD. Piper's heart fluttered. No, that was too gentle a word for what was happening in her chest right now. Perhaps *banging* was more appropriate. Yes, her heart was crashing, banging, colliding into her chestbone so hard she worried a cardiac event was next.

"I didn't know," she started to say even as she lifted her camera to snap a picture at the spectacle. She snapped again from another angle. "I mean, I can't be held responsible for everything my parents do."

He grabbed her camera and she startled at the sudden motion. "Your protests would carry more weight if you weren't taking pictures for the paper while you do it," he said in a steely tone that caused her to shiver.

"I have a job to do," she retorted, a subtle shake in her voice. She glanced at the tree-sitters, easily picking out her parents as they waved cheerfully, and she returned to Owen with a guilty flush. "I didn't know. But if I leave this place without a story, I could be fired."

He let go of her camera but his gaze hadn't softened. He looked every inch the hardened logger she'd been faced with at the newspaper, not willing to give an inch and ready to destroy any obstacle in his way. He wasn't looking very cuddly, that's for sure. So why was it her knees were weakening and her body tingled with awareness in a way that made remaining celibate seem a ridiculously lofty goal, particularly in his presence?

"You and I are going to have words," he promised her in a soft voice that did terrible things to her resolve. It was only when he stalked away that she could breathe normally again. She shaded her eyes and looked up at her parents' group and resigned herself to the part she would have to play in all this. "I really didn't know," she muttered to Timber who had ambled over to her with his tongue lolling. She gave the dog a rugged pat on the head. "Not that he will ever believe me. Thanks *a lot,* Mom and Dad."

CORAL NARROWED HER STARE at the scene below as Piper absently stroked Garrett's dog's fur. She didn't care for the familiarity at all. "Did you see the way he manhandled Piper's camera?" she said to Jasper, incensed for their daughter. "What a brute. He's Ty's son for sure. The apple doesn't fall far from the tree."

"She can handle herself," Jasper said, pride in his voice. "I hope she gets a good shot. I'm not sure that camera has the range needed to get the full—"

"Jasper, stop focusing on the minutiae of unimportant

details," Coral said stridently. "We have bigger issues. Likely he will have called the authorities by now. We need to hold the line for at least another day. That should put a serious dent in his profit margin. Perhaps with enough of these types of events, he'll leave for good."

Jasper sighed. "It hasn't worked in all the years you've been trying. I think a different strategy is called for... or perhaps just letting it go."

Coral's stare turned wintry. "Let it go? How easily you've forgotten the fallen. Mimi should ring a bell."

"Let it go, Coral," he shot back, irritably. "You're becoming obsessed and it's highly unbecoming."

Olivia hushed them. "Stop fighting. We can't have our fearless leaders showing dissention in the ranks. We're doing something important here."

Coral nodded but spared Olivia an annoyed look. Olivia had always been a sanctimonious twit but they were bound by common interests and circumstances. "Right. Stay focused, people. We don't want anyone tumbling to their death."

Light laughter followed but Coral didn't share their mirth. Jasper called her paranoid but she felt a shadow hovering over them and she couldn't shake the notion that a reckoning was coming...one that was long overdue.

She shuddered. Not yet...she wasn't ready.

CHAPTER SEVENTEEN

PIPER DOWNLOADED HER PHOTOS, picked the best one for the next issue and shut down her computer, eager to go home and bury her head under the pillows. Ordinarily, she might find her parents' political antics entertaining but tonight, she felt weighted by their actions and forced to support a cause she wasn't sure was hers any longer. She loved the environment as much as anyone else, she understood and believed in the reasons her parents championed certain causes, but this single-minded focus to drive Owen Garrett from Dayton was beginning to feel suspect.

Doubts followed her all the way home. By the time she opened her door and walked inside, she was ready to fall into a tub full of bubbles with a bottle of wine for a companion.

In fact, she knew that was exactly what she was going to do. She didn't hesitate, dropped her purse to the table, and went straight to the bathtub. She simultaneously stripped while starting the water. While the claw-footed bathtub filled, she went for the wine.

Reaching for the white zinfandel, she also grabbed a wineglass and returned to the bathroom.

After a quick test of the temperature, she sank into

the bubbles, sighing as the water lapped her tired body. Her head lolled back and she took a hearty sip of the wine, letting it soothe the rough edges and blunt the confusion making a mess of her brain.

AFTER DISCUSSING HIS OPTIONS with law enforcement and making a few calls, Owen called it a day and left the site. He hoped the people mucking up his operation with their tree-sit froze their asses off.

But as he drove away, he didn't head straight home as he'd initially intended. He made a quick call to Gretchen to let her know he'd be late and not to wait on dinner, then placed a call to Timothy asking if he'd go keep her company for a while. Once that was taken care of, he headed straight for the one person he owed a conversation.

And if she were smart, she'd listen.

Timber whined beside him and he gave the dog a good pat to let him know everything was going to be fine. He hopped from the truck and Timber followed. Owen always kept dog supplies in his truck because he never knew how long he'd be out at a site and never wanted Timber to go hungry or thirsty. Because of this, he was able to tie up Timber to the nearest tree with food and water and head for the house, ready to take care of business.

He was fully prepared to rail at Piper for her part in the tree-sit. He found it hard to believe that she'd known nothing about their plans when everything that family did was an open book.

He banged on the front door, demanding to be let in.

"I know you're in there. Your little pretend car is parked outside so you can either open this door or I'll kick it down."

PIPER, ON HER FOURTH GLASS of wine, heard the racket outside and wondered if she were imagining it. When she realized whoever it was wasn't going away, she reluctantly left her bath—albeit a little unsteadily—and tucking a towel around her wet and bubbly body, went to answer the door.

She opened the door to find Owen, plenty pissed but suitably taken aback by the sight of her practically naked.

Her first thought was how glad she was it wasn't Farley standing there, but on the heels of that thought followed another—Owen Garrett was quite possibly the most handsome man on the planet. Particularly when he looked ready to tear her head off.

"I...we...uh...what are you doing answering the door in a towel?" he demanded to know, his hands going to his lean hips in a way that made a giggle burst from her mouth. He didn't seem to appreciate the humor in the same way and his frown darkened. "You're drunk," he surmised.

"A little tipsy, perhaps," she admitted, grinning. She never drank, which would account for the alcohol going straight to her head but she wasn't going to apologize. It was after hours and she could do what she pleased in her off time. "I've had a bad day. Would you care to come in?"

"You and me both. And no, I would not like to come

in until you've put on some clothes," he retorted, though his glazed eyes said otherwise. His reaction tickled her drunken funny bone and caused her to push the envelope. She dropped the towel and his eyes nearly bugged out of his skull.

"Oh, shit," he muttered, not quite able to pull his stare from her body though he tried. She giggled and pulled him into the house, straight to her mouth. This was why she rarely drank. But what the hell? It was too late and what was done was done. Might as well enjoy the descent into debauchery. What was she saving her virginity for anyway? At the moment, she couldn't quite remember. By medieval standards, she was an old maid whose womanly parts likely had dust from neglect. Thank God, they weren't living in the 1500s, she thought muzzily. If they were, she'd likely have five kids by now. Hmm…kids. Owen Garrett would probably make lovely babies.

He stiffened against her assault on his lips until she pressed herself tightly against every inch of that firm, muscled body so that her breasts squashed against his chest, pebbling the nipples into hard nubs of aching flesh that begged for more, though more of what, she wasn't sure. She just knew that she needed something and that need was blotting out every rational thought in her head. He groaned something about *only being human* and his arms wound around her, drawing her tighter against him until a delicious friction against her sensitive skin caused her head to loll, exposing the column of her neck for his mouth. "Bite me," she instructed him in a breathy tone that would've mortified her to her toes if she'd been a bit more sober. But she wasn't, so she reveled in her hedonistic request.

He complied, greedily sucking the tender skin into his mouth, teasing it with light nips and bites. Who would've imagined that someone so rough could be so gentle? She thrilled in his touch, wanting more.

Unfortunately he tried to pull away, much to her dissatisfaction. "Piper, you're going to regret this when you sober up," he said, his voice tight with strain. He was adorable when he was trying to do the right thing. She wanted to feel those firm hands on her breasts, wanted to see if his touch would relieve the ache that seemed tethered to her private spots, driving her mad. "Piper... please..."

"I like it when you beg," she murmured in a throaty whisper. "But I like it better when you're being bossy. Come on, tell me what to do. I'm a novice, you know, but I'm a fast study."

At that, he fisted a handful of hair in his palm and demanded a kiss from her without using a single word. He devoured her from the inside, owning every single gasp and moan, his hands roamed her backside, creating waves of red-hot need cresting and overtaking her until she was writhing against him, breathless and mindless. He walked her backward until her bare back hit the wall and she gasped then giggled as she hopped into his arms, locking her legs around him so that the heat of her center rubbed nicely against his middle. His mouth descended on her breasts and she nearly swooned like a Victorian lady. Except, there was nothing ladylike about the things she wanted him to do to her. He sucked the hard tips of her nipples into his hot mouth, laving each one with equal, hungry attention. This was good, she purred to herself, loving it. "More," she demanded on a cry, wiggling against him, urging him to take her against the wall that very second and screw the consequences.

"Is this the way you want it?" he demanded, his voice a harsh growl in her ear that decimated her ability to think clearly. He reached down to cup her mound possessively with his other hand, rendering her paralyzed with painful anticipation. "Fast and rough? You want me to take you from behind and make you come so hard that you can't see straight? Or do you want me to take you against this wall, pounding into you until you shatter against me, mindless. I could." His voice dropped to a whisper, pausing for his words to sink through the lustful haze they'd created. "But you'd hate me in the morning, because your virginity is not something you would want to give to me if you were sober."

"I won't," she gasped, nearly crying, fearful that he might stop. She'd never wanted anyone like she wanted Owen right now and she didn't think she could fully blame the alcohol. "I promise."

His hand softened to a caress as he smoothed the hair he'd roughed, the lust fading from his eyes. He brushed a kiss against her swollen lips, the sweet, tender slide of his tongue barely breaching her mouth. She gasped softly and her knees trembled, threatening to buckle. She opened her eyes and stared into his, as he said regretfully, "I would." And he pulled away with a sigh. "Now, please get dressed."

An unhappy frown formed on her face as tears filled her eyes. She'd been stone-cold rejected. Turning on her heel, she tried with as much dignity as she could muster in her inebriated state to make it to her bedroom. She only made it as far as her bed before she passed out.

OWEN RELEASED A SHAKY BREATH and pushed at his rock-hard erection in the hopes of getting the randy member to settle down. He said a prayer for strength and waited a few minutes before going in to check on her. When he saw her, stretched, still as naked as a jaybird, atop her bed, he groaned softly and wondered if he were being punished for something in a past life. Not even Ghandi was tested this much in a single day. Stay focused, he told himself. Think of kittens and basketball, grandmas and broccoli—anything other than the vision of perfection lying there on the bed like a pagan offering.

He went to her dresser in search of something— anything—to put on her, but when he opened the first drawer, he found a plethora of stringy, girly underthings that made the spit dry up in his mouth and his shaft swell all over again. He shut the drawer. "Forget that. A blanket will do," he said to her gently snoring form. He wrapped her into the sheet, gritting his teeth at the alluring scent of her body teasing him with what he couldn't have, and made quick work of hiding that luscious form from view. Once safely tucked in, she curled on her side with a breathy sigh and he couldn't resist touching her hair. The smooth velvet strands slid sweetly through his fingers, leaving him aching to know more of her. He'd wondered what a bed-tousled Piper would look like. Now he knew and wondered how he was going to get through the coming days with that image in his head.

He'd have to find a way. Otherwise, the next time Piper found herself in the mood to lose her virginity... he wouldn't turn her down and to hell with the morning after.

CHAPTER EIGHTEEN

PIPER ROLLED OVER with a groan, her head splitting and her mouth dry. *This* feeling, right here, was why she didn't make it a habit to drink. Her stomach pitched and she stilled in the hopes of causing it to settle. When she felt certain she wasn't going to throw up, she cautiously made her way to the kitchen in search of aspirin and some crackers.

Midway through her first saltine, bits and flashes of memory came back to her and she choked on a swallow. Her cheeks flooded with heat as she glanced down at her nude body and realized what had happened last night.

Oh, God. Owen's hungry mouth on her breasts… up against the wall…feeling as if she were drowning on a tide of wanton goodness… She covered her face and tried not to cry from the sheer mortification of her actions.

She remembered begging him to do things to her— things she didn't even have experience with! She touched her hair, remembering how it felt to have Owen's fist firmly clenched at her scalp, how it'd made her feel deliciously possessed and her cheeks flared again.

But her memory slid into darkness after that. Had

he taken her virginity? All signs pointed to yes, given how hot and heavy they'd been going at it. But, if that were the case, wouldn't she feel…different? Perhaps sore, even? She nibbled her bottom lip, unsure. Having a sister right about now would've been handy. Unfortunately, everyone she might've asked was sitting in a tree—a tree contracted to be cut down by the very man she may have given her virginity to. *Oh, Piper. What a right mess you've made of things!*

There was only one way to find out what truly happened last night and that was to ask the man involved. She swallowed at the prospect. What was the problem? They were both consenting adults. She could handle this. Yet, her feet remained rooted to the spot. Her phone rang and nearly sent her flying out of her skin. She grabbed it and answered. Though, in hindsight, she wished she would've let it go to voice mail.

Nancy's voice sounded apologetic as she said, "Sorry to call so early but the editor just caught word that the tree-sitters are going to be forcibly taken down first thing this morning and he wants you there to capture it."

She dreaded facing Owen again, but duty called. "Tell him I'm on it," she said, without a trace of the nausea she felt.

"I will. You're a very reliable girl," Nancy said with a smile in her voice. "Have fun. I know how you love these things."

She withheld a sigh. She *used* to love these things. Now she was starting to see Owen's side of things and agreed, her parents and their friends were a bit of a nuisance. She said goodbye and hung up.

Well, she'd better shower. Time was wasting. She had a date with a situation that was guaranteed to be awkward and miserable. *Yippee.*

OWEN WATCHED WITH GRIM satisfaction as the cherry picker lifted the police officer to the level of the tree-sitters. He heard, rather than saw, Piper drive up. Within minutes she was standing beside him, snapping pictures as one by one the tree-sitters were forcibly—but safely—removed by the officer.

"Back on the job, I see," he noted, keeping his mind where it should be instead of where it wanted to be, which was reliving every moment he'd spent tasting and touching Piper's body. He scrubbed at his head as if the movement alone could shake out the memory yet it remained in full Technicolor and THX-digital sound.

"A good reporter always goes where the story is," she said, snapping another shot, ignorant of the turmoil twisting his insides into a knot. How could he simultaneously eye her like a succulent snack and want to snarl and yell at her for being such a pain in his ass? Right about now he wanted to grab that fancy camera of hers and pitch it into the woods.

Last night he'd been thwarted in his attempt to question her about her motives. He wouldn't let the opportunity pass him by again.

"Did you know they were going to do this?" he asked, her answer important to him.

She stopped taking pictures and turned to him, her eyes serious. "No." Unfortunately, his relief was short-lived as she added, "Well, I'd heard about *something* that *may have* been mentioned about it but I never got a date and then I forgot. I've been busy with other things."

"You don't think it might've been important to mention?" he asked, deceptively calm.

She had the grace to look guilty even if she didn't cop to it. "And why would I tell you? That seems inappropriate."

He held back the words he wanted to say for another time. Instead, he said, "I'm going to send them a bill for my lost time."

She surprised him when she agreed. "Seems fair and expected seeing as their goal was to shut you down for a day or two." He glanced at her, nonplussed. She shrugged, adding, "However, you'll have to take them to court to get the money and it will likely cost you more in attorney's fees than will make it worthwhile, which is something they likely already know."

Damn. She had a point. He sent a dark glower toward the group, watching with no small amount of happiness as they were marched into awaiting squad cars. One woman, before being put in the backseat in handcuffs, shouted, "Get out of Dayton! No one wants you here!" and Piper's expression faltered, clearly bothered by the woman's shouting.

"Friends of yours?" he asked.

"My mother," she answered with a sigh. She caught his startled gaze. "What? You knew my parents were involved in this. It's not like it's a secret."

No, he figured not. But her mother? If the woman hated him before, if she found out where his mouth had been last night, she'd really hate his guts. If he were a real jerk, he'd make mention of it as she was dragged off but the good manners Mama Jo had drilled into his head kept his lips firmly shut.

He glanced at Piper, taking in every last detail with silent care. The morning sun picked up the subtle strands of auburn threaded through her hair like the sparkle of the summer sand during a sunrise and he caught himself before he reached out to touch her. Suddenly, Piper turned to him a bundle of taut nerves and agitation and he was glad to see he wasn't the only one twisting in the wind over the situation between them.

"Did you and I…" Piper started then stopped, her mouth tightening with the awkwardness of the moment. She drew a deep breath and he knew what she was getting at but he waited until she threw it out there. "What I mean to say is…did we *finish* what was started last night because I don't quite, well, I don't remember."

Equal parts relief and sharp disappointment followed her admission. He shouldn't be the only one saddled with the memory. He didn't answer right away and she clearly took that as an affirmative. For some reason he didn't feel obligated to correct her. He was still mad about the tree-sitters and whether she was an accomplice or not, she was certainly involved.

"Oh, God. This is terrible," she said with open distress, which he found mildly insulting.

"Was it that bad?" he asked.

"How should I know? You could be the best lover in all of Dayton, or all of California, for all I know, because I don't have a point of reference to judge against. However, that's not the point." He waited, curious to see where this was going even though his conscience started to twinge about the deception. "The point is that…"

"You were saving yourself for marriage?" he supplied with mock helpfulness.

Her mouth firmed. "No. I wasn't saving myself for anything. I wanted to stay focused on my career not my libido. Now the seal has been broken."

He nearly choked. "The seal?" He'd never heard it called that before. "I don't think I understand."

Piper glowered, her brows crashing together with very real agitation, waiting a second for some privacy as the last of the tree-sitters were escorted away, then said, "You know, the seal. If I never know what I'm missing then I don't lament its absence. But now I know what all the fuss is about and likely I'll want to do it again at some point."

His breathing turned shallow and his mouth dried at her blithe statement. It took every ounce of willpower not to volunteer on the spot to be the one to accommodate her. He certainly didn't like the idea of anyone else helping her out in that regard. But he didn't like the obsession he was developing when it came to her, either.

She seemed lost in thought as she mused aloud. "I suppose I'll need to consider birth control now. Oh, crud. Did we use a condom?" she asked, rubbing her forehead as if trying to massage the memory free. "This is why I don't drink. Thankfully, I'm not ovulating or else we could be having an entirely different conversation because I'm certainly not ready to be a mother—not that being the mother to your child wouldn't be nice, I'm just saying, I'm not ready to be *anyone's* baby mama."

"Good to know," he said, though how he managed without sounding as if he were in pain, he didn't know.

She sighed, a very put-out sound if he ever heard one, saying, "Yes, well, the problem is, because I don't exactly remember what the actual deed was like, I'm not entirely sure if I liked it. Everyone says the first time is painful. My mother—" She noted his expression—and possibly the fact he was damn tempted to toss her over his shoulder and find a quiet spot in the woods to educate her on the finer points of what they didn't actually do—and she faltered, her tongue darting to wet her lips. The action nearly undid him. "Are you all right? You have a funny look on your face."

"Funny how?" he asked, trying to appear calm when, in fact, he was trembling with the effort.

"I don't know but—" she swallowed, admitting "—it's a bit unnerving."

He didn't know how much longer he could stand. His foreman, Wesley, hollered at him and he was glad to have a plausible escape. "Duty calls," he muttered, not waiting for her reaction. He didn't care if he seemed abrupt. He needed a little distance so he could think straight again. All the blood had drained from his head to detour south, and it'd be a miracle if he could walk at all.

PIPER WATCHED AS OWEN WALKED away stiffly and she let her gaze roam. She supposed if she had to pick someone to take her virginity, Owen Garrett wasn't a bad way to go. A hot flush followed the thought and she covered a grin. No, he wasn't bad at all. She just wished she remembered all of it. Timber ambled over to her and she gave him a good scratch on the top of the head. Good dog, solid—just like Owen. She couldn't imagine Owen packing around a Chihuahua. She sighed and tucked her camera away with her notepad, leaving without saying goodbye. She had enough on her mind; she didn't need to compound matters by lingering.

She arrived at the office, filed her photos, turned in cutlines and quickly pounded out the story, but as she reread her work, she found it lacking in spirit.

An image of her mother, spitting hatred and vitriol toward Owen, made her frown. Why did Coral despise him so much? Her feelings seemed to go a little deeper than the environmental angle. A general sense of unease settled in Piper's bones as she made the decision to talk to her parents about her feelings.

And about their connection to Red Meadows.

GRETCHEN SAT AT HER DESK, chewing a hangnail that had snagged her attention. She'd waited for Owen to come home last night but he'd hardly said two words to her before he closeted himself away in his bedroom. His dark expression just before he'd disappeared had kept her from bothering him but somehow she knew that damn reporter was the root of the problem. She hissed in pain when the skin tore as she pulled the hangnail too quickly, ripping into the soft surrounding skin. She shook out her hand then popped it into her mouth to stem the bleeding.

She imagined Piper was at the site with Owen because of those stupid tree-huggers and it made her feel left out to be the only one sitting at the office. Not to mention, every noise made her jump out of her chair, afraid that Danny had shown up after all. A twinge in her back made her suck in a sharp breath until she massaged it away. She was too early for labor but the familiar feeling made her wary. She'd been laid up with back labor with Quinn for hours. It'd been excruciating and she was hoping this baby wasn't going to emulate her big sister with her method of arrival.

The sound of a truck pulling up had her lifting from her chair in the hopes that Owen had returned, but no such luck. She sat with a disappointed frown when she saw it was only Timothy, Owen's top faller. The man wasn't much of a conversationalist, particularly around her and he had a tendency to stare a bit. It made her uncomfortable. She withheld a sigh and offered a smile for the sake of being pleasant when he came in.

"Everything all right?" Timothy asked, glancing around the office as if checking for the boogeyman, suspicious of every shadow. "Owen said he wanted me to check on you."

She warmed at Owen's concern. "That's so sweet of him. I'm fine. Just a little hungry is all," she added, mostly to make small talk but also because it was the truth. She'd forgotten to pack a snack and now her stomach was growling.

Without a word, Timothy turned on his heel and left. She blinked and frowned after him. What a strange man. So quiet. She wondered if she wanted to know what was happening behind that quiet facade. Likely not. In her experience, what went on in a man's brain wasn't something a woman needed to know. Although she wished she'd had some inkling as to how rotten Danny was behind that false smile and oozing charm. A tear escaped and she wiped at it, irritated at herself for allowing such self-pity. She'd made her bed, she'd find a way to climb out of it.

The door opened and Timothy returned with a red apple in his hand. He offered it to her with that dark-eyed stare that unnerved her. "S'all I got in the truck but it's fresh. Just put it there this morning," he said. "You shouldn't let your blood sugar drop. Here, take it."

She accepted the apple, unsure of what to do in the face of the unexpected gesture. She tried a tentative but genuine smile for his thoughtfulness. "Are you sure, Timothy? You work far harder than me…you sure you won't miss it?"

"I'll be fine."

"Okay," she said, rising to wash it off and cut it into manageable pieces. "But you have to at least share it with me. I wouldn't feel right otherwise." He shrugged as if agreeing but his eyes seemed to rest on her belly before rising to meet her questioning gaze. "What?" she asked, smoothing her hand over her stomach in a defensive motion. Why did he have to stare at her like that?

"Nothing," he said, looking away. "You feel all right?"

"My back hurts a little," she admitted, though why she didn't know. She managed a light laugh as she handed him a few apple slices on a paper towel as she returned to her seat. "I think it's this office chair. Not great for my growing behind," she said with a self-deprecating chuckle.

"Nothing wrong with your behind," he said, then seemed to blush when he realized what he'd said aloud. "All's I'm saying is that…I don't know, it seems fine to me. Good. Nice. Whatever, you know."

Now it was her turn to blush. Had he just called her fat butt *nice?* Danny had always poked and pinched at her thickening body as her pregnancy had progressed, snickering and making fun of her burgeoning belly. She risked a glance at Timothy. "Thank you. Feels good to hear even if you're just being polite," she said to him, giving him an out but he didn't take it. In fact, he seemed even more determined to heap compliments her way. Well, compliments Timothy Knox-style.

"Everything about you is bigger," he said, his stare drawn to her breasts that had indeed tripled in size since the beginning of her pregnancy. That had happened when she was carrying Quinn, too. "It's nice. Real pretty, you know? Women are supposed to be soft and curvy."

She chuckled, admitting sadly. "Danny said I was turning into a fat cow."

At the mention of her ex, Timothy's stare darkened and his mouth tightened as he said, "He's an idiot. If he comes near you or Quinn…" As if he'd realized he'd said too much, he tossed an apple slice in his mouth and mumbled a quick goodbye. Then he was gone.

Frowning, she stared after Timothy's truck as it pulled onto the highway.

She'd known Timothy for a year, almost right around the time she'd met Danny. He'd never opened his mouth around her until recently. Yet, she sensed something deeper beyond that hard faller's usual expression. And the feelings it evoked confused her.

Timothy Knox?

She bit into the apple, wiping away the sweet juice as it dribbled down her chin.

He wasn't her type. She could count on her hand the number of times he'd actually spoken to her before today. They seemed polar opposites. She liked to laugh and have a good time; he seemed to always hold himself apart from all the noise. No, he wasn't the kind of guy she would even notice under most circumstances.

Yet…he'd given her an apple from his own lunch even though fallers had one of the toughest, most physically demanding jobs in the entire operation. His concern had been her blood sugar.

She sat in quiet reflection for a long moment. It appeared there was more to Timothy than she knew.

Sad, but she'd never dated a man who put her feelings above his own. Her eyes moist, she rubbed at her stinging nose and thought of Quinn and her new daughter and wondered how she was ever going to teach her girls to look for men who will love them, instead of belittle them, when she hadn't found much luck in that department for herself. She sniffed at the tears that rolled down her cheek, annoyed at the show of self-pity but the tears kept falling. Damn hormones. She always turned into a weepy mess when she was pregnant. Owen, bless his heart, pretended not to notice but she knew it was hard to miss when he caught her sobbing over the fax machine because it had eaten her last fax. His answer had been to replace the fax machine, saying the office was due a new one anyway.

Owen was a good man, no doubt. Which was why she wanted to keep that toxic reporter away from him. Trouble was, that reporter seemed intent on being around Owen and that made Gretchen grouchy.

Owen was so good with Quinn. He treated her as a father should with strength tempered by kindness. Gretchen paused a moment to fully consider that thought. She'd known Owen for a while now but she'd never tried to attract his eye for she knew he was consumed by the job and besides, it never seemed prudent to keeping your job by messing with the boss. But, there was no doubt, he'd make an excellent father figure for Quinn. If only Owen had ever looked twice at her before she was pregnant, she might have something to build on. Now, she was seriously handicapped in the seduction department. Wallowing in self-pity and wondering what to do with her life, she wished she could snap her fingers and fix the royal mess she'd made with her litany of bad choices.

Her bladder sent a painful zing, reminding her that a tiny baby was using it as trampoline, and she waddled slowly to the bathroom. As she washed her hands, she caught her reflection in the mirror and made a face at what she saw. Everything seemed swollen. No wonder Danny couldn't stand to look at her. Timothy's bald appreciation of her curves came back to her and she wondered at what he saw. She was easily packing an extra twenty pounds on her frame including her pregnancy weight—an unfortunate side effect of her penchant for rocky road ice cream—and her face had lost the sharpness of her teenage years, rounding out a bit, particularly so now with the baby weight piling on. She tentatively cupped her breasts and groaned at how they overfilled her hands like giant melons. How could anyone find this attractive? Maybe Danny was right…there was no such thing as pleasantly plump. More tears threatened to fill her eyes but she wiped them away with determination. She'd be damned if she was going to sit here, curled up like a teenager at the prom bawling her eyes out because her date left her for someone else. She didn't have the luxury. There was work to be done and if she was good at nothing else, she was excellent at keeping Big Trees Logging moving in the right direction.

She was halfway to her desk when her back twinged again.

This time hard enough to take her breath away.

"Ohhh," she gasped when she could draw air in her

lungs. "That one really hurt…" She touched her stomach and found it hard as a walnut. She knew that feeling.

Oh, no…it can't be…

The next spasm created a band of fire around her belly and she knew there was no denying it—she was in preterm labor and alone.

Now, she realized, would be a good time to cry.

CHAPTER NINETEEN

PIPER WALKED INTO HER PARENTS' house, comforted by the familiar sounds and smells that she'd come to associate with safety and security but her nerves had progressively worsened from when she'd pulled into the driveway to the moment she stepped over the threshold.

Her parents were hiding something and she had a feeling it was terrible, which was in direct odds with everything she'd ever known her parents to be.

They weren't deceitful people. They were painfully and embarrassingly honest and blunt, particularly about things that made other people blush or uncomfortable, such as sexuality, politics and religion.

So what could they be hiding?

She pushed a sizeable lump down her throat, recognizing it as fear but she didn't turn around and skip out, even though the idea became more appealing the closer she came to the answers she sought.

Her father saw her first and the giant smile wreathing his face as he watered his prized roses broke her heart just a little. Maybe she should ask another time. The answers could wait. *No,* another voice said sternly, steering her straight to the patio chair and depositing her firmly. *Get this over with. You're a professional. Act like one. Pretend they're not your parents and get the answers you need.*

Right. Not her parents.

"Hey, peanut," Jasper called out as he adjusted the water stream to the gentle rain setting. "Fancy seeing you here. I think there's some tofu balls in the fridge if you're hungry."

Coral came from the garden shed with her shears and smiled brightly when she saw her. "Did you get a good picture?" she asked, referencing the tree-sit. "I hope you got one that accurately depicts the righteous anger and sense of indignity at the injustice—"

"I got a decent picture," she said, cutting her mother off, impatient to get to the real reason for her visit before she chickened out. "We need to talk."

At her seriousness, they both stopped and gave her their utmost attention, which is what they always did when she made dramatic declarative statements. But no doubt, they weren't expecting what was going to pop from her mouth today.

"What is it?" Coral asked, concerned. "You look all bound up like you've eaten a block of cheese for breakfast. We have fresh prunes…"

"I don't need prunes, Coral," she retorted, newly irritated. "What I need is straight answers from the people who always professed to be honest with me."

Coral and Jasper exchanged looks, but Piper couldn't tell if the look was conspiratorial in nature, as in our-goose-is-cooked or confused because their ordinarily easygoing daughter was going all psychobitchy on them without provocation. "Why didn't you tell me you were at Red Meadows?" she asked, throwing it out on the table like a big, stinky dead fish. Funny, her parents' reaction seemed appropriately aghast as if she had indeed thrown a cod their way.

"What are you talking about?" Jasper asked, twisting the valve so the water trickled to a stop. "Who told you this?"

"Classic deflection. Nice try," she said, refusing to allow her love for them to soften her questioning. "A good source has informed me that you and Coral were, in fact, at Red Meadows when the raid happened, which oddly, is something you've failed to mention in all the times I've asked you about Red Meadows."

Coral's smile faded to something ghastly as her cheeks lost the color from the sunshine and turned an ugly, unhealthy hue that made her look years older. Instead of answering, she turned a baleful eye on Jasper and said in a tone that Piper had never heard her mother use, "I told you she wouldn't stop," she hissed, letting the shears drop with a dull thud to the grass. She jerked her gardening gloves from her fingers and held them tightly in her palm. "I knew this day would come. I said I wanted to send her to New York to spend time with your awful sister but you assured me everything would be fine. Well, it's *not*." She stalked past a stunned Piper and disappeared into the house, closing the sliding-glass door so hard Piper thought the glass might shatter. She whipped around to stare after her mother, unable to process what had just happened. She returned to her father, whose usually sparkly eyes were dull, and fear came crashing down on her. Maybe she wasn't ready to know what happened.

"Dad?" she ventured, unsure of what to say in the face of her mother's freak-out. "What's going on?"

In all her years, she'd never seen her father look so haggard, so ashamed. "Why are you doing this?" he asked, his voice miserable. "Haven't I told you how much pain is associated with Red Meadows? This town wants to forget, not dig it back up again."

"William Dearborn is dead," she said. "Killed like Mimi LaRoche. Someone committed murder then and someone is doing it now. What if they're the same person and they're getting away with it?"

At the mention of William and Mimi, Jasper's eyes clouded and a mournful sound escaped him. "How'd William die?" he asked.

"Shot in the back of the head, execution style. Nothing was taken, or stolen, which rules out robbery, but it seems highly suspicious that shortly after William shared with me certain details about Red Meadows, he ends up dead."

Jasper looked at her sharply. "What kind of details?"

"I'm not at liberty to share at the moment," she said, unable to believe she was giving her father the common line she gave strangers when she wanted them to stop fishing for information that only she was privy to. His mouth pinched at her answer, clearly unhappy with her evasion. "What's going on? Is there something I should know? What was Coral talking about? I get the sense that you two are hiding something terrible and it's really freaking me out."

"You should be wary of the information given to you by William. He wasn't right in the head. That's why Olivia left him. She was afraid for Farley's safety."

She drew back. "Was he violent?"

"He was a different man back at Red Meadows."

"Sounds like he wasn't the only one," she retorted, frustrated with her father's evasive answers. She wasn't getting far and she needed more. "Help me to understand why my parents were living at a racist compound when they are plainly, at least to my knowledge, the furthest thing from racists that a person can be."

"It was a different time and we were different people, like so many at Red Meadows. Ty Garrett was—"

"Working with the FBI to bring down the Aryan Coalition," she supplied hotly, righteous anger for a man she never knew, for the son he'd been forced to leave behind bubbled to the surface. "And he took a bullet meant for his son. What do you know about that?"

"Again, if your information is coming from William, I'd say it's unreliable, at best, and grossly misleading, at worst. Ty Garrett wasn't a hero."

"What do you mean?"

"He seduced a young girl and then when she became inconvenient..."

She held her breath, not wanting to hear this but it was her father and how could she not believe him?

Jasper shook his head, a faraway look in his eyes. "She was a good, sweet person. And what happened was a tragedy and a crime."

"Are you saying Ty Garrett killed Mimi LaRoche?" she asked on a gasp.

"Nothing was proven. He died innocent...of that particular charge, but he was guilty of plenty others."

TROUBLED BY HER FATHER'S OMINOUS revelation and his reluctance to elaborate, she left her parents' house with a head full of misery and confusion. What if her source was wrong about Ty Garrett and her father was right? What if Ty Garrett was worse than just a racist but a murderer, as well? She worried her bottom lip as she thought of how devastated Owen would be to find out this new information. It certainly didn't do much for her story, either. The whole point of digging into the past was to prove Ty's innocence, putting an entirely new slant on the Red Meadows story. There was nothing to be gained from writing about a man people already considered a villain.

Unhappy and unsure of what to do, she bypassed her office and went instead to Big Trees Logging in the hopes of catching up with Owen.

When she arrived, she found a flurry of activity, including a parked ambulance. The EMS crews exited the small office building with Gretchen on the gurney, clutching Owen's hand with tears rolling down her face. She stared at Owen, surprised by the pinch of jealousy that followed at seeing him so attentive and obviously focused on the pregnant woman. They loaded Gretchen into the ambulance and Piper called Owen's name, prompting him to turn and hastily tell her to bring Gretchen's daughter Quinn to the hospital. He didn't wait for her agreement, just climbed into the awaiting ambulance and she watched as it drove away.

She frowned, coughing and waving at the dust trail that spewed behind the ambulance and realized there was someone else left behind. He couldn't be the father, otherwise he'd be the one holding Gretchen's hand instead of Owen. "Friend?" she asked the compact, intense man beside her. He looked as if granite had been poured into his muscles because everywhere she looked she saw hard, solid strength. He must be a faller, she surmised, remembering Owen's description of the various jobs on the site. She held out her hand. "Piper Sunday, *Dayton Tribune.*"

"I know who you are," he said, dismissively. "You're the one making all that trouble for Big Trees Logging. I got nothing to say to you."

She withdrew her hand, stung, though she should've seen that coming. No one, aside from Owen, had ever been overly pleasant with her. Not that she blamed them, per se, but it still sucked to play the part of the villain. "Just doing my job," she said stiffly, glancing sidewise at the man. "And you are?"

"Not interested." And then he walked away, leaving her to stare after him. Oh, that was perfect. A perfect cherry on the top of the day she was having. And he had terrible manners. She chased after him, tapping on his shoulder for his attention. He turned with a grunt. "What?"

"You don't have to like me but you could at least be civil."

"Says who?"

"Says me." She jutted her chin out. "Now, why don't

you try and redeem yourself and tell me what happened here?"

"Why should I? You gonna put it in the paper?" he asked, suspicious.

"No. I'm…worried. Gretchen is pregnant and nowhere near her due date, right?" she asked, surprised when that impassive mask slipped, revealing true concern in the lug's face. "I'm supposed to get Quinn and take her to the hospital. What should I tell her?"

"I don't know," he admitted, looking helpless, which was a strange look on a man who appeared made from steel. "I guess, the truth is a good place to start but the kid's been through so much already."

"You care a lot about Gretchen and her daughter," she said, casting for information, going on a hunch.

"'Course I do," he retorted. "She's a good office manager…and a good woman."

"I'm going to go out on a limb here and guess that you've got feelings for Gretchen. Does she know?"

He looked ready to deny it, but Piper fixed him with her best knowing stare and he crumbled like an overbaked cookie. "Is it that obvious?" he asked roughly, his stubbled cheeks coloring under the scruff.

"Maybe not to some, but I've got a sixth sense about this kind of stuff. So, why aren't you riding beside her in that ambulance?"

"Owen's taking good care of her. She needs him."

No, Gretchen needed a man who was available and Owen certainly wasn't. "Are you the kind of guy who waits for opportunity to fall in your lap or do you go after what you want?"

He scowled. "What do you mean?"

"*Hello?* I mean, the woman of your dreams is right there beneath your nose and you're letting her get away. You're the one who ought to be by her side. If you don't show a woman how you feel, she'll never know. Make a declaration and stand up for what you want."

He stared, looking caught between wanting to run after the ambulance and being rooted to the spot, but she gave him credit for stepping up when he said, "I see what you're saying."

"Excellent." She nearly clapped her hands in delight. Here she was suffering from pangs of jealousy when, in fact, this man right here had it bad for the preggers office manager. Thank God. She hated the idea of chasing off a pregnant woman for Owen's affections. She eyed him, then came upon an idea. "How about this… give me your cell number and I'll call and give you an update as soon as I hear about Gretchen."

"You'd do that?" he said, narrowing his stare at her as if he didn't entirely trust her but desperately wanted to know what was happening with Gretchen so he was willing to do just about anything. He had the look of a man who might camp out at Gretchen's door, out of sight, but within reaching distance if she needed anything. "All right," he agreed, giving her the cell number. "Call me as soon as you know. But you don't have to mention to her that you're doing it, okay? I don't want to bother her too much."

She smiled and lied, "Of course not. It'll be our secret."

He seemed reluctant to accept those terms—being

beholden to a reporter seemed a dicey deal to most—but he nodded and then climbed in his truck and rumbled down the street.

She checked her watch. School was nearly out. Time to get the kid and take her to the hospital and then find Owen.

OWEN TRIED HARD NOT TO CRY like a little girl each time Gretchen squeezed his hand in time with the contractions that, according to a monitor the nurse had hooked her up to, were registering like Mount Saint Helens right before its top blew off. "It's too early," Gretchen said between contractions, tears leaking down her face. "What if she's... Oh," she cried as another wave of pain rolled over her. "Not okay? She's too little, Owen..."

He didn't know what to say to that, because he didn't have a friggin' clue as to what could happen to a premature baby. So he just tried to reassure her with words that seemed optimistic, when in fact, he felt the urge to vomit. "She's going to be fine," he assured her, wincing as he was fairly certain she'd just crushed the bones in his hand to a fine powder. "They've got all that fancy equipment for just this occasion. It'll all be—" *holy hell, help me* "—fine."

PIPER ARRIVED WITH QUINN and she texted Owen to let him know they were there. Within moments, a white-faced Owen rounded the corner to the lobby, rubbing his knuckles as if he'd just gone a round with Ali. Quinn ran to him and hugged his waist. The easy familiarity between the two squeezed Piper's heart a bit but she ignored it. She understood Owen cared for the little girl because she was beginning to realize that Owen's heart was bigger than he liked to let on. It was endearing, this hidden component of the rugged logger and she found it entirely sexy to boot. Now that she was an experienced woman, she decided she could make those kinds of determinations.

"How is she?" Piper asked.

"She's in labor. The doc couldn't stop it." He looked down into Quinn's worried gaze and tried to put a positive spin on it. "You're going to be a big sister, so you'd better get that name figured out. Your mom's going to need it pretty soon I figure."

Quinn nodded, her face drawn and serious. "Okay."

He ruffled her hair as if she were a ten-year-old boy instead of a girl and said, "Don't worry. It's going to work out just fine."

But Piper didn't know if that was true and she could tell neither did Owen but he was trying his damnedest to appear confident for Quinn's sake. Owen caught her smile and sheepishly returned it. Caught up in the moment, she almost forgot about the promise she'd made to the surly faller, Timothy. She stepped away to make the call, leaving Owen to ease Quinn's fears and offer opinions on a name.

Moments later, she returned, pleased with the conversation, knowing that Timothy would likely risk a speeding ticket to get here.

"What was that all about?" Owen asked, wary.

"You've got a smile on your face that looks like the cat who ate the canary."

She decided to level with Owen, taking him aside so that Quinn wasn't privy to the conversation. "Listen, I don't know if you realize this but your faller, Timothy, has the hots bad for Gretchen. I told him that she needed him here pronto because she was all alone."

He scowled. "Why'd you lie? I'm here."

"Not for long. I need to talk with you."

"It'll have to wait," he said, his glower darkening. "Gretchen's baby might die. We're her family." As in *Big Trees Logging, not you* was the message left unspoken but she heard it loud and clear. "Thanks for bringing Quinn but you can go now."

And just like that, all the feel-good, gushy feelings she'd been marinating in went down the drain. Boy, he could go from endearing to uncommunicative asshole in a heartbeat when it suited him. And it hurt to be on the jerky side of that attention, particularly so because she found she cared. She lifted her chin and blinked back a sudden wash of tears at his rebuff. "You're not the only one who is concerned," she said stiffly. "But I can see that I'm not welcome. Goodbye then."

What a jerk, she thought, fuming with equal parts hurt and anger at his attitude. No matter what, she'd always be on the outside looking in when it came to him. And why did she care? She wasn't looking to build something with Owen Garrett so what was with the mopey, mournful feeling in her chest that felt like an elephant had used it for a stepping stool? She was nearly to her car when she felt an arm reach out and haul her

up against a solid chest, seconds before two strong, calloused hands cupped her face to cover her mouth with
lips that felt familiar yet strange. The contradiction,
coupled with the foggy memory of the other night, fired
her blood with the speed of a triple espresso mainlined
into her vein.

"You're driving me crazy, woman," he growled
against her mouth, sliding his tongue into her mouth,
claiming it for his own as he had before. Her knees
threatened to buckle and he pressed her against her car,
leaning into her as if he couldn't get enough. He broke
the drugging kiss and she peered into eyes she could
easily—and happily—drown in. He said with a tight,
pained voice, "I can't leave. I wish I could. You've been
on my mind since last night and we have things we need
to discuss but you have to understand that Gretchen
needs me right now and I can't walk away. I won't.
And if you're expecting me to, you're not the woman
I'd hoped you were."

She staggered under the weight of his statement,
wondering at it, too. He wanted to believe in her. She
swallowed, the echo of her father's information pressing heavily on her. She couldn't very well drop that
bombshell on him right now; he had enough pressure.
He didn't need something like that to bury him.

"I understand," she said softly, liking the feel of him
against her very much. The relief in his eyes made her
newfound knowledge a terribly heavy burden to bear but
she found she was willing to carry it for a little while
longer if only to see that look in his eyes again. That
look said he wanted her, hungered for her and she'd

never been on the receiving end of all that heated attention before. An all-over shiver caressed her body as surely as the memory of his hands and his eyes darkened as he caught the delicate motion.

He closed his eyes briefly as if questioning his own sanity and she wanted to tell him she understood because she had a few questions of her own. She remained silent, though, not willing to break the spell between them, but Owen broke it for her, pulling away with open regret that she savored like a junkie with a fix.

"Will you stay?" he asked.

If she stayed, what would people say? Someone was bound to see her and tongues would start to wag. It might get back to her editor, or the publisher. Would they care? It was highly likely. Charlie would whine into his uncle's ear that she'd lost her objectivity and he might pull her from the beat and switch her with Charlie's education beat—oh, God, the very idea sent a roll of nausea straight to her stomach—and she'd never get the chance to write usable clippings for her portfolio. She nibbled her bottom lip, caught between wanting to go with Owen and walking away to preserve her career.

But in the end, those eyes, piercing and knowing, drew her in, hypnotizing her with their warmth and depth, the way they changed with his mood and seemed to zero in on her most private thoughts with unerring accuracy. She hitched a breath and managed a smile as she slipped her hand into his and reminded herself, even as they walked through the hospital doors, that it was all for research. She needed access to Owen Garrett. And if that meant standing by his side as he went through a crisis, she'd do it—because that's what professionals do. They go after the story...no matter what.

CHAPTER TWENTY

AFTER TEN HOURS OF LABOR, Gretchen pushed out a slimy, wiggly baby girl who was immediately rushed to the NICU because of her tiny size. At barely thirty-one weeks, the two-pounder needed a little help breathing but otherwise she looked good—at least, according to the doctor.

"So, she's going to be okay?" Gretchen asked, tears in her eyes. Timothy hovered by her side, not saying much but listening very intently. "She's so small."

"She's not out of the woods yet but she's got a good birth weight considering her prematurity. You can go see her in a little while. The nurses are stabilizing her body temperature because preemies have a difficult time regulating their temperature on their own."

Owen breathed a sigh of relief and Timothy's shoulders seemed to sag a bit. He glanced at Piper standing off to the side, not wanting to intrude on the moment. But she'd remained the entire time, pacing the waiting room with the rest of them, so he figured she'd earned the right to let Gretchen know she was there. He gestured to her and she shook her head. He motioned again as if to say *C'mon, you big chicken,* and she came reluctantly into the room. Gretchen's expression registered shock, then she managed a wan smile.

"Hello again," she said.

Quinn said, "Ms. Sunday brought me."

Gretchen nodded in thanks, but Owen could tell it would be a long time, if ever, before these two women would be best friends. In spite of the exhaustion ringing Gretchen's eyes, she glanced from Owen to Piper and her mouth tightened with knowing. He figured he was going to get an earful when she was up and running again but she'd come around once she realized Piper wasn't out to destroy him. At least, he hoped. Otherwise, things were likely to get uncomfortable around Big Trees Logging with him getting cozy with Piper.

To his surprise, Gretchen offered him a smile and asked for a moment alone with Piper. He looked to Piper, who seemed equally shocked by the request and wondered if this was the mother of all bad ideas. "Are you sure? You ought to be resting...."

"It'll just be a minute," she promised.

Owen bent to hug Gretchen and Timothy moved from his designated spot.

"Is there anything you need?" Timothy asked Gretchen before leaving the room.

"I'm good." She graced him with a smile that was both sweet and appreciative and Owen saw the tiniest flicker of something pass between the two that had never been there before—at least not on Gretchen's end—and Owen bit back a tired grin. He'd never considered himself a matchmaker, but he liked to think he helped make whatever was going on between Gretchen and Timothy happen. Unless it didn't work out—then he didn't have anything to do with it. He swallowed a chuckle at his own private humor.

"All right…I guess I'll wait for you outside," he said to Piper, still not sure leaving the two women alone was prudent.

Well, he figured, at the very least, Gretchen was too weak to do too much damage. At least, he hoped that was the case.

"I—"

"He's a good man," Gretchen cut in, getting right to it. "Don't hurt him."

"I'm not out to hurt anyone," she said evenly, though a twinge of guilt poked through her fatigue. "But he's a big boy. He can take care of himself. He doesn't need a champion."

"You don't know what he needs. You don't know him."

"I'd like to know him better," Piper said. "And I think the feeling is mutual."

At that, Gretchen nodded with what looked like resignation and Piper had to wonder if Gretchen had entertained thoughts of a romantic nature in regards to Owen. She straightened and met Gretchen's stare, waiting to see which way things were going to go. Then Gretchen yawned and the fight seemed to drain out of her. "Thanks for bringing Quinn."

"Sure." A moment passed by, then she added, "You know…it seems a good man has his eye on you, in case you're interested."

Gretchen smiled and closed her eyes. "Timothy."

"Yeah, so you know how he feels about you?"

"I think so."

"Well, he seems like the kind of guy who would treat you and Quinn well. Just saying…I don't know, maybe you ought to give him a chance to try."

"Maybe I will."

Well, Piper was good with that. It was a start. It was up to Timothy and Gretchen to make it work.

Piper went to the door and then stopped, turning to say, "I'm glad your baby is okay. Quinn is going to make a great big sister."

Gretchen nodded her thanks and her eyes drifted closed.

Piper closed the door softly and met Quinn and Timothy in the hall, returning with snacks purchased from the vending machine in the cafeteria.

"Me and Timothy are going to stay with Mama, if that's okay," Quinn said to Piper. "Can you tell Owen? I don't want him to worry."

"You got it, kid," Piper said, giving Timothy a wink and a smile. "Make the most of your opportunities."

She didn't linger for a response, just headed for the exit. She found Owen waiting for her in the parking lot.

"What was that all about?" he asked.

She waved away his question. "Girl stuff." She closed the gap between them. "Kiss me before I come to my senses," she demanded in a sultry whisper.

With one smoldering look, Owen managed to sear away the fatigue and set her body to tingling. She didn't need to be psychic to discern the bent of his thoughts and she found it extremely exciting to be the source of the heat in his eyes. He responded with a kiss that left her toes curling, and at that moment she might've sold her own grandmother—if either had still been alive—if Owen asked her to.

"My place or yours?" he asked, his voice husky.

"Whichever one is closer," she answered breathlessly, then remembered her parents propensity for dropping in unannounced and changed her mind. "Yours."

"Mine it is." He kissed her again, hard. "See you there."

The twenty-minute drive to Owen's sobered her a bit. As the heady intoxication of lust and desire faded and gave way to common sense, she wondered if this part still counted as research. She questioned if she was getting in over her head, pushing too hard, with little regard for the aftermath, but then she thought of Owen and how it felt to be pressed against him and she pushed away the negative questions nagging at her.

She exited her car and followed Owen wordlessly into the house. Timber rose from his perch on the porch and followed them inside as if it were completely normal for visitors at this late hour and she almost laughed at the absurdity of the situation. She turned to say something, anything, to lighten the tension swirling around them, but he wasn't in the mood to exchange witty banter and pulled her into his bedroom, shutting the door with his foot so that his hands could be on her body.

She shouldn't be nervous, they'd already done the

deed. So why was she shaking? Was that normal? If only she knew.

"Ready to try this sober?" he asked, a devilish smile lighting up his face in a way that made him look dangerous and delectable at the same time.

"I think so," she said, licking her lips, wishing he would just launch himself at her like he did in the parking lot. Instead, he circled her like a cat, playing with its prey.

She took a step back and found the bed. She sat quickly, unsure of what to do with herself. Should she let him make all the moves or should she try a few of her own? Well, not that she had *moves,* per se, but she knew of a few things she'd like to try, such as running her tongue down the muscled wall of his chest, for starters.

Hovering over her, he claimed her mouth again, drawing out a long, deep kiss that left her clutching at his back, eager to feel more. Except, as the kiss ended, she sensed something between them—and she wasn't talking about his erection.

"What's wrong? You no longer look like you want to eat me alive," she said, her lips swollen and thoroughly kissed. She wiped at her mouth, suddenly self-conscious. "Did I do something…or not do something…"

"Oh, that's not the problem," he assured her, though the grimace that followed wasn't doing a bang-up job of convincing her of that fact. He stilled her with another kiss but the heat had definitely tapered off and she didn't know what had gone wrong. He rolled onto his back, staring at the ceiling, wrestling with something heavier and more powerful than his desire and that had to be bad, in her opinion—for, in her current state, she'd sell the farm without blinking. "I have a confession," he stated, causing her to raise an eyebrow.

"You've got some timing. Can't it wait? I mean, I'm no expert, but it seems to me that this is not the time for midnight confessions."

His mouth firmed. "It can't wait. I've already waited too long."

"Is this where you tell me that you have a wife tucked away somewhere with 2.5 children?" she half-joked, but a part of her was serious.

"No wife. No kids." Still, his expression looked grim, so whatever he was hiding must be pretty bad.

Piper sat up, wary. Man, this was not how she envisioned this happening. Disappointment tinged her voice as she asked, "Well, so what's this confession? I have a feeling I'm not going to like it."

"Probably not." He sighed.

Even wearing the weight of the world on his shoulders Owen was one hot specimen, she noted as her thoughts refused to focus. "Well, let's get it over with," she said, sighing, as well. "It doesn't look like the evening is going to end the way I'd hoped." Damn it.

"You know the other night?"

"Yeah?"

"Nothing happened. Not really."

Huh? Was he saying…? "I'm still a virgin?" she asked, grasping his meaning. Which meant he'd lied. Or wait, had he? She didn't recall him admitting to anything, she'd made the assumption and he hadn't corrected her. "Why'd you let me think…"

"I don't know," he admitted sheepishly, looking away as if he couldn't bear to look her in the eyes. Served him right, she thought with a frown. Dirty dog. "I was going to but I was distracted by the tree-sitters and your association with them and, before I knew it, it'd gone too far to pull back."

She ought to let him twist in the wind. He deserved a good flogging by his conscience, if not a literal flogging. "That was very ungentleman-like," she stated.

"I never claimed to be a gentleman, but you're right. That's why I couldn't continue until I came clean."

"How noble of you," she said wryly. "And then what did you imagine would happen?"

A twitch of a smile followed as he dared to say, "You'd appreciate my honesty and we'd continue with the slate wiped clean?"

"Not likely."

His face fell. "Yeah, it was probably a long shot. Well, look at it this way, your seal is still…intact."

Not entirely. Already a hunger curled in her tummy, at the sight of his half-clothed body. That was definitely hard to forget. "You deserve to be punished," she said sternly to his surprise. "But it's too late. I'll think of something appropriate later." She crooked a finger at him and patted the mattress beside her. "For now, let's sleep on it."

"Excuse me?" he said, his eyes widening in what looked like a little panic and shock. "You want to… sleep together?"

She grinned. "Yeah. I do." His expression said it all. He didn't hold sleepovers. Piper smothered the laughter in her chest with a yawn and shimmied out of her clothes. She rolled to her side, giving him an excellent view of her naked backside. "Don't forget the light," she called over her shoulder.

"Shouldn't you put some clothes on?" he said, his voice strangled. She grinned into her pillow, enjoying every minute of his discomfort.

"No. I always sleep in the nude, remember?" *Welcome to your punishment, Owen Garrett.* "Good night. Sleep well."

A muttered, "Not likely," as well as a stream of curse words, followed her into dreamland as she fell asleep with a smile.

CHAPTER TWENTY-ONE

OWEN OPENED ONE BLEARY EYE, feeling about as rested as a man facing his execution in the morning. No one had ever slept in his bed with him. He didn't like to give women false ideas about their place in his life. As if to question the situation, Timber walked into the room and whined.

"Yeah, you and me both, buddy," he whispered, careful not to disturb Piper. Timber licked his chops and settled with a grunt that said *buddy, I don't care what you're doing, I have to pee,* and Owen rose silently to let Timber out to do his business. When he returned, Piper had awoken and was watching him with sleep-hooded eyes. Damn, she was sexier than hell. He couldn't remember the last time he felt so out-of-control with a woman. He should've sent her packing the minute he realized the attraction but he hadn't been able to. He'd never been so utterly enthralled with someone he hardly knew, but he was helpless to do anything but stare in wonder at the body he ached to touch.

"How'd you sleep?" she asked, early-morning scratchiness giving her voice an even sexier quality. She stretched, completely mindless of the sheet as it slid away from her upper body, revealing breasts that nearly made his eyes cross.

"Not well," he answered in a low tone, sliding back into the bed and tucking her against him. "But then I think that was your intent."

He felt her smile against his chest. "You deserved it. I don't like liars."

"I'm not a liar under most circumstances," he said, tracing his fingertips up and down the bones of her spine. "But I find myself doing and saying things I'd never do when I'm with you."

She lifted her head and peered at him. "Like what?"

"Like everything," he said, leaving it at that. She evoked feelings in him that made him uncomfortable and he certainly didn't know what to do with.

She met his mouth and allowed him to roll her on her back. His erection, which he was fairly certain never fully went away, sprang back to life, straining to plunge into that sweet heat but he held himself back. Staring down into her upturned face, he wondered quietly what kind of insanity he was succumbing to that he found this moment, even as horny as he was, deeply satisfying. Touching her, feeling her, sharing the quiet morning together, it tugged at a part of him he'd shut down a long time ago for fear of it getting in the way of his business. He'd given up a lot to make his business a success, but it was only at this instant that the realization stung.

"It's easy to see why people like to do this," she murmured, her fingers threading through his hair and resting at the nape of his neck. "Being here with you…

it's difficult to remember what could possibly be more important."

He could offer a flip response to keep the mood light but he didn't. Instead, because he understood what she was saying, he offered the only bit of wisdom available to him in his current state, "You just have to remember that the moment always fades and eventually you have to deal with the aftermath."

She wrinkled her nose subtly. "True. But until then, let's pretend the moment isn't around the corner and enjoy the morning together."

He bit back a groan. "I'm not sure we should," he admitted. As much as it physically pained him, he knew he shouldn't take her virginity. It was too much responsibility, too much of a gift he didn't deserve. "You've waited for a reason. I respect that."

Her smile warmed him inside with a heat that had nothing to do with his desire. "I know. That's why I want it to be you. I wanted it that night but I handled it badly with the alcohol. And I'm grateful you had more sense than me but right now, I'm sober and I know what I'm asking. I want it to be you."

Her admission humbled him. His hands trembled as he cupped her bare breasts and brought them to his mouth. She arched against him, her breathy sighs shaking his foundation unlike anything ever before. He created a trail of kisses from her breasts to the sensitive skin of her sides, and down to her mound. He'd never been with a virgin before but he wanted her to experience as much pleasure as possible. And the best way to accomplish that was with his tongue.

EVERYWHERE HE TOUCHED, he ignited a fire. When his head dipped lower to taste her most intimate place, her first instinct was to withdraw and push him away but his growl as he nuzzled the soft, moist flesh sent goose bumps rioting across her body. She gasped aloud as he lifted her more firmly to his mouth, fitting her sex perfectly against the rasp of his chin and cleverly darting tongue. This, she realized in a haze, she didn't remember, but, oh, goodness, she was ready to give Owen whatever he wanted as long as he never stopped what he was doing to her.

She was no stranger to an orgasm—she'd been a virgin not a nun and had discovered the art of pleasuring herself on her own—but when she found her climax with Owen, it left her shaking and nearly crying with its magnitude. She thrashed on a gasping cry as wave after wave of clenching, straining muscle contracted until she felt wrung out like a damp dishcloth after a long night in the kitchen.

He climbed her body, pausing to nip small kisses on the sensitive skin of her belly and breasts, eliciting little gasps on her part.

"Are you sure?" he asked once more, his concern for her feelings so endearing she knew without a doubt he was the one she wanted to do this with. She imagined all the other times she could've lost her virginity throughout her various college escapades and thanked her stars she'd been focused *and* choosy.

She smiled up at him, deliciously languid yet hungry for more. "I'm sure. Now, come here…"

HE SLIPPED A CONDOM ON, his hands betraying him as he slid the sheath over his erection. Bracing himself on his forearms, he encouraged her to bend her knees and he nudged her opening, sweat breaking out on his forehead. Slowly, gritting his teeth and terrified he was going to hurt her, he pushed his way inside, noting the subtle tensing of her body as he broke past the hymen. She clung to him, her knees bracketing his hips, as he carefully waited for her to adjust to him.

"That doesn't feel as good as the other part," she said tightly, her breath short as if she were holding it.

"It'll get better," he assured her, barely able to get the words out, his eyes almost crossing from the strain of holding himself in check so he didn't hurt her further.

"It better, or this will be the last time I do this," she grumbled, shocking a laugh from him.

He caught her mouth, kissing her deep to distract her. When he felt her relax, he resumed the motion, grinding against her until he felt the telltale building in his testicles that signaled the end was around the corner. He pumped harder, losing the ability to be gentle, and for a second he nearly blacked out as the most intense, heart-shattering orgasm ripped through him, knocking out the lights in his brain and sending every coherent thought scattering for high ground.

Holy hell...

As he lay atop her, gathering what little he had left of his brain, he heard her muffled voice say in a breathy but slightly puzzled tone, "Is that it?" And his ego died a painful and ignoble death. Good thing, he rebounded quickly.

"Challenge noted and accepted," he murmured, rolling her on top as she shrieked with surprised delight at the sudden action. "Woman, by the time you leave this bed, you won't even remember your name."

She laughed as they rolled again...right off the bed.

Thank God for plush carpet.

PIPER WALKED INTO HER OFFICE, a dreamy smile on her face that she couldn't hide no matter how hard she tried.

That is until Charlie appeared, his smarmy mug effectively crashing her buzz with great skill.

"Got any good leads on who offed William Dearborn?" he asked casually.

"I'm not a detective, Charlie, just a reporter," she said, moving past him to her desk, hitting the power button on her computer and waiting for it to boot. "Don't you have a Student of the Month assembly to catch?"

He ignored her jab and pressed on. "How does it feel to be a person of interest?"

"Excuse me?" she queried sharply. "I'm not a person of interest any more than anyone else who had the misfortune to leave the man with a business card."

"Yes, but perhaps Old Willie didn't give you the answers you were looking for—maybe he told you that your boyfriend is the son of a monster and you didn't like it very much."

"And maybe the tooth fairy is real. Got any other wild tales of fiction to share? Honestly, Charlie, for a writer you have absolutely no amount of imagination."

"You know what, Piper? You're a bitch, and when you go down in flames I'll be there with the marsh-mallows."

"Blah, blah, blah. And if you weren't the publisher's nephew, you'd be out of a job because you couldn't write yourself out of a paper bag. Go away and let the real reporters do their work."

Charlie turned an ugly shade and she wondered if someone so young could actually have a heart attack from their blood pressure hitting the nuclear stage. Talk about a show. She'd definitely be there with popcorn. But he seemed to get a hold of himself just enough to offer her a smile that wasn't nice in any way, saying as he left, "Watch what you dig up, Piper…you won't like what you find."

That was…weird, she thought. Charlie Yertz, equal parts putz and creep. Piper shook her head and drop-kicked the annoying man from her thoughts. She had bigger issues.

She was falling for Owen Garrett.

This presented a multitude of problems, the least of them being her desire to remain single until she found her place among the greats in journalism—and that was no small thing.

She couldn't imagine bringing Owen home to her parents. If the food didn't kill him, the conversation likely would. Piper tried to picture Owen suffering through tofu and bean sprouts for the sake of her parents, and while she had no doubt he would give it a go, she wouldn't wish that on anyone. And then there was her mother's crazy behavior coupled with her father's cryptic evasiveness. Funny how just a few short weeks ago she'd been blissfully unaware that her parents harbored a deep, dark secret.

Leaning back in her chair, she ignored the flashing cursor on her word processing program, her thoughts in a tangle. And there was the biggest problem of all… what was she going to tell Owen about what her parents had shared? She felt she owed it to him, but when she thought of how crushed he'd be…there it was again… hesitation. *Damn it, Piper,* she chastised herself. *Get it together. Just because you slept with the first man in your life, doesn't mean you have to give up everything you've worked for.*

Do you still want a Pulitzer? she questioned herself ruthlessly.

Yes. God, yes. The medal would look so wonderful framed on her mantel.

So suck it up. Stop falling for Owen Garrett and get focused.

Right. She bypassed the sad little ache that created a fissure in her chestbone and returned to her computer, determined to get the newspaper work finished so she could do some more digging on Red Meadows. The problem, she realized, was that she had to determine if her parents were being truthful about Ty Garrett, and if they weren't, why?

Well, she amended, that was the problem she was willing to tackle today. The rest would have to wait.

OWEN MADE ARRANGEMENTS with his foreman out at the site and then headed for the hospital to see Gretchen.

He'd received a call saying there was some kind of disturbance involving Gretchen.

He strode to Gretchen's room, his thoughts racing. He breathed a sigh of relief when he saw Timothy standing sentinel by her side. A police officer was taking a statement, which told him something happened involving Danny Mathers, the piece of shit who'd caused all this turmoil.

"What happened?" he asked Gretchen after the officer took his leave.

She wiped at the tears flowing down her cheek, but he was glad to see the high spots of anger there. "He had the balls to come here, acting like it was all okay and he was going to see the baby. It's a good thing she's not here but in the NICU, or the jackass might've tried to run off with her, not even caring that she needs special care right now." She spared Timothy a grateful look. "If it weren't for Timothy… He made sure Danny understood the lay of the land."

She dabbed at her eyes but then clenched her fists in a show of righteous indignation. "That rat bastard. I can't believe I ever thought I was in love with him."

"So they caught him?" Owen asked, hoping that was the case. He'd sleep a lot easier knowing that asshole was sitting in a cell instead of roaming the countryside.

"Yes, thank God," she said. "Timothy wouldn't let him in the room and things got a little heated. Then the police showed up when I hollered for the nurse and told her who he was and that he was wanted for trying to kill me and the baby."

Owen looked to Timothy and he simply nodded as if

to say he agreed with her rendition of the events. "Good job, Timothy. Glad you were here," he said, not liking the thought of what might have happened if Timothy hadn't been here. But by the looks of things, you'd have to pry Timothy away from Gretchen's bedside. The man had it bad. How he'd managed to hide his feelings for Gretchen all this time, Owen didn't know but then he didn't traffic in matchmaking so he didn't much care, either. He was just relieved Gretchen and Quinn would be safe. "So how's the baby?"

Gretchen lost her ire and beamed. "She's doing excellent. She's a fighter. You can see her later if you want. Timothy was just going to help me to the NICU so I could express some breast milk for her."

Breast milk. That was his cue to leave. "Thanks, but I have to get back to the site. Do you have a name for the kid yet?" he asked, being polite and to steer the topic to safer ground.

Gretchen's mouth softened and she shared a look with Timothy. "Well, Quinn was having a hard time deciding so Timothy suggested Audrey, because it means *noble strength*. We thought it was perfect, since she's such a survivor."

"Audrey." He tested the name and found he liked it. "I agree. It's a good fit." He smiled and went to shake Timothy's hand for being there when Gretchen needed him. He sensed Timothy would always be there and he was standing where he'd always wanted to be. He envied the man's quiet resolve and patience and wondered how he'd known Gretchen was the woman for him, even though at the time, she'd been with someone else. He'd simply waited until Gretchen realized the man she'd been looking for had been right in front of her the whole time.

That was some heavy stuff. Mama Jo would've called something like this divine intervention, guiding two people who were meant to be together. He wasn't sure if he bought into that entirely, but he was glad to see two people find each other, no matter the unusual circumstances.

Inspired and buoyed by his friends after he left the hospital, Owen detoured from his office to the *Dayton Tribune* where he hoped to find Piper but had no such luck—the receptionist told him she'd already left the building.

"Might you know where she went?" he asked, to which he received a false smile but little else. "Let me guess...you don't give out that kind of information?"

She smiled again as if to say *Bingo!* And realizing she wasn't going to budge, he left. But before he could drive away, he found a man slouching against his truck in the parking lot. "Can I help you?" he asked.

"I bet I know where Piper is," he said.

"Yeah? You a friend of hers?" Owen asked, not liking the man's tone or the way he was leaning on his truck.

"*Friend* is a generous term. Colleague is more like it. So, I hear she's digging into the Red Meadows raid. I bet that puts a crimp in your date nights."

Owen narrowed his stare at the man. "What did you say your name was?"

He pushed off the truck and held out his hand, which

Owen reluctantly accepted. "I didn't. My name is Charlie Yertz. My family's been around a long time in these parts. My uncle owns this place, actually."

Owen didn't see why that was relevant but he figured even skinny nerds like Charlie Yertz needed something to crow about. "So, did you say you knew where Piper went?" he asked, bringing the conversation back to something he was interested in hearing.

"You know, I've never seen anyone more driven, more focused than Piper. When she sets her mind to something, she gets it. I mean, look at you...one minute you're ready to pull her head off and the next she's got you dropping by the office all nice-like, ready to enjoy a pleasant lunch date. She's good. I'll give her that."

Owen didn't like what this guy was implying and his scowl said as much. "What's your point?"

Charlie held his hands up. "No point, just making conversation. But man to man, I think I owe it to you to warn you."

Man to man? That was rich. Only one of them qualified by Owen's estimation but he wanted to know where the guy was going with his warning so he encouraged him with an "Oh?"

"She's just using you to write the story that she thinks is going to propel her out of Dayton and into the big-time New York scene. She wants a Pulitzer and she'll stop at nothing to get it."

He stared at the man, not sure if he wanted to deck him for being an annoying little pissant or shake more information out of him. Something about what he said made a certain amount of sense and that was the part that bothered him. Piper was undeniably driven. And she had pursued him relentlessly to gain access to him for her research into Red Meadows. Against his better judgment, he asked, "To what purpose? So what if she's digging into the Red Meadows raid? Who's going to want to read about that? It's old news."

"Maybe, maybe not. William Dearborn was killed in the same way Mimi LaRoche bit it twenty-five years ago. Seems a little suspicious that Dearborn eats it right after sharing some juicy details with Piper about the raid. You know, the cops consider her a person of interest in Dearborn's case."

That was absurd. Piper was capable of getting into a heap of trouble, but he couldn't see her killing someone for a story. However, he could see her being ruthless in her attempt to get information. Had she inadvertently put Dearborn in danger by asking questions?

Charlie's nasal voice cut into his thoughts. "Why do you think she's been digging so hard into the past? She needed you for one reason and one reason only...your memories of Red Meadows."

"That's a bunch of bullshit," he muttered, eager to get the hell away from this man and the toxic crap he was putting in his ear, but Charlie wasn't finished.

"Is it? I don't know...I'd at least check it out. You wouldn't be the first Garrett to fall victim to a beautiful woman, no matter how bad they were for you."

At the reference to his father, Owen nearly grabbed the man by the neck but he'd already turned tail and returned to the safety of the office. What the hell did he mean? He bit back a mouthful of frustration. It felt like everyone in town knew more about the past than he did, even when it came to his own father.

He tried to wipe away the stain left behind from the man's insinuations but they stuck no matter how he tried to bleach them with reassurances.

Was Piper using him?

His lips formed a grim line when he couldn't get the questions to stop. Well, if she was, she was doing a bang-up job and deserved an Oscar because she was putting on a damn good show.

Hell, he'd bought it.

But he'd never been the kind of man to go off on vague notions and assumptions. He'd go right to the source and ask her straight. Mama Jo always said it was better to hear it from the horse's mouth rather than another's back end.

He just had to find her first.

CHAPTER TWENTY-TWO

PIPER WAS BACK AT THE LIBRARY hoping to find Mrs. Huffle in a chatty mood like she was the last time she'd been in but the old gal wasn't at her post. Instead, a dour-looking matron with permanently down-turned facial lines bracketing her mouth greeted Piper with an expression that said I-hate-my-job, don't-ask-me-any-questions, so Piper didn't.

She found the archives herself and thumbed through them in the hopes of finding something she hadn't seen before but as she combed through the copious articles, her eyesight soon blurred and her thoughts wandered.

She didn't want to believe that Ty Garrett was a monster. If she were to believe her parents, Owen's father seduced a young girl and then had her killed when she got in the way. It would devastate Owen if that were the truth. Sadness crept into her thoughts. Owen was a good man. How could the apple fall so far from the tree? She couldn't imagine.

If her parents lied about being at Red Meadows, what did that say about them? Could she believe them about what they'd said about Ty Garrett?

She fished out the journal she kept in her purse and reread a few passages. Throughout, she found love and hope until the last entries. Had Mimi known something bad was coming? Had she lain awake at night, fearful for her unborn child? She swallowed the lump gathering in her throat. She wasn't sure if she was morose for Mimi's lost future or for her own turmoil. Piper tucked the journal away again, still unsure of where to turn. She needed to talk to her parents again and get them to somehow open up to her about the past but unless she had more solid proof…something to compel them to tell the truth… Her gaze returned to her purse where the journal remained hidden from view.

An idea came to her. She may have found a way to sway them.

But before she could leave, Owen walked into the library, a storm crashing behind his eyes, and she sensed she was at the heart of it. She nibbled her lip and tried a smile but he wasn't having any of it.

"We need to talk," he said without preamble. No "hello," "hey, baby," "had fun last night"…nothing. Just a curt demand for her attention.

She tried not to bristle but she didn't do well with orders. Not even from men she found desperately handsome and devastatingly sexy. "About what?" she asked, settling back in her chair.

"Tell me the real reason you're going after Red Meadows."

She gaped, her mind furiously working, vacillating between the truth and total fiction and she was troubled by how quickly her first instinct was to offer up a fish tale. Just like her parents had given her. She chafed privately at her own drawn parallel and went boldly with truth.

"I want to write about it."

He swore. "Why?"

"Because it's the biggest story no one has ever told, sitting right here in Dayton. Imagine, if I can prove Ty Garrett wasn't the monster everyone thought he was… it would change history. And it wouldn't hurt for you, either. For once, you could talk about your father without censure in this town."

"I could give a rat's ass what anyone thinks of me or my father. I know who he was and that's all that matters."

"You're lying. It matters a lot. You've always wanted people to forgive your father for his part in Red Meadows but that's kinda hard to ask for when the man's been painted as the villain all this time."

"No one in Dayton is going to change their minds no matter what you find," he shot back. "Besides, I don't believe you have Dayton in mind for this story. Am I right?"

She hesitated. It was true, she'd been thinking of a bigger, national stage for her story but in the face of Owen's anger, she was reluctant to admit to it. "I don't know," she flung back, anxious to turn the focus away from her. "But if you'd just stop thinking emotionally for a minute, you'd see that it's a win-win for you and me." He drew back, as if stung, and she reacted defensively. "I don't need your permission to write this story."

"No, you just needed my memories," he said bitterly.

"And what better way to get them than to pretend your motivation was purely altruistic."

"Come on, Owen, you and I both know you didn't really buy that story. But you wanted to believe it, so you did."

"What about this morning?" he asked.

She colored, glancing around to see if anyone had caught their conversation. She lowered her voice, saying "What about it?"

"Was that part of the investigative process?"

This time she was the one who felt slapped. "Excuse me? I won't even dignify that with an answer. No, wait, I will because that was the most vile thing anyone has ever said to me. I didn't give you my...my...most precious gift because I was doing *research*."

Unmoved by her answer, he simply shrugged and said in the most infuriatingly flip manner, "So that was just a bonus?"

"You're a jerk," she said, mortified to feel tears stinging her eyes. Damn, she was crying over a man— something she swore she'd never do. She gathered her papers to her breast and fixed her purse on her shoulder, needing to get the hell away from him. "You know what? I'm going to write this story and I don't care what you think about it. I don't care if you think I used you to get information—which, for the record, I did not— and when I win a Pulitzer for busting open the biggest scandal Dayton has ever seen, I'll send you a Starbucks gift card for all your *help*."

OWEN STARED AFTER PIPER, willing his feet to chase after her, but he was stymied by his anger over her admission. That slime colleague of Piper's had been right. She had been using him, even if she didn't care to admit it. Her focus had been Red Meadows all along, but in the beginning, she hadn't denied that fact, either. Maybe he was the idiot, not her.

But even so, it rubbed him the wrong way.

He liked her. Hell, he might even feel more than that for her but he was loath to admit to something that she didn't share in the least.

For the first time since he was a kid, he felt lost. An awesome wave of homesickness overcame him and he wished he were back in Bridgeport, sitting at Mama Jo's table, eating cornbread and ribbing his brothers. He was too old to cry but the sucker punch to his gut was enough to make his eyes sting. Maybe it was time for a trip home. He'd put it off too long and Mama Jo had been after him for quite some time but he'd always had too much on his plate to commit. He'd give it some serious thought. His foreman could run the operation while he was gone. And Piper? She could go to hell, for all he cared.

TEARS BLINDED PIPER as she drove to her parents' house, determined to get answers, no matter how hard they tried to dissuade her. She'd do whatever she had to to get them to open up, even if it meant threatening to walk away and never speak to them again. She dashed the salty moisture from her eyes, turning her attention to the road before she ran into a tree as she cried the tears of an idiot.

She drove up her parents' drive and parked. Taking

a full minute to compose herself, she took several deep breaths before she could exit her car.

I will not accept anything but the truth, she told herself as she marched to the door.

She let herself in and found her parents sitting at the breakfast nook, speaking in low but urgent tones. They stopped as soon as she entered, their guilty expressions fueling her resolve.

Piper reached inside her purse and slammed the journal to the table, causing both to jump at her sudden action. "This is the journal of a woman who was in love with Ty Garrett, the man you claim was a monster. Her words don't support that claim. Now, either you level with me and tell me what you know or I'll walk away and you'll never see me again because I can't be around two people who have blatantly lied to me my entire life. You have a chance to redeem yourselves right now."

Coral's mouth trembled and she looked ready to lose it. She looked to Jasper. "You were supposed to throw that away years ago," she said, blinking back tears.

"I thought I did." Jasper stared at the journal as if it were a snake about to bite him. "Where'd you find that?" he asked, his lips white.

"Does it matter? The fact remains that I have read it and I know more than I did before, and your stories are smelling like fiction. How did you know Mimi La-Roche and how did you happen to gain possession of her journal?"

"Piper—" her father started, but Coral interrupted, seeming to collapse in on herself, as if the strain of whatever secrets she was hiding had suddenly become too much.

"It's time to come clean. We took a chance that this day would come eventually," Coral said dully, giving in, causing Jasper to stare at her in alarm. She waved away his protests with a weary motion. "She's not going to stop. We've raised an independent woman, who is very focused and driven." At that, she spared Piper a smile that made her feel terrible for pushing so hard but Piper had to know what they were hiding from her. She couldn't pretend everything was fine when it wasn't. Acting had never been her strong suit. Coral leaned back in her chair and sighed, saying, "I'd do anything for a cigarette right about now."

Piper's eyes bulged. "Since when do you smoke?"

"I gave it up years ago, but it doesn't mean I don't wish for one now and then," Coral answered. "And for the record, we're not the only ones who've been hiding things. Did you think we wouldn't notice that you've stopped being a vegetarian?"

"Says who?" she said, being evasive, though she wasn't sure why. She was an adult. It was her choice. But still, she'd have preferred to keep that knowledge from her parents. "Did Farley tell you?" she asked, ready to pummel the man for snitching, but Coral shook her head, further confusing her.

"Darling, I can smell it on your pores."

"Are you telling me I have meat stink?" she countered.

Jasper's mouth twitched with a tired smile. "I think we're getting off topic here."

Ever the professor, but Piper was grateful. "No, you're

right. Okay, back to the point. I will share my secrets if you share yours."

Coral made a resigned sound and nodded. "What I'm about to tell you may change the way you feel about us. Are you willing to take that chance?"

She swallowed. "Yes. I have to know."

Coral and Jasper linked hands and the single action said without words that, no matter what, they'd face the situation together. For two nonconformists, they were surprisingly—and endearingly—traditional when it came to the love they felt for one another.

Coral began, taking the lead, while Jasper provided emotional support. "We were young college professors at the city college when we heard of the Aryan Coalition. Of course, we were disgusted by their tenets but intrigued, too. As students of human behavior we were fascinated by the way the *purists* perceived their place in society. We decided to infiltrate the group and then write a book about our findings." A sad, contrite smile followed. "We were so naive and arrogant. We had no idea what we were getting ourselves into."

Piper could imagine her parents, young and confident, yet hungry for the accolades publishing such a book would create. However, the image clashed completely with the one she'd associated with her parents her entire life.

"It soon became apparent that we were in over our heads. The Aryan Coalition was a hub of criminal networking, from drugs to guns, and they were making money hand over fist. Ty Garrett was at the center of it all. He had a way about him that drew people in and made them think that his ideas were their ideas. It was dangerous.

"Before long, there were so many within Dayton who secretly followed the Aryan Coalition. As you can tell from your research, when it all came crashing down, a lot of people were arrested or killed in the raid. It was shocking how many people were involved." She drew a deep breath as if for strength. "There were some who chose to band together after the raid to create something good to make up for the terrible things they were associated with at Red Meadows."

"Like a penance?" Piper asked.

"I suppose. Your father and I invited a few people we'd known at Red Meadows to come here to the farm so we could start rebuilding fresh and clean, without the stain of what we'd done."

Piper could hardly manage the words but she managed to ask the single question that haunted her. "Did you become a racist?"

"God, no," Coral gasped, shaking her head. "Never. But we did things we aren't proud of in the name of research. And we carry the knowledge of that every day."

Piper imagined it was a very heavy burden. She was carrying a pretty hefty load herself at the moment. She could still see Owen's pain reflected in his stark gaze when she'd admitted she was going to write the story, that she'd planned to all along. "So why all the secrecy?" she asked.

Coral and Jasper shared looks. Jasper decided to take it from there. "Honey, when the raid happened...it was never supposed to happen like it did. When we realized something big was going to happen, we tried to contact the FBI, to let them know secretly but they brushed us off."

"Maybe because they already had a man on the inside," Piper interjected, continuing in a rush when her parents didn't agree. "No, you see that's what I found out… Ty Garrett was working for the FBI, under deep cover, to bring the Aryan Coalition down. But something went wrong and Ty ended up getting killed along with a score of other innocent people—one of whom would've been Owen himself if Ty hadn't stepped in."

"An FBI agent wouldn't gun down an innocent child." Coral scoffed at the idea.

"According to the documents, two children died that day," she reminded her mother. "The youngest one being only six months old."

Coral's eyes misted. "Tabitha Aberline," she remembered, a hitch in her voice. "It was a terrible accident. The bullet ricocheted and hit Patience, who happened to be running to safety with Tabitha in her arms. They both died that day. It was so awful. She was only a little younger than you. I used to babysit her."

"I'm so sorry," Piper offered, feeling her mom's pain. "But that's what I'm saying…kids did die that day. And you don't know for certain that Owen's life wasn't in danger, particularly if someone was trying to cover their tracks and figured Owen was old enough to understand his father's business."

"Honey, I know you're looking for ways to clean up

the past, because for some reason you've gotten soft on Garrett, but we were there…he was no angel."

"I'm not saying he was perfect. He probably had to keep up the facade in order to keep things kosher so no one suspected."

"I saw a man beaten because of Ty Garrett's orders," Coral said quietly, shuddering at the memory. "It was horrific."

Piper closed her eyes briefly to shut away the image but she stuck to her guns. She believed William Dearborn. "I think William's shame and regret caused him to pull away from society, from his family. He shared a few things with me…things that were never in the reports."

"Such as?" Jasper asked.

"Well, he was close to Ty, sort of his right-hand man, but he didn't figure out the deception until right up to the raid. He said he heard Ty arguing with someone in the storeroom where they kept the drugs ready for shipment. He peeked inside and saw Ty with a guy he didn't recognize but the expressions on their faces were intense. Ty said something like, 'This wasn't the deal' but he didn't catch the guy's response, because gunfire erupted on the compound. Within minutes, the whole place was filled with smoke, bullets flying and people screaming."

Coral looked as if she were trying to put it gently as she reminded Piper, "William wasn't a good source of reliable information, honey. He had problems with reality."

"Not about this," she insisted. "Just because he was a

recluse doesn't make him crazy. Trust me, Mom. My instincts are right. William may have been a lot of things, but he wasn't lying about the stuff he told me about Red Meadows." Coral was clearly doubtful but she let it go, freeing Piper to continue with the last bit of damning evidence that she felt was proof positive that William had secrets to tell that someone wanted quiet. "Someone killed him not two days after I talked to him about Red Meadows. Someone knew he'd talked. And I think it was the same someone who killed Mimi LaRoche all those years ago."

Coral's eyes softened. "Oh, Mimi…such a beautiful, talented girl. I tried to warn her away from Ty Garrett in the safest way possible without outing ourselves but she was infatuated and my efforts were lost. Of course, she didn't know he was leader of the Aryan Coalition because they'd met at the college where he worked as a carpenter."

"But she had to know something was up by the time the end came near, because her last journal entry talked about the purists when they came to visit her." She looked at Coral. "Do you know who killed Mimi?" she asked, afraid of the answer.

"No," Coral answered, dabbing at her eyes. "We assumed it was Ty because we knew he couldn't afford to have the information come out about his relationship with a black woman."

"So how'd you get her journal?"

They exchanged glances. "Mimi didn't have any family and, since we knew her from the college, after she died we volunteered to go through her effects to find what could be donated to charity and what could be thrown out. We found the journal between the mattress and the box spring. We'd considered giving it to the police but by that point, the investigation had simmered down and everyone was ready to close the door on the whole sordid affair. People needed to be able to grieve and move on. They wouldn't have been able to do that if they'd known Mimi's death was also possibly connected to the *purists*."

Just saying that word made Jasper and Coral cringe. Piper could feel the shame radiating from their pores. She reached out to them. "Why'd you hide this from me all this time?" she asked.

"Because our shame was our burden. Not yours."

"Why do you blame yourself so much? Your crime was pride and arrogance, but you weren't like those people."

"It left a stain, sweetheart," Coral said with a sniff as Jasper nodded, his head bowing under the memory. "We almost moved out of Dayton completely but then we were offered positions at UC Santa Cruz and we figured it was best to try and rebuild, to help those who also shared the burden. We also felt we owed it to the fallen…to honor their memory in some small way."

"Did you ever write your findings?" she asked.

Coral and Jasper paused, each waiting for the other, then Coral nodded her head, as if just admitting it was bad, as well. "We never published it," she added in a rush. "It's sitting in a box in the closet. It hasn't seen the light of day since we put it away twenty-five years ago."

"May I see it?" She held her breath. A first-hand account, written for posterity, in her parents' possession. It was almost too much to hope for.

"Why?" Coral asked, pained. "It's like digging up the dead."

"Because it might have something you've forgotten about that day. Something that might help prove that Ty wasn't the monster, that maybe he was the victim, too."

Distaste registered on her mother's face but she rose with a stiff nod. "I suppose, but I think you should prepare yourself for disappointment."

Coral left and Piper went to her dad. He looked older, worn. She pressed a kiss on his receding hairline and hugged him tight. "I don't think less of you for being at Red Meadows," she told him. "I love you more for being honest with me."

He patted her arm. "We tried to outrun the past so it wouldn't touch you but it did anyway. I'm sorry, peapod."

She grinned. "You have nothing to apologize for, Dad."

Piper returned to her seat and he gave her a mock stern face. "So...eating meat, huh?"

She gave a sheepish grin. "Yeah. I'm actually quite the carnivore."

He chuckled and offered a wistful sigh. "Ah, I remember the days of steak and potatoes. Now it's just potatoes. I miss a good rib eye. Soy burgers and tofu balls just don't cut it sometimes. Can you keep a secret?" he asked in a conspiratorial whisper. She leaned forward to listen. "When your mother is gone on her educational summits…once in a while I eat a good, drippy burger, for old times' sake."

She clapped a hand over her mouth to contain her laughter, enjoying the sparkle that had returned to her father's eye. This was the man she knew. And she was relieved to have him back.

"Any other deep dark secrets we should know about?" her father asked, his gaze speculative. "Like you've become a conservative or you've joined a spacey cult that thinks the next comet is going to wing them to heaven as long as they're wearing the right shoes?"

Her father was joking but Piper knew he was asking for anything else she might want to come clean about. She toyed with the idea of telling him about Owen, but seeing as she didn't know where that stood, she figured why risk blowing the feel-good moment over something that may be a nonissue, so she simply shrugged and shook her head. "Just the same old me. Except for the meat-eating part."

"I guess I can live with that but I'd keep it on the down low with your mom. You know how she feels about that stuff."

Yeah, she knew. She imagined if she came out and said, "Mom, I eat meat and I've given my virginity to Owen Garrett," it'd be a toss-up which declaration would cause Coral to fall in a faint to the floor.

Her mother came back to the room and handed a thick manuscript to her. But as Piper began to scan the pages, eager to start, Coral stopped her with a gentle hand. "Not here. Take it and read it at home. Frankly,

I'm relieved to see it go. It's been under our roof for too long."

Piper nodded her understanding and leaned in for a kiss on her mother's cheek. She inhaled the sweet scent she associated with her mother and smiled.

"This is in good hands," she promised, and then gathered her purse. She couldn't wait to start reading. Hopefully, something stood out…something that might point her in the right direction.

CHAPTER TWENTY-THREE

OWEN RETURNED HOME at the end of the day, surly and tired. Even Timber kept a wide berth as he sensed Owen was not in the mood for much of anything aside from a cold shower and a few beers before bed.

He managed the shower part but as he toweled himself off, his cell went off and he saw it was Thomas.

He picked it up, the first real smile of the day finding him, but it died when he heard the somber tone of his foster brother's voice.

"What's wrong?" he asked, fear eating his gut. "It's Mama, isn't it?"

"Yeah," Thomas answered. "You need to get a flight home. Now."

"What's wrong?"

"You know those tests the doc ordered? Routine, she said. Well, turns out maybe they weren't so routine but she hadn't wanted to worry us. They found something. A tumor. It looks like cancer of some sort."

The strength went out of his legs, and luckily, he was near the sofa when it happened. Cancer? Mama Jo? She was tougher than rawhide. He wiped his palm down his jeans leg and swallowed the damnable lump that kept rising to choke him. "How bad?"

"I dunno. Just come home. She needs to see you, man."

"Of course. I'll take the next flight."

"See you then. Call me with your flight details. I'll pick you up at the airport."

"You got it." He clicked off and sat for a long moment, staring at his phone, unable to process the horror and fear of what was happening. Mama Jo…she was their anchor point, their touchstone. If she were gone… Tears gathered and fell. He wiped at them but they kept coming until he was sobbing, the sound hoarse and rasping as his heart poured out all the terror he'd known as a small boy alone in the world until Mama Jo filled the empty space with plenty of love. He couldn't imagine her not being in this world, making it a better place.

He should've made more time to visit. Hell, he should've dragged her stubborn butt onto the plane so he could show her a slice of his world here in California. But he hadn't. He'd been consumed with all the things that cluttered his life with crap. He'd forgotten what was important: family.

And damn it, all his family was back east…not in Dayton.

He went to his closet and pulled out a suitcase and started throwing clothes into it. When it was full, he zipped it up and placed it outside his door. He dialed up Timothy and asked him to look after Timber for a few days, maybe even a week, and then after placing a key under the mat for Timothy to pick up later, he threw his suitcase in the back of the truck and climbed inside to leave. But Piper, driving like a madwoman, pulled in beside him.

"What are you doing here?" he asked, not in the mood to chat. He didn't wait for her answer. He had a plane to catch. "I was just leaving."

"Wait," she called out, her voice a high screech. She clutched a sheaf of papers to her breast as she chased after him. "I have to talk to you," she said breathlessly, climbing into the truck in spite of his unwelcoming glare. "It's about your dad. I think I've found what I was looking for that will prove your father's innocence."

"Get out," he demanded, startling her with his curt response. "I have to catch a plane."

She looked hurt—wounded even—but she covered well. "Where are you going?"

"Home."

She frowned. "To…Bridgeport?"

"That's right."

"Why?"

He gritted his teeth, unable to even say the words without tearing up. Man, what a big sissy he'd turned out to be. "My family needs me. Mama Jo…she's sick. I've got bigger problems to deal with than your single-minded focus to earn a Pulitzer," he added with a healthy dose of sarcasm.

"Okay, I might have deserved that one," she allowed, even though her stare narrowed. "But I really think you should hear this."

"It can wait," he said, reaching across and opening the door for her in a not-so-subtle motion that said *get out.*

She glared at him and purposefully shut the door, placing the papers firmly in her lap. "If you want me out of the this truck you're going to have to do it yourself."

"Damn it, Piper, I'm not messing around."

"Neither am I."

Holy hell, how'd he get messed up with this crackpot? "Fine," he said, getting out and going around to the other side of the truck to jerk open the door and grab her by the waist and flip her over his shoulder. She shrieked in surprise and barely managed to hold on to her papers, but that didn't stop her from jabbering as she started making her case to his backside. "My mom wrote a research paper on the behaviors of the purists with the hopes of publishing it for her PhD when they were at Red Meadows."

"Figures," he grumbled. "Another person trying to capitalize on Red Meadows."

He deposited her firmly on the ground and started to walk back to his truck but she refused to let him go. She jumped in front of him, blocking his door. "My parents were pretending—like your dad—to get inside information, but for different reasons. They managed to document some of the events and people involved without anyone's knowledge." She lifted the papers in her hand and shook them at Owen until he batted them away with a scowl but she didn't quit. "Now will you listen to me?"

She posed a persuasive argument even if he wanted to walk away and leave the experience with Piper Sunday as an unfortunate memory but he had a commitment to Mama Jo. "We'll talk about it when I get back," he said, giving a little. But that wasn't enough, and Piper countered with her own idea.

"Let me go with you," she suggested. "We can read on the plane. Besides, didn't you tell me your brother Thomas works for the FBI? That's perfect. He might be able to answer some questions I have about the investigation part of the case." She scrambled to her car and pulled an overnight bag that was in her trunk. He stared, dumbfounded and she explained with an efficient grin. "I'm always prepared at a moment's notice. You never know when the next big story is going to break or where it will take you. Besides, my dad always insisted I keep emergency stuff in my car, like flashlights, water, granola bars and a change of clothes in case I find myself in a predicament."

How could he argue with that logic? "I don't know, Piper…this is my family and they're going through something terrible. I think I should do this alone."

Her lovely, stubborn mouth firmed as she shook her head, tossing her bag into the truck alongside his. "That's exactly what you shouldn't do. Being alone isn't a badge of honor or courage, Owen. And there's no shame in admitting that you don't want to be alone."

Had he admitted that? He canted his gaze at her, realizing she wasn't going to quit. It was either take her along or fight her all the way to the airport, where she'd probably end up finding her way on the plane anyway.

"Oh!" she said suddenly, beaming, as she pulled her cell phone from her purse. "I happen to have some frequent-flyer miles I never found time to use so you don't even have to worry about a ticket. I'll log on while we drive so that by the time we arrive at the airport, it'll all be set." She hopped into the truck and motioned to him. "Well, c'mon, slowpoke. We're going to miss our flight!"

Owen couldn't quite believe it but he was going to Bridgeport…with Piper Sunday in tow.

PIPER CURLED HER TOES inside her tennis shoes, glad she exchanged her strappy sandals for the sensible Nike sneakers that were in her bag. She sent a text message to Nancy at the paper letting her know she was taking some personal time and then a similar text to her parents about needing some time to reflect and get away from Dayton. She put her phone away and settled back in her seat, ready for takeoff.

She loved flying but lately she'd been so busy with her investigation into Red Meadows that everything else had fallen by the wayside and that included private time for herself. She risked a glance at Owen. The tension rolling off him dimmed her enjoyment, reminding her that they weren't on a pleasure trip.

"So tell me about Mama Jo," she said, hoping to break the ice between them. There was still plenty that needed to be said but she figured a plane cabin wasn't the most appropriate location, so she sought to distract him for now. "Tell me what it was like when you first came into her home."

Owen shifted in the tiny seat, clearly uncomfortable with their accommodations but he seemed grateful for something to focus on aside from whatever turmoil was in his head.

"I was the first in Mama Jo's care. I was twelve and she'd been taking in troubled kids for a while by that point but her home was empty when I arrived. I was a mess when I got there," he admitted.

"I can only imagine. How did you cope with a black caregiver, given your background?"

"Ah…not well," he said, his gaze clouding. "I was a real jackass for a few weeks. But she wore me down with kindness and firm discipline. And in the end, I was still a brokenhearted kid who'd been abandoned by circumstance and she seemed to understand that somehow." He cracked a grin as he shared a memory. "Mama Jo had a belief that anger was an emotion that had to be physically worked out or else it just festered beneath the surface to show up later. So you can imagine how three messed-up kids acted when they got hot under the collar. Her answer to that kind of stuff was to send us out back to chop wood."

Piper smiled, finding that little bit of information delightful. "Did it work?"

"Hell yes. By the time we were finished chopping wood, our arms felt about ready to fall off and we didn't want to bother with anything else." His smile deepened. "She's one smart woman. She knew a thing or two about raising boys."

"She didn't have any children of her own?"

"One. Cordry. He died in a group home for troubled youth. I guess that's why she got into foster care in the first place. She wanted kids who had nowhere to turn to have a safe haven somewhere. But she said when she met me and my brothers, Thomas and Christian, she'd found her true purpose for being a foster parent and that was to find her boys."

"Wow. That's so awesome."

"Yeah. She's something else."

"So what's going on with her right now?"

He looked away, out toward the view across the wing and into the clouds below. "She's sick. Cancer."

"Oh, that's awful," Piper said softly, reaching over to tuck his hand into hers. "It'll mean a lot to have you all there for her."

He nodded, his gaze finding their entwined hands and he gave her fingers a soft squeeze. "I should've done this earlier. It's been too long since I've been home."

She remained quiet, sensing his admission didn't require a rejoinder. Taking a risk, she leaned against him, resting her head on his shoulder. She resisted the urge to sigh contentedly. There was still an ocean of problems between them but for now, she was going to enjoy the moment. Within minutes, she'd fallen into a blissful sleep.

CHAPTER TWENTY-FOUR

OWEN AND PIPER DISEMBARKED from the plane and met Thomas outside the terminal. Any questions he might've had at the unexpected guest he kept to himself and simply introduced himself to Piper and then wrapped Owen in a tight, effusive manly hug that still brought tears to Owen's eyes. He'd missed this. Wiping at his own eyes, Thomas ribbed him saying, "You big crybaby. You always were a softy."

Owen tucked him in a headlock, grinning. "I'll show you soft…"

They messed around for a minute as they loaded the luggage but soon they were in the car and driving to Bridgeport.

The sights and smells took him back, and the trip into the past was powerful stuff. He'd left so soon after high school and it'd been a long time since he'd even come home for a visit. Sobering, he asked after Mama Jo. "So, what's the word? What kind of cancer are we talking?"

"Breast. But the doc says we caught it early so there's a good chance she's going to beat this."

"Is she getting good care? What's her health insurance like?" he asked.

"Well, she's on Medicare and that's at least better than nothing, but me and Cassi have been picking up some of the tab for her treatments."

"I want to pitch in, too," he volunteered immediately. "What about Christian?"

"Yeah, he's helping, too."

"Good."

Piper remained quiet in the backseat of Thomas's truck, observing their interaction with something of an enigmatic smile on her face.

Thomas glanced at Piper in his rearview mirror. "So you two friends or something?" he asked, fishing for details that Owen wasn't ready to share.

"Or something," Owen answered for her making her frown. "She's that reporter I told you about."

Thomas's brow inched upward in surprise. "The same reporter who…"

"Who was trying to make my life a living hell," he supplied for his brother. "The very same."

"I wouldn't say I was trying to do that. We have a difference of opinion on that score," she retorted, pausing to give Thomas a blinding smile. "Piper Sunday. So pleased to meet you."

Thomas was likely dying to know why he'd brought the "yellow journalist" home with him but Owen would have to fill him in later. Right now, he wanted to focus on Mama Jo, so he gave the basics of his association with Piper. "We're working on a project together and time was an issue, so she offered to come with me."

She opened her mouth to add her own twist but he quelled her with a look. He didn't need his brother knowing their personal business. She snapped her mouth shut and turned to gaze out the window, effectively closing him out and promising an earful later, but he'd deal with her ire behind closed doors.

"What project?" Thomas asked, curious.

"Later," he promised. "I'm beat from the flight and the peanuts I ate on the plane didn't go very far. Mind if we stop and get a bite before we head to Mama's?"

"If I bring you home with a bag of fast food I'll be disowned. You know better than that."

He scowled. "Mama Jo doesn't need to be worrying about feeding people right now. She needs to consider her health. She should be resting."

Thomas cut Owen a sidewise glance. "Man, it has been a long time since you've been home. Have you ever known Mama Jo to slow down even when she ought to?"

"No, but maybe that's the problem. She's run herself into the ground taking care of others."

"Cassi is back at the house, helping Mama Jo. When she heard you were coming, she set to making enough cornbread to feed an army."

His mouth watered at the memory of Mama Jo's cooking but he felt like a toad for the jump in anticipation. "Cassi's helping out?" he asked.

"Yeah, she's about the only one Mama Jo lets in her kitchen these days."

"Things good between you?" he asked.

Thomas cracked a wide grin. "They're good." The self-satisfied smile said more than good. Owen shared his brother's happiness. They all loved Cassi. For him and Christian, she was the sister they never had. For Thomas, she was the one.

"Who's Cassi?" Piper chimed in from the back.

"My wife," Thomas answered. "Don't worry, you'll get to meet her when we get to Mama Jo's."

Owen chuckled to himself, imagining how Piper's jaw would drop when she found out how Thomas and Cassi got together. It made for interesting conversation when your brother was tasked with arresting his secret first love when she was on the run from the law. Owen still couldn't believe how they ended up happy and in love after they'd both traded punches before the "you're my soul mate" part started. And according to Thomas, Cassi had a wicked left hook.

BY THE TIME THEY ARRIVED at the small cottage belonging to Mama Jo and the place where Owen and his foster brothers had finished growing up, nervousness had set in. Perhaps she'd been a little rash in jumping on board with this trip. She hadn't been thinking clearly. All she'd known was that she was riding high on her findings and Owen was leaving town. She couldn't fathom watching him leave and waiting for him to return. The obvious answer had seemed to be that she go with him, but now, she wasn't so sure. She wasn't anything to him. How could she face his family as if she belonged?

They filed into the house and Piper purposefully hung back, definitely feeling like a third wheel amongst the clan who was hugging and kissing and making up for lost time. As she watched Owen with his brothers, their wives and Mama Jo, genuine joy unfurling in his expression, she knew she was finally seeing the true Owen. Before, she'd always seen the businessman, the logger, the opponent. Now she saw the man underneath all the personas he projected for everyone on the outside. The people here right now, in this small but cozy room, were the privileged few who got to see the real Owen. The realization humbled her. She'd never been a particularly private person, having grown up surrounded by a community of people on the farm, but she knew, watching the interactions between these people, that allowing someone in your inner circle was a gift. A gift Owen had inadvertently given to her.

She swallowed and waited to be introduced but before Owen could do the honors, the matriarch who ruled the roost stepped forward with a strong, assessing gaze that Piper felt compelled to meet without flinching, no matter how she might want to run and hide.

"Owen, who is your friend?" she asked.

"My name is Piper Sunday," Piper answered for herself, putting her hand out for a handshake.

Mama Jo cracked a smile on her softly worn face and cackled with laughter. "Honey, if Owen brought you home, you're more than a friend. Now, come here and give Mama Jo some love. Here, you're family. We don't stand on ceremony." And then Piper was gathered into a warm embrace much the same as the rest and she delighted in the warm and fuzzy feelings it evoked. She'd never been shorted in the love department—her parents, though academic, were still affectionate—but there was something about a hug from Mama Jo that fed the soul.

She risked a glance at Owen, perhaps to apologize for horning in on his private circle but he looked anything but unhappy to have her there. Puzzled, but certainly warmed by it, Piper was released by Mama Jo and she went to stand by Owen while Mama Jo returned to the kitchen in a blur of motion.

"She certainly looks pretty healthy," Piper offered hopefully. "I've heard a good attitude accounts for a significant part of a person's recovery when it comes to cancer."

"Mama Jo is a force of nature. I can't imagine something like an illness taking her down," he murmured softly. She leaned toward him and smiled as his arm reached around and anchored at her waist. "I wasn't sure if this was a good idea at first but I'm glad you're here."

She looked up at him. "Me, too," she said with sincerity.

The rest of the night was spent talking, laughing, sharing stories and eating until their guts felt ready to pop.

By the time Cassi, Thomas, Christian and Skye left, everyone was ready to turn in. Mama Jo turned to Piper with a warm but firm smile that brooked no argument as she said, "In this house, the only ones sleeping together are the ones bound together in front of God. Blankets are in the linen closet, sugar."

Mama Jo reached up on her tiptoes to place a smacking kiss on Owen's cheek, then pinched his cheeks for good measure, murmuring with a warm smile, "Feels good to have all my boys home for a change. Good night, honey."

"Night, Mama Jo," he returned with love in his voice. "You get some rest. No getting up to fix breakfast, you hear?"

Mama laughed softly and closed the door behind her, leaving them alone for the night.

"Why do I have the feeling I'm going to wake at the crack of dawn to the smell of breakfast cooking no matter what you say?"

"Because that's exactly what she's going to do. Stubborn woman," he said with affection. He gestured outside. "Want to sit on the porch swing for a little while?"

She smiled. "Yeah, I'd like that."

Owen led the way and they took up residence on the creaking wooden swing. Thoughts and questions raced through her brain, each clamoring for attention but she was reluctant to ruin an otherwise fabulous night with the things that were left unsaid between them.

"I understand your devotion to Mama Jo," she said, breaking the silence. "She's amazing. She manages to make you feel like you're a part of something bigger than yourself within the first five minutes of meeting. I imagine when you were kids that was something more precious than gold to feel accepted and loved like that."

"More than you know," he answered gravely, the light from the moon reflecting in his eyes. "She's the epicenter of our family. Without her… I don't even like to think about it."

She couldn't even imagine the fear he had bunched inside. She'd never lost anyone close to her but she sensed his need for closeness and she was happy to give it to him. She leaned forward and brushed her lips against his. He reacted slowly, as if savoring the kiss, then drew her to him, deepening the contact until she felt as if she were happily falling. His tongue teased hers and then he broke contact. Their breathing had become shallow, as the intensity of the moment robbed them of the ability to think, much less breathe normally.

"What are we doing?" she whispered, almost afraid to hear the answer.

"I don't know," he admitted with a sigh. "But you're so beautiful sometimes it hurts to look at you. I've wanted to kiss you since the moment you showed up in my driveway."

Delicious heat warmed her from the inside as she said, "Me, too." She grinned until she remembered with a frown. "That is, until you started yelling at me. Where did that come from?"

Pulling away, he said, regret in his voice, "I ran into that colleague of yours—Charlie Yert. He put a few worms in my brain that I couldn't seem to lodge loose. I didn't mean to lose my temper. Everything got to me at once."

"Charlie's always looking to stir up trouble when it comes to me and if you're not on guard, he can get under your skin."

"Well, he definitely managed to do that. Why does he want to stir up trouble for you?"

She shrugged. "He hates me. I think it all started

when I shot him down romantically when I first came on staff. He thought he could impress me with the fact that his mother's brother owns the newspaper." She made a gagging noise. "But the thought of even sitting across a dinner table from Charlie was more than I could stomach. I tried to let him down easily but he wigged out. And from then on, he was on a mission to catch me screwing up. When he discovered I was nosing around the Red Meadows story, he got really weird. I just chalked it up to Charlie being Charlie but he started to get really mean about it."

"Mean how?" he asked.

She shrugged off his concern. "Charlie is a wuss. He couldn't hurt a fly. Doesn't have the stomach for it. But he can be pretty snotty."

She yawned and he rose from the swing. "Let's hit the hay," he said, reaching out to help her up. She climbed to her feet and even though she loved the comfort of Mama Jo's house, suddenly she wished they'd gotten a hotel room.

CHAPTER TWENTY-FIVE

THE NEXT MORNING BROKE EARLY with a threat of a springtime shower. Jet lag messed up his internal clock but he rose in the hope of catching Mama Jo before she hit the kitchen. No such luck. He followed his nose to the savory smell of hickory-smoked bacon and eggs frying. He went to the coffeepot percolating on the stove and poured himself a cup. "Good morning," he said from above the rim of his mug. "You are bound and determined to kill yourself, aren't you? Thomas said the doctor told you to rest. I'm pretty sure that doesn't include slaving over the kitchen stove at the crack of dawn."

She smiled and moved the bacon to a paper towel to absorb the grease. "When's the last time I got a chance to spend this kind of quality time with my favorite boy?"

Sneaky woman. He smiled into his cup. She called them all her favorites when in private. He did enjoy spending this quiet time with her—it reminded him of when he lived at home. He'd always been an early riser, a man after her own heart, she'd said.

She slid an egg, perfectly cooked, onto a plate and finished it off with a generous serving of the bacon.

She handed him the plate and gestured toward the table where they could sit and catch up.

"So tell me about this girl you've brought home," she said. "She's a curiosity for sure."

"That's no lie," he agreed, setting his mug down to chew a piece of bacon. Lord, have mercy, that was good. He paused a minute to savor the good old-fashioned cooking he'd forgotten and then said, "Mama Jo, we started off as adversaries but somewhere along the way…things changed. Now I don't know where we stand. It's complicated, I guess."

"No doubt." She sipped her coffee. "Why don't you start from the beginning. I have a feeling it's a good story and I'd love to have something to think about aside from how my body is failing me."

He sobered at the mention of her illness, even if it was offered in jest. "Mama…why didn't you tell me sooner?" he asked, pained by her silence when her health was concerned. "I would've come running if I'd known."

Her soft mouth, responsible for countless kisses that soothed infinite injuries caused by overconfident boys with little to no common sense, tipped in a knowing smile. "Which is exactly why I didn't call. There's nothing you could've done, save sit here with me fretting about things you can't control. It's in God's hands, sugar." She reached over and patted his hand. "But don't you worry…I still have too much to do in this life to be going home just yet. Now, back to the girl. Tell me how you met."

Owen spent the next hour pouring out his heart to the

one woman who had always understood him, and when he was done, she simply chuckled and rose to start the dishes.

"What should I do?" he asked, hoping for some guidance. "I never felt like this before. It—"

"Makes your stomach queasy and your heart ache like you've just caught something contagious and don't know whether you want to puke your guts or break out into song?"

He laughed. "Well, definitely something along those lines. Not sure about the singing part because I can't carry a tune like Christian but I think you nailed the other part."

"You're in love, boy."

He shook his head. "No, I don't think love is supposed to feel this messy."

"Owen, that's the best kind of love. Let me tell you something, love isn't so easily defined like the stuff they put on greeting cards. Sometimes it makes you act crazy and stupid but as long as you have that person in your life, everything is good."

"She wants to write about the Red Meadows raid," he said, the heaviness in his heart coming out in his voice. "All my life I've been connected to this terrible thing…I thought I was all about clearing my dad's name but now…I think I was doing it for myself. If people no longer thought of my father as a monster, maybe I could live a more anonymous life."

"Honey, what she writes isn't going to matter. People are going to think what they choose."

"That's what I told her, but she's determined to write it anyway."

"Then let her."

He stared at Mama Jo. "I don't want her to."

"Sometimes we have to let the people we love do the things they feel they must in order to find what they're looking for inside of themselves."

Mama Jo's wisdom settled down deep as it always did and he realized it'd always been about Piper and, to a lesser degree, himself. His father was gone and it didn't matter to him whether or not people whispered about what had happened twenty-five years ago. His father had died knowing Owen loved him. That's all that should matter between a father and a son.

Mama Jo came and smoothed a lock of his hair the way she used to when he was a boy and refused to cut it. "Owen, you were always my thinker. Do yourself a favor and stop thinking this time. Go with your heart, sugar. You've got a good one…it won't steer you wrong."

TWO DAYS HAD PASSED and Piper was starting to catch the rhythm of Mama Jo's house, but with her back complaining from sleeping on the sofa, she was looking forward to staying a night or two with Cassi and Thomas. Apparently, before Cassi had turned into a wanted felon, she'd actually been quite rich. Now that Cassi had returned to polite society, she and Thomas had moved into Cassi's family mansion. The thought of fine sheets and a soft bed were a big draw, though she'd miss hanging out with Mama Jo.

"So what's on the agenda today?" she asked, her

mind moving in excited circles over what she'd discovered last night with Thomas's help. She wanted to talk to Owen about it but she was a little wary after their last blow-up, so she decided to wait for the right moment.

"Let's talk for a minute," Owen offered.

"What would you like to talk about?" she asked, curious.

"I don't know…stuff people talk about when they're trying to get to know one another naturally and not with the aid of government files."

"Ask away. I'm an open book."

Put on the spot, he floundered a little. Then he started off with simple questions that felt a lot like a dating-game questionnaire. "Do you like animals?"

She sipped her coffee. "I do. As long as they don't require too much care. A fish is probably about my speed."

"How about kids?"

"Same."

"Same?"

"Well, I mean, I love kids as long as they go home with someone else. Kids are a lot of work. Worse so than a puppy, I hear."

He chuckled but she heard a little disappointment, too, as he continued, "So no kids for you, huh?"

"I didn't say that, necessarily. Just none for me, *right now*. My parents gave me a wonderful childhood. I want to be able to do that, too, and I can't when I'm focused on my career." She peered at him. "Are you trying to see if we're compatible or something?" she joked.

"Maybe."

Her heart warmed at his admission and the jolt of happiness it caused nearly made her forget what she needed to say. Her smile faded and she drew a deep breath before saying, "Owen...I'm still going to write about Red Meadows."

"I know."

She met his stare. "And you're okay with that?"

"Yeah. I know who my father was. Anything you write isn't going to change that."

She let out a shaky breath and waited a minute for her nerves to settle. Now she could tell him what she'd been itching to tell him since last night. "I'm so glad to hear that because I have news to share that I think you're going to want to hear."

"Like what?"

"Remember how I told you my parents wrote about their findings and experiences within the Aryan Coalition? Well, there was a name in the findings that was listed in the names of the deceased. Up till now I hadn't been able to find a paper trail for the mysterious guy who'd been seen arguing with Ty before he died. William Dearborn said he didn't recognize him, but apparently someone had noticed his comings and goings, right around the time the shipments were heading out. I think he was an FBI agent on the take. If so, he'd do anything to make Ty look like the monster to throw the attention from him, even kill innocent people."

"What was the name?"

"Richard Stark."

He searched his memory but came up with nothing. "I don't remember that name. It might've been a cover."

"Exactly. Which is why I had your brother look into it. He was able to do a search for aliases within the FBI system for their agents."

"When did you have time to talk to Thomas?" he asked.

She waved away his question. "Immaterial. The fact is, he was willing to help and he found answers that would've taken forever and a lot of paperwork to find out on my own."

"So what'd he find?" he asked.

"Well, here's the best part…turns out Richard Stark— the man who orchestrated the raid—is actually Hank Yertz."

"Yertz…why is that name familiar?"

"Because he just happens to be the father of one Charlie Yertz, the number one pain in my butt at the paper. But wait, it gets better. Hank, under the alias of Richard Stark, had been listed as one of the deceased in the raid but that'd just been to avoid questions later as he resumed his life, rich and fat from the millions of dollars he skimmed from the Aryan Coalition's illegal activities." She made a show of checking her watch. "Right about now, Charlie Yertz and his scumbag father are probably getting arrested by federal agents on a host of charges that range from murder to accessory to murder. All in all, it's news that I find extremely gratifying. Seems Thomas ran with the information as soon as it became clear that there was something dirty going on. Your brother is pretty cool. Very Johnny on the Spot. I like that."

"Yeah, he's always been a stickler for the rules," he murmured, appearing a little dazed by the sudden flow of information after decades of silence. "So, what now?"

She sobered and straddled his lap, wrapping her arms around his neck. "Now I let the FBI dig around in Yertz's life and when they finish, I scoop up the dirt and write about it, win an award and then become a famous journalist."

"And where do I fit in with that plan?" he asked.

She bit her lip, glancing at him from beneath her lashes. "I was hoping we could figure that out together."

"Are you sure? It might not be easy," he said with a sweetly vulnerable expression that spoke to her heart and created a riot of warm and toasty feelings.

Owen Garrett was a good man, who cared deeply for others and put the welfare of those he loved above his own. That was why he worked punishing hours and never let a call go to voice mail no matter the hour—unless the call had been hers. She regretted railroading him in the beginning to get what she wanted and pursuing him relentlessly—even using a wee bit of extortion to persuade him to talk to her. Yes, she realized, she hadn't played fair or nice.

And yet, he'd still helped her.

If her parents could stomach the idea that she wolfed down burgers and steaks with the unapologetic abandon of a true carnivore, they'd eventually get over the fact that she was in love with Owen Garrett.

Imagine how awkward those tree-sits were going to be…

Suddenly she gripped his face, staring into his eyes. "I'm pretty sure I'm in love with you. I don't have a lot of experience with this sort of thing, so I'm not sure if I'm doing this right. I don't know if I'm supposed to be coy and make you chase me but to be truthful, I'm an impatient person and I want to skip the part where I make you run after me and I want to get to the good stuff."

"The good stuff… And what might that be?"

"Well, I like to do something until I feel I'm quite *proficient,* which means I'm going to require plenty of practice in the carnal department, that is if you're *up* for it."

His voice sounded strained as he said, "Careful or you'll end up on your back before you even realize what happened."

She tightened her arms around his neck and whispered in his ear, "What are you waiting for?" Smiling when she felt his muscles tense, she added in a husky, suggestive tone. "I've heard of this thing called a quickie…?"

As Owen educated her in the joys of fast and dirty, she closed her eyes and knew she'd found her rightful place…in Owen's arms no matter where they might end up in the future. She wanted to be by his side as he weathered every storm, to be his rock during a crisis, because she knew, in her heart, that he would always do the same for her.

And that was pretty damn awesome—perhaps even better than a Pulitzer.

EPILOGUE

OWEN BEAMED WITH PRIDE as Piper accepted a national newspaper award for her investigative piece on Red Meadows.

It was hard to reconcile how different his life had become from six months ago.

Thanks to Piper's insistent belief that Ty Garrett had been innocent, a twenty-five-year-old secret had been brought to light and two people had been brought to justice.

Both Charlie and his father, Hank, were taken into custody when it was discovered Hank had killed Mimi LaRoche to scare Ty into keeping quiet when Ty threatened to blow the lid off the Red Meadows case.

Once the FBI reopened the investigation—again, thanks to Piper—it was discovered Hank had been pocketing gobs of dirty cash raked in from the Aryan Coalition's drug and gun sales. When Hank discovered William Dearborn had started sharing details about what went down the day of the massacre, he convinced Charlie to put the guy down in the hopes that no one would care what happened to a crazy old recluse and the past would die with him.

And while it felt good to have some closure on

something that had torn his life apart for so long, he was most grateful that his father had gained the respect he deserved for trying to do the right thing, even if no one had been allowed to know his part.

And he had Piper Sunday—soon to be Piper Morning Dew Sunday-Garrett—to thank for it.

He glanced at his watch. Almost time for Mama Jo's appointment. Piper came from the stage, clutching her plaque with bright eyes but she also checked her watch. "Time to go?" she asked, grabbing her purse.

"You should stay. I can take Mama to her appointment."

"Mama Jo is my family, too. I'm not going to miss her first chemo and radiation appointment at this fancy new cancer clinic you insisted on taking her to. Besides, I told her I'd read her my *award-winning* article while she got juiced up, and she's looking forward to it."

He chuckled. "Sounds like a plan."

Life wasn't too shabby. He'd finally managed to convince Mama Jo to come to California, wooing her with the promise of innovative cancer treatment as he appealed to her stubborn and welcome belief that she was going kick cancer's can and he'd managed to convince Piper to marry him—and maybe even have a kid or two.

Now, if only his soon-to-be-inlaws would stop forcing him to choke down tofu—life would be perfect.

* * * * *

COMING NEXT MONTH

Available June 14, 2011

You can find more information on upcoming
Harlequin® titles, free excerpts and more at
www.HarlequinInsideRomance.com.

HSRCNM0511

Harlequin® Blaze™ brings you
New York Times *and* USA TODAY *bestselling author*
Vicki Lewis Thompson with three new steamy titles
from the bestselling miniseries SONS OF CHANCE

Chance isn't just the last name of these rugged
Wyoming cowboys—it's their motto, too!

Read on for a sneak peek at the first title,
SHOULD'VE BEEN A COWBOY

Available June 2011 only from Harlequin® Blaze™.

"THANKS FOR NOT TURNING ON THE LIGHTS," Tyler said. "I'm a mess."

"Not in my book." Even in low light, Alex had a good view of her yellow shirt plastered to her body. It was all he could do not to reach for her, mud and all. But the next move needed to be hers, not his.

She slicked her wet hair back and squeezed some water out of the ends as she glanced upward. "I like the sound of the rain on a tin roof."

"Me, too."

She met his gaze briefly and looked away. "Where's the sink?"

"At the far end, beyond the last stall."

Tyler's running shoes squished as she walked down the aisle between the rows of stalls. She glanced sideways at Alex. "So how much of a cowboy are you these days? Do you ride the range and stuff?"

"I ride." He liked being able to say that. "Why?"

"Just wondered. Last summer, you were still a city boy. You even told me you weren't the cowboy type, but you're…different now."

He wasn't sure if that was a good thing or a bad thing. Maybe she preferred city boys to cowboys. "How am I different?"

"Well, you dress differently, and your hair's a little longer. Your face seems a little more chiseled, but maybe that's because of your hair. Also, there's something else, something harder to define, an attitude…"

"Are you saying I have an attitude?"

"Not in a bad way. It's more like a quiet confidence."

He was flattered, but still he had to laugh. "I just admitted a while ago that I have all kinds of doubts about this event tomorrow. That doesn't seem like quiet confidence to me."

"This isn't about your job, it's about…your…" She took a deep breath. "It's about your sex appeal, okay? I have no business talking about it, because it will only make me want to do things I shouldn't do." She started toward the end of the barn. "Now, where's that sink? We need to get cleaned up and go back to the house. Dinner is probably ready, and I—"

He spun her around and pulled her into his arms, mud and all. "Let's do those things." Then he kissed her, knowing that she would kiss him back, knowing that this time he would take that kiss where he wanted it to go. And she would let him.

Follow Tyler and Alex's wild adventures in
SHOULD'VE BEEN A COWBOY
Available June 2011 only from Harlequin® Blaze™
wherever books are sold.

Finding Her Dad

Janice Kay Johnson

Jonathan Brenner was busy running for
office as county sheriff. The last thing on
his mind was parenthood...that is, until
a resourceful, awkward teenage girl shows
up claiming to be his daughter!

*Available June
wherever books are sold.*

SPECIAL EDITION

Life, Love and Family

LOVE CAN BE FOUND IN THE MOST UNLIKELY PLACES, ESPECIALLY WHEN YOU'RE NOT LOOKING FOR IT...

Failed marriages, broken families and disappointment. Cecilia and Brandon have both been unlucky in love and life and are ripe for an intervention. Good thing Brandon's mother happens to stumble upon this matchmaking project. But will Brandon be able to open his eyes and get away from his busy career to see that all he needs is right there in front of him?

FIND OUT IN

WHAT THE SINGLE DAD WANTS...

BY *USA TODAY* BESTSELLING AUTHOR

MARIE FERRARELLA

AVAILABLE IN JUNE 2011
WHEREVER BOOKS ARE SOLD.